The Uncomfortable Dead

The Uncomfortable Dead

(what's missing is missing)

A NOVEL BY FOUR HANDS

Paco Ignacio Taibo II
& Subcomandante Marcos

Translation by Carlos Lopez

Akashic Books
New York

This is a work of fiction. All names, characters, places, and incidents are the product of the authors' imaginations. Any resemblance to real events or persons, living or dead, is entirely coincidental.

Published by Akashic Books
Originally published in serial form in Spanish in *La Jornada* with the title *Muertos Incomodos (Falta lo que Falta), Novela a Cuatra Manos*

Cover design by Pirate Signal International
Author photos by Marina Taibo

ISBN-13: 978-1-933354-07-1
ISBN-10: 1-933354-07-0
Library of Congress Control Number: 2006923112

Printed in Canada

First printing

Akashic Books
PO Box 1456
New York, NY 10009
Akashic7@aol.com
www.akashicbooks.com

TABLE OF CONTENTS

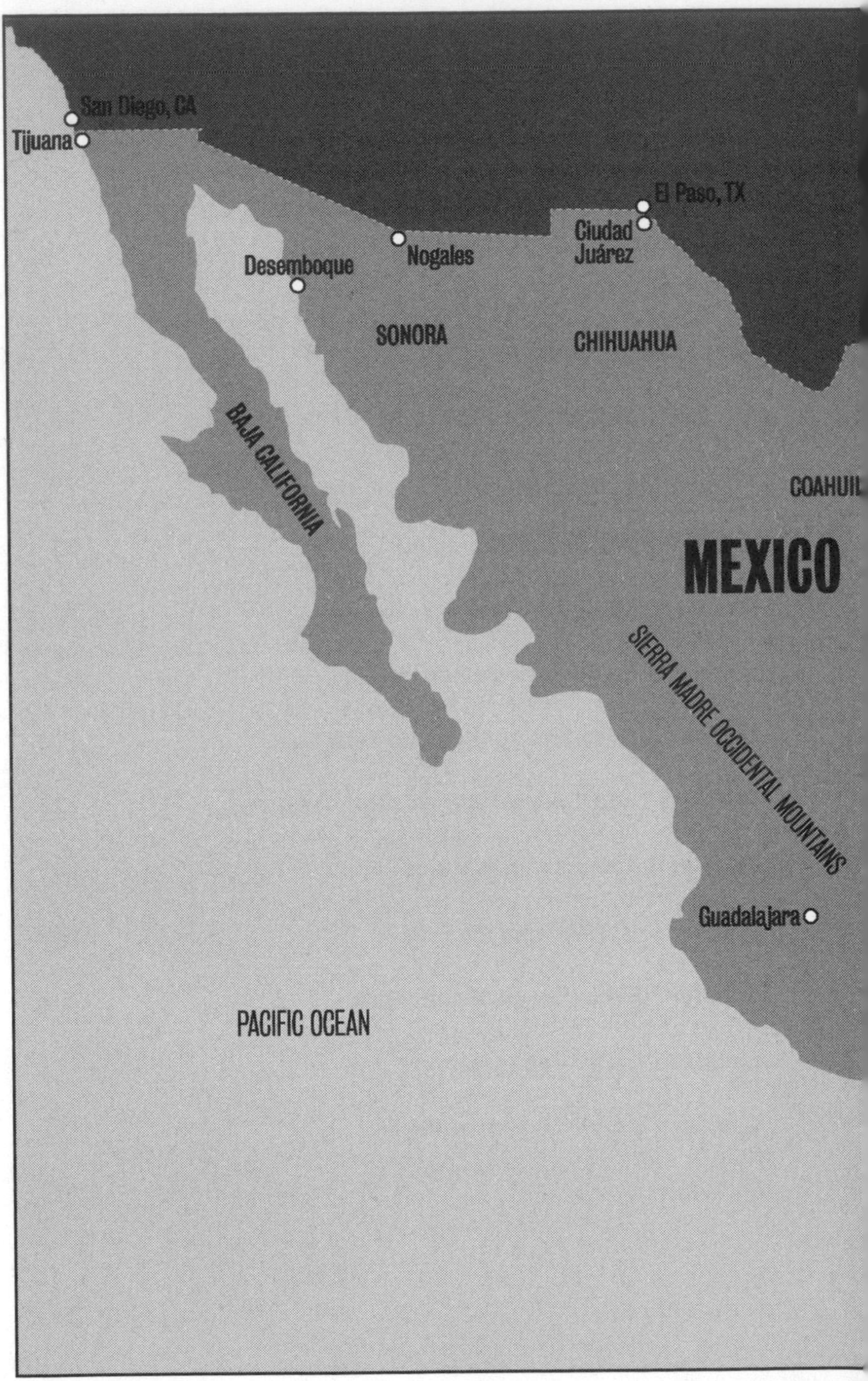

San Diego, CA
Tijuana
El Paso, TX
Ciudad Juárez
Nogales
Desemboque
SONORA
CHIHUAHUA
BAJA CALIFORNIA
COAHUIL
MEXICO
SIERRA MADRE OCCIDENTAL MOUNTAINS
Guadalajara
PACIFIC OCEAN

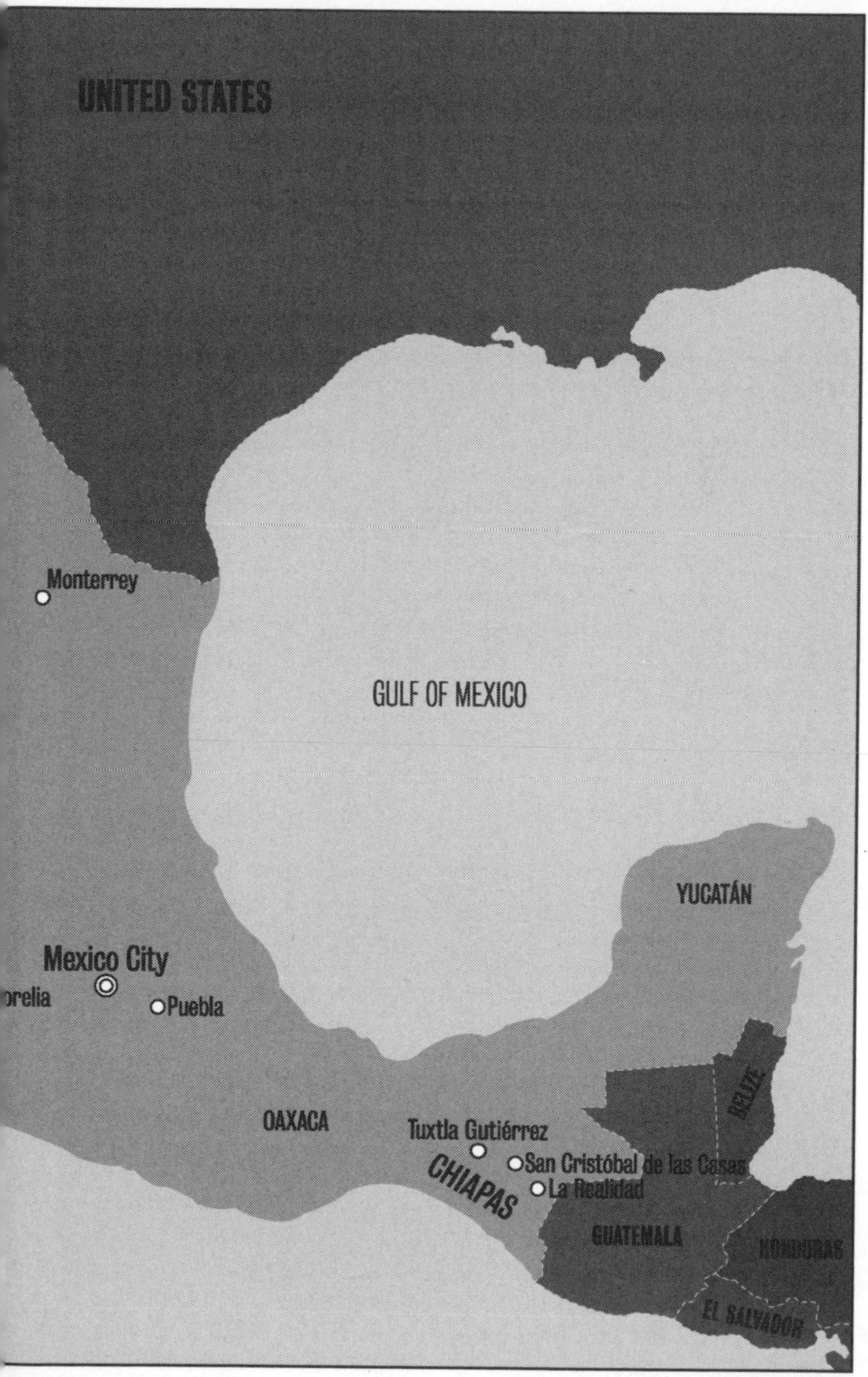

UNITED STATES

Monterrey

GULF OF MEXICO

YUCATÁN

Mexico City

orelia

Puebla

OAXACA

Tuxtla Gutiérrez

San Cristóbal de las Casas

CHIAPAS

La Realidad

BELIZE

GUATEMALA

HONDURAS

EL SALVADOR

Note from the Authors

The odd-numbered chapters (1, 3, 5, etc.) in this novel were written by Insurgent Subcomandante Marcos and the even-numbered chapters by Paco Ignacio Taibo II.

The authors' share of the proceeds from this book will be donated to the Mexico-U.S. Solidarity Network, a non-governmental agency that works to improve relations between Mexico and the United States.

CHAPTER 1

SOMETIMES IT TAKES MORE THAN 500 YEARS

A*nything that takes more than six months is either a pregnancy or not worth the trouble.*

That there's what El Sup told me, and I just looked at him to see if he was joking or what. Cause the thing is, El Sup sometimes mixes things up and jokes with the city folk like he's talking to us, or he jokes with us like he's talking to the city folk. And then nobody much understands him, but he don't really care a whole lot. He just laughs to himself.

But wasn't that way this time. El Sup wasn't joking. You could tell from the way he just stared at that pipe while he was trying to get it to catch. He was just staring at that pipe like he was expecting *it* to answer him instead of me.

He told me he was going to send me into the city; that I had to do a couple a things for the struggle and I had to hang around picking up city ways, and then I could do the job. That there was when I asked him how long I had to hang around picking up city ways and he told me six months. So I ask him if he thought six months was enough, and that's when he said what he said.

El Sup said this after he spent some time talking to a certain Pepe Carvalho, who'd just got into La Realidad with a message from Don Manolo Vázquez Montalbán and asked to see El Sup. Well, that's what I heard from Max, the guy who got the message first. Now me, I knew Don Manolo well. It was just a few days ago he'd come up to interview El Sup. He'd brought with him a bunch of sausages, which is some kinda meat, in his knapsack. Now, I didn't rightly know what in hell sausages was, but when I rode out to meet him, I saw how the dogs was all around him going wild and I asked him if he had meat in that there bag and he said he had sausages, but "they're for Insurgent Subcomandante Marcos," that's what he said. And right then I knew he really respected El Sup, cause that was the way he was called by city people who really respected him and liked him a lot. But like I was saying, that's how I found out what sausages was, cause I asked if he had meat and he said he had sausages, so sausages must be a way they fix meat in the country where Don Manolo's from.

Don Manolo don't like to be called "Manolo," but "Manuel." That's what he said when we was on the way to Headquarters. It took us awhile to get there. First, cause Don Manolo didn't take to horses really well and he was awhile getting into the saddle. And second, cause the horse they got him was a little skittish and didn't really take to being rode and all, so he kept making for the pasture instead of heading along the road. Since we spent some time getting the horse to go where we wanted him to go, Don Manolo and me got to talking and I think we even became friends. That's how I found out he don't like to be called Manolo, but me, you know, all you gotta do is tell me something is "no" for me to go "yes," and I don't do it outta being ornery or nothing, no sir, it's just the way they made me, or that's the way I am, you know, contrary: Contreras. That's what El Sup calls me, "Elías Contreras," but not cause that's my name. "Elías" is my fighting name, and "Contreras," well, that's what El Sup named me cause he said I had to have a fighting last name too, and seeing as how I was so contrary, a last name like Contreras was just right for me.

Now, all of that happened some time before I went to Guadalajara to pick up a mail pouch in the public baths at La Mutualista and met the Chinese guy Fuang Chu. And it was also a long time before I ran into the Investigation Commission guy called Belascoarán over by the Monument to the Revolution, down in Mexico City. Now, I say *Investigation Commission*, but this Belascoarán feller says *detective*. In our Zapatista territories there ain't no *detectives*, only *Investigation Commissions*. But this Belascoarán says that in Mexico City there ain't no *Investigation Commissions*, only *detectives*. So I says to each his own. But like I was saying, all this was a lot after El Sup said what he said about the six months. And it was even later that he ran into Magdalena in Mexico City. Oh, that Magdalena honey! But I'll tell you more about that later . . . or maybe I won't, because some wounds just don't heal even if you talk them out. On the contrary, the more you dress them up in words, the more they bleed.

Anyway, a long time before El Sup told me about the six months, I'd already investigated some things in the Zapatista autonomous rebel municipalities. You have to say *cases*, not *things*, this Belascoarán told me later, and the thing is, he kept riding me because according to him I talk very different, and whenever he felt like it he would go on correcting the way I talked. But me, instead of changing the way I talked, I just went right on . . . Contreras, you know? And it was from one of them *cases* that we got the name of this chapter in this here book, which, you're gonna see, is very different.

But let me tell you a little about who I was. Yeah, *was*, cause I'm deceased now. I was in the militia when we went up in arms back in 1994 and I fought with the troops of the First Zapatista Infantry Regiment, under the command of Sup Pedro, when we took Las Margaritas. Hell, I'd be sixty-one now, but I ain't, cause I'm dead, which means I'm deceased. I first met Sup Marcos back in 1992, when we voted to go to war. Then later I ran into him in 1994 and we were together when the federal troops chased us out in February of 1995. I was with him and Major Moses when they came at us with war tanks and helicopters and special forces and all, and yeah, it was tough, but as you can see, they didn't get us. We high-tailed it, as they say . . . although we spent a bunch of days hearing the *thwack-thwack-thwack* of them helicopter blades.

Okay, that's enough talking. All I wanted to do was introduce myself. I am Elías Contreras and I'm Investigation Commission. But I didn't used to be Investigation Commission; before I was just a supporter of the Zapatista National Liberation Army over here in Chiapas, which is in our country that's called Mexico. You wanna know where that is? Well, you can take a look at a map and you'll find it right over by the . . .

EZLN General Headquarters

High up on the trunk of a bayalte tree, a lonely toucan polishing his beak. Below, Lieutenant Hilario is checking to see if the horses have finished off the little corn patch, and Insurgent Martina is reviewing the list of state capitals. The guard detail is sitting in front of the little shack cleaning their weapons. On one side, tacked to a pole, the old black flag with the five-pointed star and the letters, *EZLN*. The star and the letters are a faded red. El Sup steps out of the door. The guards spring to attention.

"Call Lieutenant Colonel José," says El Sup. José arrives. El Sup hands him some papers. "This just came in."

After reading the papers, the lieutenant colonel asks, "What are you going to do?"

"I don't know," answers El Sup, both of them standing there thinking, as the toucan takes off in a flurry of flapping wings that draws their attention.

After a moment, they look at each other and say in a single voice: "Elías."

The last rays of sunlight are just fading away when the silhouetted figure of the lieutenant appears riding over the hilltop. He skirts the town, avoiding mud holes and stray glances, until he gets to where Adolfo has his post.

"The major?"

"He's in a meeting with the municipal authorities."

The lieutenant goes in to see him.

The major takes the papers and reads.

"Get hold of Elías," the lieutenant says, "and tell him to drop around he-knows-where to have a chat with the old man, tomorrow, if he can make it; if not, when he gets a chance. That's all."

Grabbing the radio, the major barks, "Lama gama. If you copy, tell the big eye to buy his telescope tomorrow, or whenever he can."

High up on a hill, the operator receives the message and relays, "Lovebird, Lovebird, if you copy, there's a forty for Elías, and Cloud says he's to go tomorrow."

In the town, the man in charge of the post relays to the CO, "They want you to get Elías and have him go to La Realidad tomorrow."

The sun has long since taken cover behind the rolling

hills when Elías shows up at the door of his shack, a bundle of pumpkins hanging from his head sling. In one hand he holds his *chimba*, and in the other . . .

The Machete

Yeah, El Sup didn't actually show me the paper, but he told me what it was all about. There was a disappearance. The message said that one of the women had disappeared and that El Sup should write up a paper blaming it on the bad government. Which is actually what El Sup is sposed to do, the problem being that the citizens, that is, the city folk, are already used to the Zapatistas telling them the truth, that is, that we don't lie to them. So like I said, the problem is that if El Sup writes his communiqué accusing the government and then it turns out that the woman ain't disappeared at all and the bad government didn't harm her, what happens is our word begins to look weak, and what happens is people stop believing us. So then, my job was to investigate to see if she really was disappeared or what, and then I was to report to El Sup what it was that happened so he could decide what to do.

I asked El Sup how much time I had and he said I had to do it in three days. I didn't ask why it was three days and not one, ten, or fifteen. That was for him to know. So I went to saddle up a mule, and that same afternoon I headed out for Entre Cerros, which is what they call the town where they had the disappearance of María—or the former María, cause what if she's deceased?—who is/was the wife of the local Zapatista rep in that town.

Soon as I got to the town I talked to the rep, whose name is Genaro and who is or was the husband of the deceased María. Well, she ain't deceased, not yet anyway. That's what we had to find out. So Genaro told me that she went out for firewood and that later, well, she didn't come back again. Didya look for her? Yes! Ya didn't find her? No! He said how if he'd found her he wouldn't've called Headquarters. That was three weeks ago. So why didn't he call then? Cause there was still a chance she'd turn up. So, did he know which way she headed? No! Maybe she was taken by the Army or the paramilitaries and she was already deceased. Who was going to make his *pozol* and his tortillas? And who was going to take care of the kids?

So I says goodbye to Genaro, thinking how he was more worried about who was going to do his cooking than about the deceased, or not, María, and thinking that what he was remembering was not that he loved her or nothing like that, but all the work she did around the house and all. Then I went down to the stream where the women did the washing and I ran into cousin Eulogia. She was with Heriberto, my godson, and she was washing something. I decided to talk to her cause she was naturally real nosey, and she told me that just before she disappeared, the deceased María, who wasn't really deceased yet, had quit going to the meetings of the Women for Dignity Cooperative just when they were fixing to name her to the bureau, and that she, Eulogia, had gone to see her, the alleged deceased, to ask why it was that she wasn't going to the meetings, and that she, María, answered, "Who's gonna make me?" and didn't say no more cause just then Genaro showed up and María shut up and just went on grinding corn. I asked if María could have got lost in the woods, and Eulogia went, "How's she gonna get lost when she knows every path and every trail?"

"So she didn't get lost," I says.

"No!" she says.

"So then what?" I says.

"You ask me, I think it was that demon with the hat—*El Sombrerón*—who hauled her away," she says.

"Shit, cousin, you're old enough to not be believing those stories about *El Sombrerón*."

"All I know is that things happen, cousin, like what happened to Ruperto's wife," Eulogia insisted.

"Ah, c'mon, cousin, that wasn't no *Sombrerón*. Don't you remember how they finally found her all cuddled up naked behind the fireplace?"

"That may be," Eulogia said, "but there's a whole lot of other *Sombrerón* stories I figure are true enough."

Well, right then I didn't have time to explain to cousin Eulogia how those stories about *El Sombrerón* were just that, stories, so I headed for the trail that lead up to where they go for firewood. I was just about leaving the town when I heard a voice behind me: "Is that Elías Contreras?"

And I turned to see who it was, and it was Comandante Tacho, who was just getting into town—to talk up the citizens, I think.

"So how're you, Tacho?" I said.

I wanted to hang around and chat with him about neoliberalism and globalization and all, but I remembered I only had three days to clear up the matter of the deceased María, so I bid him goodbye.

"I'll be moving along now," I said.

"Oh, so you're on a mission?"

"That's about it," I said.

"Go with God then, Don Elías" he said.

"And you, Don Tacho," I added and hit the trail.

As I was getting to the sunflower fields it started raining. I wasn't carrying nothing to keep the rain off, so I started hollering and cussing, which don't keep you dry, but it does warm you up a bit. I followed the firewood trail every which way and back again, cause the thing spreads out like the branches of a tree, but no matter how far I went up any one of them branches, I didn't find nothing to tell me what could have happened to the alleged deceased María. I went over by the stream and had my *pozol* sitting on a rock. Night falls hard and fast in the woods and although there was a big old moon, I had to use a light to get back to the trail. *So now what?* I asked myself, just staring like a dummy at the branches cut by a machete . . . machete . . .

Machete! That's it! There was no sign of the machete the alleged deceased María had used to cut firewood. And then I remembered that back at Genaro's I'd seen a machete by one of the piles of firewood stacked up against the side of the shack. There was a goodly amount of wood there, so why would the right now not-so-deceased María have gone out to chop more, seeing as how she already had plenty? And that was when I got to thinking that María had not been disappeared, but had disappeared herself. What I mean is that, like folks around here say, she just up and left.

So I got myself on the road and headed back to Entre Cerros. After a cup of coffee at cousin Eulogia's, I made myself as comfortable as I could on the grain bin to get some sleep. It turns out I didn't get much sleep, what with the drumming of the rain and the worrying about finding María. Now, when I don't sleep I get to thinking too much. Mara always scolds me for thinking too much, and I tell her there's no way to stop, that that's how they made me. So I went on thinking about what if María ain't deceased, what if she wasn't disappeared, what if she disappeared herself, and where could she have got to, and if she disappeared herself it musta been cause she didn't want to be appeared, so then she musta gone where nobody could appear her.

In the morning it was still raining, so I borrowed a nylon poncho from cousin Humberto. I left him the loaded mule and went to the local government at La Realidad.

Soon as I got there, I asked to talk to the head of the Good Governance Board. They took me first to the Vigilance Commission. Míster and Brusli were there. I told them I was on the Investigation Commission and that I needed to talk to the Good Governance Board. Then they sent me in. I asked the Board if they had information about the women's collectives in the towns. They handed me some lists. It took awhile, and I couldn't find anything I wanted in the lists, so I gave them back.

"So what is it you're looking for?" they asked.

"I don't know," I answered, cause it was the pure and simple truth. I didn't know what I was looking for, but if I found it, I'd know.

"Looks like you're all mixed up," the Board guys said.

"That's about right," I said.

"So you couldn't find what you were looking for?" they went on asking.

"That's right," I said.

"Well, that list has all the women's collectives," one of the Board guys told me.

"Yeah, all of them except a brand new one that's just getting started," another one added.

"Oh yeah, that one, but it's in a new region and it barely hasn't even started up yet. They don't even have an autonomous municipality, but the women are organizing their collective," the first one said.

"That's the way it is," the only female Board member said, "the women are the first to get organized, and if the fight is taking too long it's because of the men; their minds are too narrow." None of the men said anything.

I got the feeling that I was about to find what I didn't know I was looking for, so I asked, "Where is that collective that's just getting started?"

"It's over in the Ceiba region, in the town of Tres Cruces, along the Comitán road," the woman said.

Brusli loaned me his mare and I set out for Tres Cruces. Along the way it grew dark and the mare kept getting spooked at every shadow, so I put her up in a town along the way, but seeing as how the second day was running out, I walked it—fact of the matter is, I think I practically ran the rest of the way.

I got to Tres Cruces when the moon was halfway across the sky. I went to see the local headman and introduced myself. He went off for a while, I imagine to radio in and see if I was who I said I was, cause he came back real happy and even invited me to dinner. We had coffee and *guineo* bananas. When we got through I asked him how the work was going and he said it was fine, that the collective sometimes lost a bit of push, but that with a little political talking-to they perked right up again.

"The one that's getting along just fine is the women's collective, and it's that April who's providing the spark," the headman said.

"Who's this guy April?" I asked.

"Not a guy, but a gal," he answered.

I took another sip of coffee and waited on him. Soon the headman continued.

"April's a woman who came in about three weeks ago, said she was Women's Commission. We put her up at Doña Lucha's, seeing as how she's alone after Aram went deceased.

So that's where the April woman is living and I think she's got a good head on her, cause the other women in town really like her. Every week she comes in for the political work and stuff, and I think they already asked to have their collective registered with the Good Governance Board.

So I said goodbye to the headman and told him I was going to spend the night over at the church. Making believe it was just out of curiosity, I asked him where that Doña Lucha lived. He said it was on the outskirts of town facing the hill. So I left him, but instead of going to the church, I went right on. There was only one shack on the side of town by the hill, so I figgered that must be Doña Lucha's place. I stood around awhile waiting, but not for long. The door opened up and the first thing I saw was a shadow that by the light of the moon became a woman.

"Good evening to you, María," I said, stepping out from behind the water trough.

She sorta froze up a second, but then she bent over, picked up a rock, and looked me in the eye.

"Who says my name's María? My name's April."

I just stood there not saying a word, and thinking how any other woman would've gotten spooked and would've screamed or run away or both. This here one was ready to face down a stranger, though. A woman like that don't shut up when things aren't right. She don't stay with a man who treats her bad, either.

I kept my eyes glued to the hand with the rock and talked to her real slow: "My name is Elías; I'm Investigation Commission and I'm looking to find out what happened to a woman called María who disappeared from the town of Entre Cerros, and the thing is, her husband is real worried."

Still holding onto the rock, she asked, "Am I supposed to

know this town Entre Cerros or this María or her husband Genaro—"

Right there I butted in, "Now, I didn't say her husband's name was Genaro."

Well, I'm imagining she went pale, but I could barely make out her face so it was hard to tell if she actually changed color or not. Then, after a long silence, she picked up a stick with her free hand and said real slow, "Nobody's taking me where I don't want to go."

"Not my job to take anybody anywhere, ma'am, not by hook and not by crook. I'm just investigating." I turned around to take my leave but had hardly moved when I heard her voice.

"You like to come in and have something to eat? Doña Lucha made tamales."

After dinner, as María-April or maybe April-María told me her story, Doña Lucha offered me . . .

Some Coffee

"El Sup is right there waiting on you," said the insurgent combatant standing guard outside the command post, and sure enough, there was El Sup by the hitching post, smoking his pipe. He gimme a hug, offered me some coffee, and we sat down on a log. Lieutenant Colonel José was there as well. I told them the whole story. Cause the thing is, this María, who is actually April, her husband, who's called Genaro, mistreated her a lot, didn't let her participate, and was very jealous. And when Genaro, her husband, found out that they were going to name her to the Board of the Women's Collective, well, he even beat her. Then she took it up with the town assembly but they couldn't come to any decision, and things went on the way they were. Now, her children are all grown and all and don't really depend on her, and the Revolutionary Law on Women says she has the right to progress. And with every word she said, Doña Lucha kept nodding her head like saying she agreed, and she kept clenching her fists like she was real mad. And so April, who is María, got tired of being treated like a dog, but before disappearing herself she left a good stack of firewood for Genaro so he would never think she left cause she was lazy. She said that she had disappeared herself cause she couldn't take it no more. That the Revolutionary Law on Women says that she has a right to choose the man she wants to have—or if she wants to have one at all. That she left for Tres Cruces because she had already met Doña Lucha at a women's meeting and she knew she would back her up. That she knew it was wrong to have lied about being Women's Commission and all, but that's the only thing she could think of to get them to let her into town. That she changed her name and called herself April cause that was the month of women who fight. Now, I didn't mention that the month of women who fight is not April, but March, cause they were pretty mad right there and it might be better for somebody else to explain later on when they were a bit more settled down. And that April accepted that she should be punished for lying about being Women's Commission, but that she was not going back to be mistreated again, that she was a Zapatista and she was acting like one.

El Sup and the lieutenant colonel listened in silence, El Sup only refilling and lighting his pipe now and again.

When I finished reporting, he said, "Well, that's a surprise. I met that Genaro *compa* once at a meeting of headmen and he spoke very well, he sounded very Zapatista."

And I said, "Hey, Sup, you ever heard of anyone who

couldn't be a Zapatista for a little while?" El Sup moved his head like he was doing some thinking.

"So, how long does it take to become a Zapatista?" he asked as he was helping me saddle up the mule.

"Sometimes it takes more than 500 years," I said and hurried up to get going, cause my town is actually a ways off.

And the sun was hurrying along like there was something it was . . .

Missing

The sky bit off chunks of the darkness billowing among the treetops. Distracted by a flying cloud, El Sup chewed on his cold pipe stem.

"There's still a whole lot missing on the question of women," the lieutenant colonel said.

"Yeah, *missing*," said El Sup, putting the case documents into a thick folder that read, *Elías: Investigation Commission.*

Someone, very far away, received a sealed envelope on which the sender had written:

From the mountains of Southeast Mexico,
Insurgent Subcomandante Marcos
November 2004

CHAPTER 2
LEAVING AN IMPRINT

Were there more antennas or fewer? There were many more, he told himself. Many more television antennas. Many more than when? More than before, of course. And he let that *before* just linger. With every passing day, there were more *befores* in his conversations and in the thoughts that flitted through his mind; he was turning into a pre-retirement adult. But the fact was, he had that antenna thing nailed right. There were a whole lot more antennas than before, and they were part of the jungle canopy. The jungle of television antennas of Mexico City. The jungle of antennas and lampposts and buttresses that wove in with the trees, stretched over the rooftops, hung off lines, climbed up broomsticks: glorious, arrogant. The jungle of Mexico City, along with its mountains, the polluted Ajusco hills.

The afternoon was fading away; Belascoarán lit his final cigarette and gave himself the seven minutes it would last before leaving his perch. Over the last few months, he had begun to prefer seeing Mexico City from above. From the highest roofs and bridges he could find. It was less harmful that way, more like a city, just a single solid thing as far as the eye could see. He liked it and still likes it.

When he was about five and a half minutes into his cigarette, his office mate, Carlos Vargas the plumber, came whistling through the metal door that led to the roof. He was whistling that old Glen Miller piece that had become so famous at sweet-sixteen parties in Mexico City during the '60s. He was whistling in tune and with a great deal of precision to boot.

"You know, boss, I've got half a notion that these disappearances of yours up here on the roof might mean you've begun smoking grass on the sly. You've gone pothead, you're getting high and flying low."

"You're wrong and I'm going to show you," Belascoarán said, offering him the chewed-up butt of his filtered Delicado.

Carlos shook his head. "There's a progressive official looking for you."

"And what is a *progressive* official?"

"Same as the others, only they're not on the take, and this one's got a chocolate stain on his tie and a crippled dog."

Héctor Belascoarán Shayne, independent detective, accustomed to absurd enigmas because he lived in the most marvelously absurd city in the world, climbed down the seven stories asking himself what the hell a "crippled dog" might mean in upholsterer's crypto-language, only to find out that "crippled dog" meant a goddamn dog with a splint on one of its front legs, a timid face, and ears hanging to the ground. The animal was resting serene and sad at the feet of this progressive official. Carlos paid them no mind and was already back in his own corner of the office stuffing a pink-velvet easy chair.

Belascoarán dropped into his seat and the wheels carried him elegantly, until he hit the wall. He stared at the progressive official and raised his eyebrows, or rather his eyebrow—

ever since he had lost one of his eyes, he found it difficult to move the other eyebrow.

"Are you a leftist?" the official asked, and God only knows why, but Belascoarán did not find that icebreaker at all strange in these times when the nuns of the Inquisition were flying back on their broomsticks, conjured up by the administration of one Mr. Fox, who wasn't foxy at all.

He took a deep breath. "My brother says I'm a leftist, but a natural one, which means unawares," Héctor said, smiling. "And that means I'm a leftist but I never read Marx when I was sixteen and I never went to demonstrations to speak of and I don't have a poster of Che Guevara in my house. So, well, yes, I'm a leftist."

The explanation appeared to satisfy the official. "Can you guarantee that this conversation will remain confidential?"

"Well, if God knows it, why shouldn't the world?" answered Héctor, who hadn't guaranteed anything for a long time.

"Are you a believer?" the progressive asked, a bit taken aback.

"There's a friend of mine says he quit being Catholic for two reasons: one, because he thought that with so many poor people the Vatican treasures were a kick in humanity's balls; and two, because they don't let you smoke in church. And I imagine that goes for all religions. And I agree—the very idea of God annoys the shit out of me," Héctor wound up very seriously.

Taking advantage of the moment of silence, Héctor checked out the progressive official and found that, as opposed to what Carlos had said, the guy had no tie, although he did have a stain on his yellow shirt, a shaggy beard, and the glasses of the terminally short-sighted. He was tall, very tall, and when he got excited he shook his head sideways in a perpetual no. He looked like an honest man, the kind his mother used to call "a good person," referring always to workers, plumbers, milkmen, gardeners, and lottery hawkers. If memory didn't fail him, his mother had never said that any bourgeois, grand or petit, was "a good person." She must have had her reasons.

"There's a dead guy talking to me," the man said, breaking in on Héctor's mental evaluation of him and his past.

Héctor opted for silence. Just a couple of months before, he had gone to a video club and rented a series created by Alec Guinness based on a novel by le Carré, *Tinker, Tailor, Soldier, Spy,* produced by the BBC, and for six continuous hours he had watched in fascination as Smiley-Guinness used the most effective interrogation technique in the world: putting on a stupid face (if the guy weren't British, Héctor would say he was the biggest jerk he'd ever seen) and staring at people languidly, not too interested, like he was doing them a favor, and people would just talk and talk to him, and once in a while, a *long* while, he would drop a question, as if not really caring much, just to make conversation.

And the method worked.

"For about a week now I've been hearing messages on my answering machine from a buddy of mine, only this buddy died in 1969. He was murdered. And now he's talking to me, leaving me messages. He tells me stories. But I don't rightly know what it is he wants from me. And I think he's calling when he knows I'm not home so he can just leave a recording. Maybe it's a joke, but if it is, it's a hell of a joke."

Héctor kept up his Alec Guinness face.

"My name's Héctor," the man said.

"So's mine," Belascoarán replied, kind of apologizing.

"Héctor Monteverde."

"How about the dead guy?"

"His name's Jesús María Alvarado, and he was really something."

Héctor went back into silent mode.

"So, how much do you charge?"

"Not much," Belascoarán said.

That appeared to quiet the man down . . . the dog too.

"Here's the tape. You can listen to the whole thing in five minutes. You decide and we'll talk later."

"I don't have an answering machine in this office. If you can lend the tape to me, tomorrow we can—"

"No! Not tomorrow. In a while. Take my address," Monteverde said, handing over a piece of paper. "And here are some notes I prepared about how I met the dead man. I'll be at home . . . I don't sleep."

"I don't either," Héctor said.

And he watched as same-name Monteverde stood up and left the office, followed by his limping dog.

"That's one hell of a story!" said Carlos Vargas with a mouthful of tacks, shaking his hammer over the pink easy chair.

"The phrase that comes to mind is the one about reality getting extremely strange," Belascoarán answered.

Hours later, sitting at home, Héctor listened to the voice of the dead man coming from the tape.

"Hello. I am Jesús María Alvarado. I'll call you back, buddy."

The voice did not sound familiar; it was gravelly and didn't reveal any anxiety, urgency . . . nothing. Just a toneless voice offering a name. It was not cavernous or put through special effects; it wasn't intended to sound like a voice from the grave. What's a voice from the grave supposed to sound like? This talking to dead people . . .

Yet Jesús María Alvarado was indeed dead, although not in 1969 like the progressive official Monteverde said, but in '71. So it was prehistoric, thirty-four years ago. He had been murdered as he left prison. A bullet in the back of the head for the first political prisoner to be freed after the 1968 movement. Execution-style . . . and no official explanations.

Monteverde and Alvarado had met at a school where they both taught literature. They were just nodding acquaintances. A couple of coffees together, a couple of faculty meetings. The 1968 assemblies, the founding of the coalition of teachers in support of the student movement. Monteverde was a little absent-minded, lovesick, a bit timid . . . the son of an undertaker who had made his fortune on the luxury of death, something that Héctor Monteverde (according to his meticulously drafted notes) thought was not only immoral, but thoroughly shameful and reprehensible in the year of the movement. World literature was the antidote to the funeral parlors. Alvarado was the child of peasants who had come to literature through some incomprehensible conception of patriotism, and by the sheer force of rote repetition of "Suave Patria" and the memorization of verses by Díaz Mirón, Gutiérrez Nájera, and Sor Juana, for recitation to the town people. Forever poverty stricken, he couldn't even afford to have his clothes washed at the end of each month, his tab at the corner store was overflowing, and he was filled with anger.

Apparently, during those magical and terrible years, Héctor Monteverde had followed the life of Alvarado from a distance, up until the man was murdered.

Héctor figured that he had to think the matter through

calmly; he put aside the answering machine and the peach juice he had been drinking, and climbed back up to the roof with a packet of letters he had found in his mailbox. With infinite patience he set out to make paper airplanes and place them in a row along the parapet around the roof. Down on the street, the new day's noise was just getting started in Condesa, the bikers, the teenagers having fun.

There was the slightest of breezes, and every once in a while it managed to blow one of the paper planes off the parapet, sending it into marvelous acrobatics before crashing to the ground. But very rarely did one succeed in floating away on the updraft. When the planes were all gone, he returned to his room. He had left all the lights on, the best antidote to loneliness, turning the damn house into a Christmas tree. He rewound the answering-machine tape. What he heard was what he had heard, and the voice said again, *"Hello. I am Jesús María Alvarado. I'll call you back, buddy."*

Another Jesús María Alvarado, the son of Jesús María Alvarado, the ghost of Jesús María Alvarado, an alter ego of Jesús María Alvarado with the same name, some table-dancer trying to attract attention, the police trying to drive Monteverde nuts for reasons known only to themselves, he summarized.

The second call was even better:

Listen, man, this is Jesús María Alvarado. I hope you've got a long tape, cause I have to tell you what happened to me. It's a really rat-shit story, crazy. There I was in Juárez, in a bar, and since all the tables were taken I just stood around drinking my beer and watching the goddamn TV. The noise was a pisser and I couldn't hear a thing, but there was bin Laden, with his stony expression, in one of those communiqués he keeps sending out over the TV. This guy's a real pain in my balls, so I wasn't listening much, but then a couple of guys behind me started hollering something like, "Das Juancho, das freekin Juancho!" So I turn around to see what was up with this freekin Juancho and there were these two half-drunk muscle-bound studs going on with their mantra: "Das goddam Juancho, Juancho!" pointing at the TV. I flipped around to make sure I wasn't the one who was nuts, as usual, but it was still bin Laden, all elegant with a field rifle in his hand and the rag around his head and that dopey face of his. So I flipped around again to talk to the Juancho fan club. "What's with this fuckin Juancho?" I says, and them, half slurring because of the booze, they tell me that there on the TV was none other than their buddy Juancho, and just lookit how the prick had done himself up. And I kinda found out that Juancho ran with these guys, he had been a taco vendor in Juárez and got tired of his crappy life about three years ago and wetbacked it over to open a butcher shop in Burbank, California. Me, I couldn't make heads or tails of the whole thing, so I turn to the TV again and, sure enough, the sonovabitch was still there, so I went to ask the two drunks what else they knew about Juancho, and were they sure it was him, and when had he grown that shitty beard, but the guys had disappeared, gone, nada. *I searched the bar and the sidewalk and all, but there was no sign of them. And I says to myself,* Now ain't that a pisser. Bin Laden's alter ego is a taco vendor from Juárez. *But then I started getting it all together and I says,* Alvarado, what do you know about Burbank? *And the thing is, I do know something about Burbank. It's the skin-flick capital of the United States, a shit town near Los Angeles, triple-X companies and motels . . . Fuck, fuck, film, film, long live savage capitalism! And I put*

> *two and two together, and I ask myself, like, what if it was the Bushes who've been making the bin Laden communiqués, those messages from hell, in a porno studio in Burbank, California, where they even have all the desert you might want? What if they concocted the whole thing? What if it's all a dream factory starring a Mexican taco vendor by the name of Juancho? But to tell the truth, even I couldn't believe that crock, and I kept telling myself,* You can't be serious . . . *But it does make a cool story, doesn't it?"*

Héctor turned off the machine. He went into the bathroom, looked in the mirror, and splashed cold water on his face. Like a lot of people who live alone, he was in the habit of talking to his mirror persona, but now he couldn't think of anything to tell himself. He thought it over again and broke out into roaring laughter. Kafka swimming in his briefs in Xochimilco. Bin Laden played by Juancho in Burbank. And, of course, when he wasn't doing communiqués, like Alvarado said, Juancho spent his free time fucking on film and getting paid for it. A free version of *A Thousand and One Nights*, as told in a taco emporium in Juárez: crazy but funny, the dumbest prick on the border.

The third tape started as always—"*This is Jesús María Alvarado*"—like he was trying over and over again to establish that he had come back from the valley of the shadow of death. After the name, there was a pause and a cryptic comment, "*Maybe I shouldn't have come back,*" and then a long silence and a click that put an end to the call.

There was a fourth call that started off with the usual, "*This is Jesús María Alvarado,*" then without a word of explanation went into some verses:

Where I will only be
a memory of a stone buried under briar
over which the wind flees its sleepless night.

And that was all. The poem sounded familiar, but Héctor couldn't remember where or when he had heard it.

The progressive Monteverde lived in the Roma Sur neighborhood about twelve blocks from his home, so Héctor decided to take a walk, strolling along the promenade on Alfonso Reyes Avenue, which was better when it was Juanacatlán and lined with unionized whores or those hoping to join. He stopped at one of the taco joints to have a couple of cheese *arracheras* with lots of green salsa, then went on his way, smiling to strangers, every once in a while saying good evening just to see how the well-mannered Mexicans of the capital would recover their basic manners and reply.

The character seemed to live alone. Alone except for the dog with the splint, which, just as Belascoarán passed through the doorway, came over and licked his hand, either to identify him or simply to express solidarity between two cripples. There was no sign of children in the house, no pictures, but the walls were covered with reproductions of paintings of mountains and volcanoes, from a Velasco to Atl's *Paricutin,* and rather attractive photographs of Everest in the style of *National Geographic*.

Monteverde was wearing the same chocolate-stained shirt from a few hours earlier. Héctor asked to use the bathroom, which was pristine, spotless. In his free time, Monteverde must be a detergent and Windex freak. A touch of incongruent humor among such hygienic fundamentalism moved him: On one of the walls there was a poster that read,

Constipation Promotes Reading. Héctor decided he had to get one of those for his own home. The idea wasn't new and he wasn't constipated, but it was another good excuse to read in the john.

The floor in the hallway was filled with books for lack of bookshelves. Monteverde had arranged them on their sides so that all you had to do was bend over slightly to pick one up. Héctor recognized many of his own favorites: Remarque, Fast, Haefs, Ross Thomas, Neruda, Hemingway, Cortázar. They were all there.

"So tell me it ain't strange, man."

He didn't answer, but he figured he would have to give the Alec Guinness method a rest. It was time for questions. He dropped into a rat-gray rocker, and before Monteverde could do likewise, he blurted out, "Did you recognize the voice?"

"No, but you can't tell. It's been so many years."

"Were you guys friends? Friends enough that if he were alive he would—"

"I went to his funeral. He's dead. I saw him lying there dead in his coffin, with a patch that you could see sticking out from the back of his head where they had shot him," Monteverde interrupted.

"Were you good friends?"

"Just friends. He was always raring to go about everything. I was more timid. But there we were, in the movement, teaching literature in the preps, and we had a sort of a girlfriend, him first, then me, and we only ate street food, the cheapest we could find."

The bit about teaching literature in the preps reminded Belascoarán of the poem, which he began to recite:

Where I will only be
a memory of a stone buried under briar
over which the wind flees its sleepless night.

"*Where forgetfulness may dwell/in the vast dawnless gardens/where I will be . . .*" Monteverde added.

"Of course, the Cernuda poem, I thought it sounded familiar, but I couldn't . . ." Belascoarán paused, slapping his hands together to applaud his own memory.

"A marvelous poem," Monteverde said, and resumed:

Where sorrow and fortune will be only words,
a native sky and land enveloping a memory;
where I will finally be free without even knowing it,
dissolved in a mist, an absence,
an absence soft as the flesh of a child.

"*There, far away; where forgetfulness may dwell,*" they finished in unison.

Now *that* was a real poem, one of those that grabs you by the nuts and squeezes softly until the pain becomes an idea. That was one hell of a poet, the old Spaniard exiled in Mexico. Héctor lit a cigarette; he used the moment to organize his ideas, while the dog, who must have been nervous about secondhand smoke, limped to a safe distance.

"That one scared me more than the other messages; it was Jesús María's favorite poem—he would recite it for his students every so often. I wound up doing the same because of him."

Héctor lit up another with the butt of the prior; the dog didn't protest.

"Why would Alvarado, Alvarado's ghost, or someone trying to pass himself off as Alvarado, be sending you these messages? Who are you, Monteverde? What do you do for a living?"

"I work for the government in Mexico City. I'm a special investigator for the Department of Oversight. It's kind of a delicate job, particularly these days, that's why I freaked. Otherwise I would have laughed it off. You can't imagine, recently things have become very murky . . ."

"What are you working on now?"

"I'm sorry, that's confidential, and furthermore it doesn't seem to have anything to do with the dead guy's calls. I sound like some half-baked Charlie Chan," Monteverde concluded with a smile, "don't I? But the fact is, it's delicate, what with all the goddamn corruption they had during the PRI administrations and the shit those bastards left us."

"And are *you* corrupt? Forgive me for asking, but since we don't actually know each other . . ."

Monteverde squeezed out a sad smile. "You can only buy what's up for sale. Me? I'm made of steel, friend, stainless steel, incorruptible, a bit of a jerk and very far to the left. I don't insult our dead."

The sad expression was becoming something else and there were a few sparks in his eyes. Even the dog seemed to respond and lifted his head.

"So, are *you* for sale?" he asked the detective.

"My friend, I don't want to wake up one of these days with my mouth full of ants. Me, I bend but I don't go down," Belascoarán answered, tapping his knee where he had a steel spike implanted that set off every metal detector in every airport around the world. "Who have you told about this?"

"Only Tobías," Monteverde said, pointing to the dog.

"And the bin Laden story, do you believe that?"

"No. But it's a hell of a story. I'm just sorry I didn't come up with it myself."

Belascoarán returned to the Alec Guinness routine, but it didn't work. Monteverde was off thinking about something far, far away.

"How about you, when did you become an insomniac?" the detective finally asked.

"When we lost the elections in '88, the day the system crashed, the election fraud. For some reason I got the idea in my head that during the night they were going to come and kill us all . . . How about you?"

"It was a few months ago. One night the woman who sometimes comes over to sleep with me didn't show up, but I waited all night for her, and now I don't sleep," the detective answered, a little embarrassed. His own explanation couldn't stand up to Monteverde's; his insomnia paled in comparison to the historic insomnia of the literature-teacher-turned-progressive-official. "Who gave you my number? Who suggested that you contact me?"

"We have a common acquaintance working in the office of Cuauhtémoc Cárdenas; his name's Mario Marrufo Larrea. I told him I had some really weird things going on and he said you specialized in weird things."

"Well, I ain't the only one in Mexico."

And they celebrated by downing a couple of Cokes, Belascoarán's with no ice.

It's already becoming a cliché, this notion of being tied to the city by an umbilical cord, trapped in a love-hate relationship. The sleepless Belascoarán was looking out his window on the neon night and reviewing his own words. He was feeling like the last of the Mohicans. He averred, confirmed: There is no hatred. Just an immense, infinite sensation of love for this ever-changing city that he lives in and that lives in him, that he dreams of and that dreams of him. A determination to love that goes beyond all the rage, possession, and sex, and dissolves into tenderness. It must be the demonstrations, the golden hue of the light at the Zócalo, the book stands, the meat tacos, the currents of deep solidarity, the friends at the gas station across the way who always say hello when he passes. It might be that marvelous winter moon. It might be.

Héctor sat in a rocker to smoke. He spent the night smoking and listening to the sounds of the street. For no apparent reason, the image of Héctor Monteverde's limping dog came to mind. It was dawn when he fell asleep.

CHAPTER 3

WHICH IS A LITTLE LONG

. . . cause all of a sudden it tells about the Broken Calendar Club; it explains how Elías solved the case of the woodpecker; it addresses the dangers of ignoring customs and mores; it warns that the dead have no company; and it relates how Elías traveled and arrived in Mexico City, with all the marvelous adventures that befell him, besides reflecting on the Bad and the Evil.

I'm not the murderer— *A match burned, lighting up a cigarette and the face surrounding it: haircut like a skinhead, face with shining eyes, silver rings, unshaven cheeks.* I think I should explain this right now to avoid confusion.

Neither am I the butler. I suppose I should say this right at the beginning, because, you know, in mystery stories the murderer is the butler . . . or the other way around. I've never been a housekeeper, but I have been a goalkeeper, and I sometimes played that position in the soccer games at the local government in La Garrucha. In the beginning I didn't know what was going on, but every Sunday, after praying at church, there was a big noise among the children and a lot of talking in Tzeltal among the adults. I only understood the part about "Zapatista campamenteros," and then everyone went out on the playing field. Though it's not really a playing field. From Monday through Friday it's the paddock, but on Sundays it's the soccer field. As if they knew it was Sunday, the cows would move to the neighboring field, leaving us a minefield of cow shit. Then some people from the town would come carrying pews from the church and benches from the school and improvise the grandstands. The field we used is on the side of a hill so one goal is higher than the other, which is an obvious advantage for the team that plays on the high side. However, in the second half they change goals and everything evens out. Or so they say. Then the teams are organized; a town person, always someone in authority, is referee. I was saying that sometimes I was a goalkeeper for the "campamenteros" team, as the town people say, or the "campamentistas team," as we say. Basically, men and women from different parts of the world were in a peace camp—we joined together in a soccer team and we played against the Zapatista towns. When I played we almost always lost. But don't you believe that it was because the Zapatistas were so good, no. It was a breakdown in communication. We used to shout at each other (cause the team was always mixed, men and women) in French, Euskera, Italian, English, German, Turkish, Danish, Swedish, and Aymara. Nobody understood nothing and, like they say around here, it was an unholy mess and the ball always went where it shouldn't.

In that soccer thing I learned what those Zapatistas call "the resistance." At least I think I did. What happened was that in one of the games our side had two huge Danes, about six-foot-six and terribly good at soccer. Their height, plus their extra-long strides, left the Zapatistas far behind, cause they're smaller and have shorter legs. Within the first few minutes it was obvious that our patent superiority would soon be reflected on the scoreboard. And fact of the matter is, after about ten minutes we were ahead two to zero. It was then that it happened. I saw it because I was the goalkeeper and because, furthermore, around here I learned to pay a lot of attention to things beyond the obvious. There was no indication from anyone, no meeting, no conversations, signals, or looks among the Zapatistas. And yet I think they had a way of communicating, because after our second score all the Zapatistas moved back to defend their goal. They left the whole field to our huge Danes, who were happily rushing back and forth. But with all those people on the Zapatista side, the field became a mudhole. The ball would stick, like in cement, and you needed several internationalist kicks to even make it roll.

They're going to stall, I thought, *so they don't get stomped,* and I sat back to watch the game, which was on the far side the whole time. A few minutes went by and then what happened, happened. Our team, which was doing all the running around, began to show signs of fatigue. In the second half it was evident that we were getting bogged down. Our Danish stars were gasping for air, stopping to breathe every two or three steps. And then—again without any overt signal—*wham,* the whole Zapatista team hit me. They scored seven goals in twenty minutes and the spectators went wild, cause you know they were all rooting for the local team. The game ended seven to two, and half of our team took an hour to recover and three weeks before they could walk right.

So I been a goalkeeper but I'm not the doorkeeper and I'm not the murderer. As you probably guessed, I'm a campamentista, and I'm from another country. I've been in peace camps in five autonomous municipalities, even before they were called *caracoles*, and in a few other communities that suffered militarization or paramilitarization. You might be asking me what exactly a foreign campamentista is doing in this mystery novel. Actually, that's what I keep asking myself,

I can't really help you out with that. While we check out what's going on, I can tell you a bit about myself. Maybe that way we can, together, figure out what the hell I'm doing in this book.

The Broken Calendar Club

I'm a Filipino and my name is Juli@ and my last name is Isileko. Somebody once told me that Isileko means *secret* in Euskera. I'm a mechanic and I work in an auto repair shop in Barcelona. I write my name with an @: Juli@. I write it that way because . . . . Do I really have to say I'm gay? Okay, yes, I'm gay, homosexual, queer, fruit, queen, faggot, or however it is you call us in your own world. But actually, I don't think I should mention it because then they associate *homosexual* with *criminal*. So. Maybe we should leave out sexual preference altogether and stick with the fact that I'm from the Philippines, that I have a Basque name, that I'm a mechanic in Barcelona, Spain, and amateur goalkeeper in Chiapas, Mexico . . . And in my home town they call me Julio.

For more information, I got a skinhead haircut and a few tattoos. On my back, between my shoulder blades, I have a notice tattooed in gothic letters that says, *THIS SIDE BACK*, and one on my chest that says, *THIS SIDE FORWARD*. That's just in case they cut me up in pieces. I have another one somewhat below my belly button that says, *HANDLE WITH CARE*, with an arrow pointing to my dick. I have another on my butt saying, *NO RETURNS*. I'm also a ringer, which means I have piercings and I wear earrings, but not too many: one on my left eyebrow, two in my right ear, three in my left ear, one in my nose, one each on my nipples, and . . . that's it.

I came to Zapatista country because I got tired of reading

communiqués. Yes, I began to get interested in the Zapatista movement because I read about it in a book by Manuel Vázquez Montalbán. It's not as if I was personally acquainted with the author, it's just that once I was working on a car and I found this book in the backseat. After reading it, I asked one of my buddies in the shop if he knew anything about the Zapatistas in Chiapas. He said he didn't, but that there was this café near his house where some young guys used to get together, some of the ringers like me, to try to raise support for those Zapatistas. So I went; I got some books and some website addresses where I could find the communiqués, and I read all of them, until I finally came over to Chiapas. I got tired of reading because I could tell that they were only fragments of a bigger story, as if they only gave me a few pieces of a jigsaw puzzle and hid others, the most important ones. Yes, I got angry at El Sup without actually knowing him. I began to ask myself why they mentioned certain things and not others. What right did that guy in the ski mask have to only show me some things and hide the rest? I had to go over there, I thought.

So I quit going to the professional soccer matches—Barcelona wasn't doing so hot, anyway. That's how I got a few dollars together. So I came over. I was right and I was wrong. I learned that the Zapatista messages do tell certain things and hide others—the biggest, the most terrible, the most marvelous. I learned that they are not trying to fool people, but rather to invite them . . .

Just a moment. Give me a second here . . .

Okay, I've just been informed that I'm not in this novel, so it's probably just an unfortunate mistake that the newspaper or the publishing house will have to sort out, or so I'm told. Since its likely that this is going to take awhile, I'll use the time to tell you about some people I met at La Realidad Peace Camp, and about how I met Elías.

Another flame lights another cigarette.

Want one? You don't smoke? In this novel everybody smokes. Belascoarán smokes, Elías smokes, I smoke, El Sup, well, what can I tell you? They should attach a fire extinguisher to each copy and announce on the cover: *Tobacco may be harmful to your health*, or, *Smoking during pregnancy may increase the risk of premature delivery and low birth weight*, or any of those things they write on the cigarette packages that nobody reads. That way, even if the book doesn't win a literary award, at least it will get one from the *Society of Active Nonsmokers*, if there is any such society.

So then. In the camps I've met people from many countries, although not many from Mexico. Some stay only a short time and others stay for years. Of course, there are those that come and go, like that Juanita Dot Com who comes from I don't know what country or even if his name is what he says it is, the only certain thing being that he has a website. Every time that guy comes, he brings a stack of magazines and newspapers and leaves carrying no more than a smile. So what I'm saying is that although we're from different countries with different languages and most of us differ on our take on Zapataism, all of us campamentistas develop close, more or less stable bonds of camaraderie. In fact, I had a close fraternal relationship with three campamentistas. Together we founded what we called the Broken Calendar Club, which might have been a good name for a mystery novel or a secret esoteric society, or for a group of unemployed *Playboy* bunnies, but it was a group of people who called ourselves this for reasons I will now explain.

The Broken Calendar Club includes a German woman

who worked for a pizza joint delivering food on a motorcycle to raise the money to make the trip over here. I don't think it's necessary to mention that she's a lesbian, for the same reason I gave earlier, but what I *can* tell you is that her name is Danna May and her last name is Bí Mát, which is a Vietnamese name that means *clandestine*. Danna May plays defense on our soccer team and she came to Zapatista lands on something like a honeymoon with her friend, a woman with a doctorate in mathematics, who is not here right now because she went back to Berlin to raise more money to prolong their stay here in Chiapas. In town they call Danna May "May."

There's also a French woman, a school teacher from Toulouse, whose name is Juin Hélène and whose last name is Protuzakonitost, which means *outlaw* in Serbo-Croatian. Juin Hélène loves jazz; she says her life is like a piece by Miles Davis, and she came, she says, to learn about this autonomy thing, because on her return to France she intends to get together with her pupils and start an autonomous rebel municipality and name it after Charlie Parker. Juin's job on our team is to be a deterrent, because of her precise kicks—not at the ball, but at the other team's ankles. In town she's known as Blondie or Frenchie.

Our fourth element is an Italian, a cook by trade, whose name is Vittorio Francesco Augusto Luiggi and whose last name's Nidalote, which in Albanian means *forbidden*. He's a firm believer in extraterrestrials, and according to what he told us one night in the forests of Chiapas, there are good extraterrestrials and bad extraterrestrials. The bad ones already landed a long time ago in Washington, London, Rome, Madrid, Moscow, and Mexico, and they took over everything and started the fast-food craze. The good ones, well, the good ones haven't arrived yet, but if there's any place where they are going to land, it will be on Zapatista soil. And they won't be coming to conquer us or teach us their high technology, but how to defeat the bad ones. Vittorio Francesco Augusto Luiggi figures that the good extraterrestrials are going to need a cook, and that's why he's here. Vittorio Francesco Augusto Luiggi plays left end on our team because he says you have to be consistent with your political positions, even in sports. In town they call him Panchito, something for which he, and all of us, are thankful.

So that's it. We're what you might call an *original* group, and if we Zapatify our names you get: May Clandestine, June Outlaw, July Secret, and August Forbidden. So we have perfect names for characters in a porn novel, or a spy novel, or a porn-spy novel, but not a mystery novel. And even if we add the April from the first chapter, the calendar is still incomplete, broken.

Don't pay me too much mind now. Maybe El Sup put us in the novel like a random sampling of people—because the Zapatistas, you know, maintain that the world is not unique, that there are multiple worlds, and that's why they're sticking the book with a gay Filipino mechanic, a German pizza-delivering bike dyke, a jazz-loving French teacher, and an Italian cook who believes in extraterrestrials. So it's not just men and women, and it's possible that later on we might even get a few more odd characters.

Although, actually, I think the Italian cook is only in the book because in mystery novels the detective usually winds up having culinary adventures. The other day, for example, I found Vittorio Francesco Augusto Luiggi (August Forbidden in our broken calendar) trying out a recipe that he said El Sup had given him. It was called Marcos's Special and he did it up just the way they told him: mince and fry one ration of beef; add a small can of Mexican salsa and cheese; mix thoroughly and serve hot.

When August Forbidden finished his concoction, I told him, "It looks like dog barf."

Then he tasted it himself and added, "It tastes the same as it looks."

But August is one of those people who believes the Zapatistas are never wrong, so he claimed the problem was that the salsa brand he used was Herdez and "El Sup actually told me it had to be La Costeña."

In any case, begging the pardon of Pepe Carvalho and Manuel Vázquez Montalbán, the fare in this novel is not going to be all that good. And now that I have discussed eating, give me a second so I can go to the john.

Elías and the Case of the Woodpecker

A dummy, because aside from being a woodpecker, the bird was a dummy, like you're gonna see from what I'm gonna tell you.

Okay, the thing is, they sent me on an Investigation Commission to the Morelia *caracol* (you remember that's what they call the autonomous municipalities) in the Tzots Choj region, and the thing, or rather the *case*, was a man who had been deceased by some guys who said they weren't the ones who deceased him. The Good Governance Board from those parts had sent a request for assistance to the EZLN Staff Headquarters. El Sup wasn't there but they told him over the radio, and then they told me that he told them to send me. The local officer in charge at La Realidad gave me some money for the trip, some toast, a ball of *pozol*, and some papers. I read one of them:

WRIT OF REMOVAL

Nich Teel Community, Olga Isabel Autonomous Zapatista Rebel Municipality, Chiapas, June 25, 2004.

I, Pedro Sántis Estrada, Autonomous Municipal Honor and Justice Commission, 9:25 p.m., do hereby submit the following description of the removal of the body:

1. That the deceased is Francisco Hernández Solís, thirty-eight years of age, joined in common law marriage, father of nine.

2. That on the 25th day of June of 2004, the deceased left home to work at his milpa at 6 a.m. in the so-called Ba Wits, at a distance of five kilometers from his home.

3. That at 13:00 hours (1:00 in the afternoon) he was returning, together with his younger brother Santiago Hernández Solís, twenty-one years of age, accompanied by his son Pedro Hernández, ten years of age, and when he was 300 meters from his milpa, Francisco Hernández Solís was ambushed and shot from a distance of two meters, four shots having been fired from a .22 caliber automatic weapon.

4. That two of the shots entered the same hole on the right side of his chest, another more to the center, and yet another in the right buttock.

5. That from the place where he was ambushed he ran forty-eight meters, shouting the names of the ones who shot him, and he was able to show his comrade the places in his body where the bullets had entered, and there he dropped dead: on his back, facing south, his eyes open, with his right hand on his chest and his left hand and his feet stiff.

Personal Information: The deceased, Francisco Hernández Solís, was carrying half a sack of corn, a machete, a sharpening file in his belt, a backpack, and wearing a white-striped shirt, white denim pants, black belt, and rubber boots; he had straight black hair, thick eyebrows, dark eyes, large nose, black mustache, round face with a dark complexion, large ears, and he was 1.6 meters tall.

THIS WRIT OF REMOVAL IS HEREBY CLOSED ON THE AFOREMENTIONED DATE.

Pedro Sántis Estrada
Honor and Justice Commission

So I left for the Moisés Gandhi community, where I was met by the Tzots Choj Good Governance Board. Soon as I got to Morelia, which is where the *caracol* is, I got together with the autonomous authorities of the Ernesto Che Guevara and Olga Isabel ZARCs (Zapatista Autonomous Rebel Communities).

They reported that on the day of the murder, they arrested two people who had quarreled with the deceased, and that the quarrels were about a parcel of land, a coffee plantation, and firewood. That the quarrels had started long before. That the two individuals arrested, the alleged perpetrators, were named Sebastián Pérez Moreno and Fausto Pérez Gómez. That those were the names the deceased had shouted when he wasn't yet deceased. That they claimed it wasn't them, that is, that the arrested alleged perpetrators claimed it wasn't them that were the killers of the deceased. That they had gone to work in their coffee plantation on their own property. That they were carrying hunting weapons in case they ran across some animal. That they saw a woodpecker out in the bush. That they fired four shots at it and missed. That later they went home because of the heat. That it was there they found out about the deceased.

I asked them to take me to the place where everything happened. They took me, but it was already late so we just had some coffee and bread. They put me up in the community school. The next day, real early, we went to the place. I looked around where the deceased was killed—that is, I examined the terrain. Just bush on one side and pasture on the other. There were a few hills and tall trees close to the coffee plantations. I followed the steps of the deceased to the place where he finally died. I also checked out the whole way where the alleged perpetrators claim they walked.

Something wasn't right and I couldn't find what I was looking for, so I kept on looking without really knowing what I was looking for, but thinking that when I did find it, I'd know. We had some *pozol* when it was getting late. I asked the guys with me if on the day of the tragedy it rained. Yeah, they said, it rained a whole lot, the whole damn day, matter of fact, didn't stop till night. I stood there thinking it over for a long time. Then I saw that I was not going to find what it was I was looking for—that is, that I was looking *not* to find what I was looking for. The other guys said my head wasn't right just then, and I said they got that right.

So we headed back. I went to see the authorities and told them that I didn't find what I went to find and that's why the alleged perpetrators wasn't alleged no more, cause they did it. The authorities also said my head wasn't quite right. Bout that time I was figgering I should get myself a bunch of cards saying, *You got that right,* so I wouldn't have to be saying it all the time. But since I didn't have the cards saying *You got that right,* I told the authorities that they got that right, but that the thing was, I didn't find the woodpecker. And so what? says the authorities. It probably went deceased like the deceased. So I told them that the woodpecker was a dummy who went out pecking when it was raining, in an *acahual* where there was no trees to peck at, and it just hung around when they fired four shots at it—or maybe there wasn't no woodpecker. So how about there wasn't no woodpecker? the authorities say. So how about that? I says. So without any real knowledge of the fact, but sposing there was no woodpecker, then what were they shooting at? So I says that's what I says, but without that lawyer talk, and it's real clear that they was telling a lie, I said again. So how about there's someone else in this business? I says again. So they says they're gonna check it out, and I says I'm going for a swim in the river because I picked up a bunch of burrs in the *acahual.* Goddamn burrs get into everything, I thought, but didn't say it out loud. So I went to the co-op store for some cigarettes. What kind? the guy says. Gratos, I says. Ya want them with menthol? he says. Do I look like I want candy? I says. And later that night, they came to tell me that the authorities arrested another suspect by the name of Pascual Pérez Silvano, sixteen years of age, single, living with his family. That he came clean on the facts. That they were already taking the statement from the accused. And later they brought me the . . .

PRELIMINARY PUBLIC STATEMENT

Pascual Pérez Silvano states clearly that his actions were done together with the other perpetrators. At the crossroads he ran into Fausto and Sebastián, who were carrying .22 caliber weapons and a 16-gauge pump action, and he was invited to go hunting but didn't accept because he had to pick up some corn.

"In the end I agreed to go with them and we took the road to Corostik, then the road to Mustaja, and down to Xaxajatik, and I was already tired and we hadn't found anything. I told them I couldn't go on walking and Sebastián told me I'm not a man if I can't keep walking, so we kept walking until we got to a place where there were no roads, and I decided to stay there and he started telling me that if you say something ahead of time I'll shoot you. I just stayed back about fifteen meters and they reached the road to the milpa, and I didn't see where they went and started firing their weapons. I ran off cause I was afraid and I didn't know what they were gonna do. There was a few shots—if they had told me I wouldn't a gone with them. Then I ran off alone back down the same path we found, but I didn't see Fausto and Sebastián. I had to search around awhile to find the path that goes to my milpa to pick the corn, but I was so scared I couldn't fill my sack, and I came home as soon as I could, and I didn't tell my family. After a while, when they began talking about how somebody got killed on the road and that it was Señor Francisco Hernández Solís, I got to thinking that it was them that did the shooting on the road, cause I didn't know nothing about it, I didn't even see what they shot at. So people started getting ready to go see him, and far as I know he didn't do anything."

Fausto and Sebastián couldn't say nothing, they were just looking in their friend's eye because of the statement Pascual Pérez Silvano had given. And finally they admitted that it was them that were responsible for the murder of Francisco Hernández Solís.

THERE BEING NO OTHER BUSINESS, THE PRESENT PRELIMINARY INVESTIGATION REPORT IS CONCLUDED.

Pedro Sántis Estrada
Honor and Justice Commission

The next day they told me I was going back to La Realidad. They thanked me and gave me travel money, some toast, and *pozol* to eat along the way.

It was raining. The cigarettes got all wet. Right there in Cuxuljá I caught a ride to Altamirano and from there to Las Margaritas. I got to La Realidad real late, it was night already. At Max's house they had tamales, coffee, and plantains. Max gave me some more cigarettes. And then it rained again. I holed up at a store called Don Durito. I couldn't sleep much. I was full of burrs everywhere.

Elías and the Broken Calendar Club

Okay, now I can tell you how it was that Elías met the Broken Calendar Club.

One night there was a small riot in the hut where the campamentistas were staying. What happened was that Juin Hélène, the French woman, has trouble sleeping, and from her hammock she saw something moving in the thatch. She lit her lamp up and it turned out to be a snake. Of course she started screaming and of course we all woke up, and then there was generalized panic, but disguised as a cross between an ecological debate and group therapy. The first thing we discussed was if we should kill it or not. The snake, not Juin Hélène. Danna May made a naturalistic case against killing it, calling attention to the danger of altering biodiversity; Vittorio Francesco Augusto Luiggi argued to kill it for culinary reasons, extolling the gastronomical benefits of snake meat—and he had read in a communiqué from El Sup how roast snake tastes like fish. Juin Hélène was in favor of altering the biological balance by killing it, and I don't much like fish, so the overwhelming majority of the jury came back with the verdict of a death sentence.

Course, the first problem was getting it down out of the thatch, and the second problem was killing it. Danna May said we should find a chair and that Vittorio Francesco Augusto Luiggi should climb up there and knock it down with a soup ladle. With a perfect Mexican accent, he answered by asking if she was out of her freakin mind.

So that was the state of things when Elías walked in, got quickly informed on the situation, went out, and came back with a long pole that he used to knock the snake on the floor, then whipped out his machete and sliced its head off.

"It was a nauyaca," he explained, and he took both pieces and carried them off somewhere.

Awhile later he came back and asked if we were going to go out and when. We said that we were and that it would be on Sunday. Danna May had to withdraw money from the bank, Juin Hélène was returning to France, Vittorio Francesco Augusto Luiggi had to buy a few things, and I had to renew my tourist visa.

We all had to go into Mexico City. Elías asked if he could come with us. We said yeah, sure, of course, that we would be honored, and so on.

"That's real nice of you."

We asked where he was heading and what for.

"I'm going into Mexico City to buy some medicine, but

don't go publishing it," he answered, fading into the shadows of the night.

After the nauyaca scare nobody could sleep, so we convened a special meeting of the Broken Calendar Club. Subject? Elías's trip.

June Outlaw said that Elías was not going in for medicine at all; that he was going to buy tickets for the jazz festival in Mexico City and that El Sup was going disguised as a saxophone, and after that he was going to do some table-dancing at a "girls only" club to raise money for the cause. May Clandestine alleged that it was something else, that Elías was going to find the address of a hospital where they do gender-reassignment surgery because El Sup was a lesbian, which means he likes women, but the women don't pay him any mind so he was going to become a woman so that they would.

Me, July Secret, I figured that Elías was going to find out when the Gay Pride Parade was being held so that El Sup could participate and come out of the jungle and the closet in one fell swoop. Forbidden August was just listening quietly, and when we had all finished arguing, he spoke. "You don't know a damn thing," he said disdainfully. "El Sup is as macho as Pedro Infante and Lando Buzzanca rolled into one, and he listens to music like the *son* and the *huapango*. Besides, if you read the papers you would know that Elías is going to see about that Wal-Mart thing in Teotihuacán."

We just stared at him, not understanding a thing, until finally he sighed and stooped to explain: "Wal-Mart opened a store in Teotihuacan so they could steal the Pyramids of the Sun and the Moon. They're going to steal them stone by stone. For every stone they take away they're gonna substitute a fake one, but made out of sheetrock. The genuine stones get packed in the used cardboard cartons. That's why if you're moving or doing something like storing books, records, clothing, or humanitarian aid, and you go ask them for some cartons, they always say they don't have any. The first one they're going to take is the Pyramid of the Moon, so that on March 21 the original Pyramid of the Sun will still be there and they'll have a whole year to dismantle it without anyone finding out."

We just went on staring at him and still couldn't understand what the hell he was talking about. June Outlaw asked why Wal-Mart would want to steal the Pyramids of the Sun and the Moon from Teotihuacan.

August Forbidden answered in his most polished *elementary, my dear Watson* tone: "So the good extraterrestrials won't be able to find the place to land. The good extraterrestrials are waiting for the Zapatistas to extend their territory and organize a *caracol* in Teotihuacan. Then they're going to land on the pyramids and *wham*! No more McDonald's and no more Pizza Huts. But if the pyramids are not really the pyramids, then the good extraterrestrials won't land and then we'll really be stuck forever with Bush, Blair, Berlusconi, Aznar, and the IMF. *Ci siamo capiti?*"

May Clandestine asked where Wal-Mart was going to take the Teotihuacan pyramids. July Secret—me, that is—joined in on the question. June Outlaw had already fallen asleep.

"That's what Elías is going to investigate," Forbidden August answered.

We all came to the conclusion that we'd had enough of nauyacas, pyramids, fast-food joints, and extraterrestrials, and that we needed some sleep.

In the hammock, as I was dozing off, everything started to get confused. Because the thing is, as opposed to every other month in our Broken Calendar, I had already read the first chapter of this book, *The Uncomfortable Dead,* and although there was a lot missing, I already knew why Elías was going into Mexico City.

And I was afraid, very afraid.

But it wasn't the fear of the unknown. No, it was something more rational. It was the fear of the known. Fear of the long history of defeats. Fear of becoming resigned and getting used to those accounts where we're always on the minus and divide sides and never on the plus and multiply sides. I was afraid that Belascoarán and Elías would lose, that we would all lose together along with them. Because it is a known fact that the murderer always returns to the scene of the crime. But just suppose that Elías and Belascoarán are going after a murderer, after THE murderer. And if it's who I think it is, THE murderer is not going to return to the scene of the crime, simply because the murderer *is* the scene of the crime. The murderer is the system. Yes! The system. When there's a crime, you have to go looking for the culprit upstairs, not downstairs. The Evil is the system, and the Bad are those that serve the system.

But the Evil is not an entity, a perverse and malevolent demon looking for bodies to possess and turn into instruments for creating more evil, crimes, murders, economic programs, frauds, concentration camps, holy wars, laws, courts, crematoriums, television channels.

No, the Evil is a relationship, it's one position against the other. It's also an election. The Evil is to choose the Evil. To choose to be the Bad unto the other. To transform yourself, of your own free will, into the executioner. And to transform the other into the victim.

We're screwed. Campamenteros should not enter into

metaphysical considerations. Campamentistas are supposed to count battle tanks and soldiers, they're supposed to get sick from the food, they should fight among themselves over nothing, they should play soccer, they should lose to the Zapatistas, they should help with the projects, they should listen to Radio Insurgente, they should criticize El Sup for not being or doing what they think he should be and do, they should plan how they're going to export Zapataism to their own countries, they're supposed to be bored most of the time. All those things and many others—but they should definitely *not* enter into metaphysical considerations. Neither should they wetback their way (no one has asked the Broken Calendar members for passports yet) into mystery novels, especially those that are written by four hands, twenty fingers, two heads, many worlds.

These damn Zapatistas fight against a monster with the help of a detective and a Chinese guy. It won't be long before some Russian shows up. Yeah, and the Chinese one will turn out to be a Trotskyite and the Russian a Maoist. Sonovabitch! Fuck Wal-Mart! Fuck the nauyaca! Fuck the fucking pyramids! Fuck fast food! Yes, and fuck me, because just as there are good extraterrestrials and bad extraterrestrials, there's also good fruit and bad fruit, and I'm one of the good fruits. I'm one of the good ones because I chose not to be one of the bad ones. Fuck this hammock! We're screwed . . . and I can't fucking sleep . . . and I'll be fucked if I ever have *pozol* and beans for dinner again. And about then I fell asleep.

Elías and Customs and Mores

Just let me have a cigarette and I'll go on telling you about the things that happened before I met up with Belascoarán at the Monument to the Revolution, over there in Mexico City.

Me, I smoke Gratos. Or Alas. That's all there was around here to smoke, so I got used to them. What I mean is that even if there's the other kind, I smoke Ingrates or Scorpions, which is what we over here call em when we wanna be funny. So then, let me tell you about the days before I went into the city to pick up city ways. I went over to Headquarters so El Sup could give me a few things and I could head to the city. I went off with Major Moses and after passing the guard post we ran into a bunch of insurgents. Captain Noah was sitting there with a guitar singing a song to the tune of "The Little Roe," the one that goes, *I'm just a poor little roe, living in the mountains*, but the words to this one were a lot different:

I'm just a poor captain, who has no one to talk to.
I'm just a poor captain, who has no one to talk to.
And I may be married, but I ain't been fixed,
and that's why I want you, little light of my eyes.
How I'd like to be your blouse to be close to you always,
to brush up against your breasts and circle your waist,
the two for being so firm and the other for being so yielding.

Well, El Sup was not in the office but over by the side of the barracks. He was with Comandante Tacho, in a shack with walls but no roof and a half-built frame. We said hello and they said it back.

"Lookit here, Elías," El Sup said, "we have this argument going with Tacho. We're building this sanitation shack and he says it has to have a cross bar or something like this," and El Sup waved his arm at the roof that wasn't a roof yet, just a bunch of sticks.

Then El Sup pulled out his pipe, lit it, and went on: "So then I ask Tacho why it has to have that cross bar. I mean, whether it's something scientific or something that has to do with customs and mores, cause if it's something scientific, then there's a reason to put up the cross bar, so I ask him what the reason is and he answers that he doesn't know, that this is the way they taught him and otherwise the whole thing would cave in."

By that time, Comandante Tacho was doubled over. And Major Moses joined in the laughter. You could tell they'd had the argument a lot of times.

El Sup went on talking as he climbed up the roof frame. "I'm gonna apply the scientific method to see whether the cross bar has to go here or not. I am going to proceed by trial and error, which means that you do it one way and if it doesn't work, it's wrong, and if it does work, then it's right. So if I climb up onto this beam and the frame caves in, it means that it isn't going to hold the weight of the roof on its own."

El Sup was already up and straddling the beam like it was a horse, and while he tried to keep his balance, he asked me, "So, Elías, what do you think? Is it scientific or is it customs and mores?"

Bout then I got out from under the beam, and barely got out: "It's on account of customs—" And there was a crack and the beam broke and El Sup was flat on his back and I finished, "—and mores."

Comandante Tacho was bent over with laughter. Major Moses couldn't hardly talk he was laughing so hard. Captain Aurora came running up to El Sup and asked, a little concerned, "Did you fall, Comrade Subcomandante?"

"No, this was just a dry run to see how long it would take the Zapatista sanitation services to arrive at the scene of an accident," El Sup said, still flat on his back, and the captain walked away laughing.

And El Sup was still there, looking for his pipe and lighter, when another insurgent woman arrived.

"Comrade Insurgent Subcomandante Marcos!" she barked, snapping to attention and saluting.

"Insurgent Comrade Erika," answered El Sup, saluting back from the ground.

"Comrade Subcomandante, may I speak . . . ?" Erika said, twisting a *paliacate* in her hands.

"You may speak, Comrade Erika," El Sup answered, as he pulled over a piece of the broken beam to use as a pillow and lit up his pipe.

"It's just that I don't know what you're going to say, but Captain Noah keeps hitting me," Erika said.

El Sup inhaled the pipe smoke, coughed, and asked, "He whaaaat?"

"He keeps hitting me, you know, he does this with his eye," Erika said, winking.

"Well, now," El Sup said, breathing a little bit easier, "you don't mean hitting you, like beating you, but hitting *on* you, like flirting, right? So do you want me to reprimand him?"

"It's not that," Erika explained, "it's that I don't know if it's allowed, cause if it's allowed, well, that's fine then, but if it ain't allowed, well, then first he should see if it can be allowed and then he can hit me all he wants."

"Hit ON you, Erika, hit ON you," El Sup drilled.

"That's it, whatever," she said.

"Very well. I'm going to look into that and I'll let you know," El Sup replied, still lying on the ground smoking.

"That was all, Comrade Insurgent Subcomandante Marcos," Erika said, then saluted and marched off.

El Sup just lay there thinking and biting the stem of his

pipe. Then there was a cracking noise and he rolled over, spitting pieces of pipe on the ground.

"Sonovabitch! I think I'm getting too old for this job," El Sup said, and you couldn't tell if it was because of the broken beam or cause he fell and didn't get up or cause the pipe kept going out or cause Erika said *hitting* instead of *hitting on* or cause he had just ruined another good pipe with his biting or because of the damn customs and mores.

"So I'm heading out," I said.

"Did you get someone to go with you?" he asked.

"Yeah, I did," I said. "I'm traveling with some campamenteros who were going into Mexico City anyway, and—"

"Into the Monster, remember that we call Mexico City the *Monster*," El Sup corrected.

"That's it," I said.

What I didn't say was that I had told the campamenteros that I was going into Mexi—into the Monster—to buy some medicine. I don't rightly know if they believed me, but that's what El Sup told me to say. He said that his granny used to tell him to invent a story when he wasn't sposed to say what he was doing, the first story that popped into his head, and then tell it like it was some big secret. That way they'd believe you. That's what El Sup said his granny told him, El Sup. Now who woulda thought that? I always figgered El Sup didn't have no grandmother.

"That's good," El Sup said. Looking at Major Moses, he went on, "Turn those envelopes with the letters over to Elías."

Then Major Moses gave me some envelopes and I stuck them in my backpack. It was already starting to rain again when I asked, "Say there, Sup, there anything you need?"

"Yes," El Sup answered, "there's a few things. The first is that little nylon bag over there."

So I give El Sup the nylon bag—him still flat on the ground—so's he could cover the pipe from the rain.

"And the second thing is, I want you to bring me back one of those soft drinks from the Monster, the one called Chaparritas El Naranjo, the kind that tastes like grape. Oh, and there's another thing. Tell Belascoarán that if he don't manage to teach you how to play dominos, it's because he's an imbecile. No, not an imbecile; that's too strong a word around those parts. Maybe you'd better say it's cause he's an asshole, which isn't so offensive and he'll get the drift of what I mean."

"So what's that good for?" I asked El Sup, cause I didn't know what that dominos was.

"Except for demonstrations and earthquakes, couples dominos is the closest thing citizens have to working collectively. You learn and then come back and teach us, cause just maybe we'll be needing it someday to keep us from getting stuck with the six, isn't that right?" El Sup said, turning to Tacho and Mo, who were laughing again. Well, they seemed to know what he was talking about.

"Dominos?" I asked. "Not chess?" Cause the thing is, I see people playing chess in the towns, even with the campamenteros.

"Nope. That stuff about how military commanders and detectives play chess is bull. Military commanders play cards—solitaire, to be precise—and they do puzzles. Detectives play dominos. So you tell him to teach you, hear?" El Sup said, finally getting off the ground.

"Okay by me," I says.

Major Moses bid me goodbye cause he was going somewhere else. He hugged me and said I should have a good trip. Then I hugged El Sup and Comandante Tacho, too. And they said the same thing about having a good trip and taking care of myself and all. El Sup reminded me that I shouldn't forget what he told me; that through the communiqués he would let me know what to do.

As I walked away, El Sup was climbing on the part of the roof frame that hadn't caved in and telling Comandante Tacho, "Okay, Tachito, now we're going to test the other beam. What method should we use? Scientific method or customs and mores?"

When I passed the guard post, I could still hear Comandante Tacho laughing his ass off. I put the letters in a plastic bag so they'd stay dry.

Elías's Trip According to the Broken Calendar Club

We left very early Sunday morning. The five of us climbed aboard a three-tonner: May, June, July, August, and Elías. We got there in time to catch the bus for Mexico City. June sat next to Elías and gave him the window in case he got bus-sick. I had May next to me and August sat behind us. When we got to La Ventosa, the bus stopped at the immigration checkpoint. An officer got aboard and walked by May and me with hardly a glance. August made believe he was asleep and snored. Then, on the way back, the officer stopped next to June and Elías, who was leafing through a French edition of *Le Monde Diplomatique*.

"Identification, please," he said.

June reached for her passport.

"Not you, madam, the gentleman," he said, pointing to Elías.

Elías never raised his eyes or broke concentration on his reading. "American citizen."

Although Elías had a wetback accent, the immigration officer hesitated. After a few seconds, which I suppose is long enough to keep the suspense high in a mystery novel, he did an about-face and walked off the bus. The driver got the bus on the way again and June, without a word, took the newspaper Elías was reading and turned it right-side up.

"Right! Musta been why I couldn't find the sports page," Elías said, and promptly fell asleep.

That night and during the whole trip, the Broken Calendar Club monopolized the bathroom in the back of the bus. Without ever consulting each other, we all blamed it on the *pozol* we'd had the evening before.

As we left the bus terminal, we said goodbye to Elías and took off in different directions.

When I returned later to La Realidad, I passed the message Elías had given me to the person in charge of the *caracol*: *The one with the big eye is already with the doctor.*

I asked El Sup the other day, when I ran into him by the stream, if he was going to use us as Elías's team in the book. He said he wasn't, that we were only going to be in one chapter. I asked why, and he answered, "Cause dead people don't have teams."

So this is as far as we go. If we want to know what happens from now on, we have to wait to read the following chapters in the book. Sonovabitch! I don't know about you, but me, I've had it with these mystery novels where all the characters are so intelligent and cultured and the only ignorant asshole is the reader. Well, I don't know about being assholes, but we sure are ignorant, cause we're always missing what's missing.

Elías's Trip According to Elías

So I did it: I went into the Monster. I woke up just as we were going down this very steep hill. The campamenteros were fast asleep. And then I saw the city. It was sitting there, it was still far away.

And it's true what Belascoarán says about there's lots of antennas, like skinny little hairs growing on the heads of the houses. When we was close I saw that besides antennas there was people, lots of people, and I didn't count em but I think there was more people than antennas, although there was about as many cars as antennas. How to find my way?

Back home I could tell where a town was by looking at the trees. So I figgered the city people must find out where houses are by checking the antennas. Later I found out they don't. What they have is streets with names and numbers. Then there's also very tall houses, so tall you'd think they wanted to get up over the antennas, and they put numbers on those houses too.

When I got to the station, there was Andrés and Marta. They were the city comrades that was sposed to wait for me, but they were alive, you see, not deceased like me. I saw them from far away and I said goodbye to the campamenteros real quick so's they wouldn't recognize Andrés and Marta. Those campamenteros were real pale and kinda didn't have any color, but I think that's the natural color people have back where they're from.

"Well, I'm here," I said to Marta and Andrés.

Andrés asked if I had a suitcase and I said I only had my backpack, and he said let's go and I said let's go. And we got on one of those metro things they've got.

So, how did it go? Marta asked. No big deal, I said.

Then Andrés told me that it was going to take about an hour to get there, depending on traffic, which depends on whether there's a soccer match, and that his team used to be the UNAM Pumas, but when he heard how that Rosario

Robles and a Televisa announcer also went for the Pumas, he decided to change teams and he quit the Pumas for the Chiapas Jaguars, but they have fruity uniforms. So what team did I go for? I said the Underdogs, and that ended the soccer talk.

Finally we got to this house way up high in one of those buildings. I gave them the letter from El Sup and they read it. They asked how long I was gonna stay with them and I said about six months, learning how city people do things and maybe getting some jobs until El Sup's communiqué comes out telling about the deceased Digna Ochoa and the deceased Pável González.

"Ah, some more uncomfortable dead," Andrés said.

"Yes," Marta said, "the downstairs dead are never quiet."

"You got that right," I said.

That was in July and August, I don't rightly remember, but it was before the communiqués about the Good Governance Boards. We still hadn't set out to find the biggest sonovabitch of all the sonovabitches in the world, including the bitch herself. I mean that sonovabitch Morales, who was like the Evil itself had married the Bad and they had an evil child who was that sonovabitch Morales. So a certain amount of time had gone by. I had forgotten until I got the letter from El Sup that closed with . . .

From the mountains of Southeast Mexico,
Insurgent Subcomandante Marcos
December 2004

CHAPTER 4

SHEER FORGETFULNESS DWELLS

The Black Palace of Lecumberri, the ancient prison of Mexico City, a pillar of the old city's shadows, had been turned a few years earlier into the General Archives of the Nation. This political whitewash, this facelift, had not succeeded in freeing the enormous building from its malignant aura, especially on one of those days at the onset of winter when the whole city becomes a kaleidoscope of grays. Thunderheads, smog, and a chill wind, somehow emanating from its past: The ominous building was crowned by clouds that were somehow blacker than the rest.

He saw Fritz cross over from the main entrance of the palace, dodging cars, trying to keep from getting run over and lighting a cigarette at the same time. They sat in the park before the statue of Heberto Castillo.

"Years, old buddy. It's been years I haven't heard from you. And something tells me I'm not going to learn anything about you now either. You're undoubtedly going to ask me about some bullshit."

Belascoarán smiled. For historical, political, and personal reasons, Fritz Glockner had spent the last four years digging into the history of the Dirty War, combing through the records of the secret police agencies of the old regime.

Records that chance had sent to the National Archives in the old prison. Chance had made a good turn, for once—after the collapse of the PRI era someone had gotten them confused with the records of the old Commission for the Development of Territorial Waters, or something like that.

"What do you know about Jesús María Alvarado?"

Fritz studied Belascoarán for a moment before answering. And that was logical, because in spite of the Austrian name, Fritz was a country boy and naturally suspicious.

"He's dead. They killed him in '71, like they killed my father . . . a bullet in the back of the head."

A cold draft flowed between them. Héctor stared at the silhouette of the palace where Alvarado had spent the last days of his life. The building sprawled out in all directions, heavy and somber.

"Why'd they kill him?"

"Go figure. Those days, they shot first and asked questions later. Maybe they thought he was in contact with, or was the lynchpin of, one of the armed resistance groups that sprang up after '68 . . . or that he ran a group that was dormant but would get back into the action as soon as he got out . . . That might have been it. Or maybe some kind of personal vendetta by the prison authorities, because he was one of the organizers of the hunger strike in '69."

"Did you know him?"

"I saw him a couple of times, from far away."

"Did he have children?"

"When I used to visit my father, Alvarado used to get visits from this very big older woman and, yeah, she had a kid with her, a bit younger than me. If I'm forty-two now, the kid would be about thirty-eight, or something like that. But I don't know if it was his son, I don't remember seeing a young woman with the child. Maybe it was a nephew, or a younger brother. I do remember the kid because during the visit he would be hanging around the fountains in the inner courtyard fooling around with a yo-yo."

"During the investigations you guys have been doing, have you found out who killed him? Do any of the documents you've been reading mention his death in any way, or those responsible?"

"Let me check around and ask some of the other bookworms digging into those records. If anything turns up, I'll call you."

They embraced and Fritz repeated his suicidal ballet across the avenue. Suddenly, he stopped and turned around amidst the wildly honking cars.

"Why don't you look up the Chinaman? That was his cell mate."

"What Chinaman is that?"

"Fuang Chu, the only Chinese member of the movement of '68. It was just him and the Mao Tse-tung posters. I think he's living in Guadalajara now."

Héctor Belascoarán Shayne had his office on Donato Guerra, near the corner of Bucareli, in the heart of hearts of Mexico City. And as it turns out, this was a heart, like in Juan Luis Guerra's song, unaware of what it was, amassing little glory and making lots of noise. Mornings, the corners were overrun with newspaper distributors, making their bundles and their noises. Then the afternoons were taken over by the record shops and lunch counters.

The elevator was out of order, so he limped up the three flights. This made his limp worse and the pain stuck to the bone.

Bones hurt?

Only when it's cold, he answered himself.

He ran into Carlos Vargas at the door.

"You've got your progressive official in there, boss."

But it was Tobías the dog that welcomed him first. He was limping, of course, his leg still in the splint, but it was probably on account of the cold as much as the broken bone. He took one look at Héctor, reared up, and hit him with a foot of slobbery tongue that left the detective and his new cigarette drenched. Héctor tossed the wet cigarette to the dog, who swallowed it, and would have smiled if he could.

"He likes them. He hates it when I smoke, but he likes to smoke himself, or at least to eat them," Monteverde said.

Now that he thought about it, both of them, dog and master (you figure which was which), had faces like Droopy.

Héctor pointed to a black leather couch for the other Héctor to sit on, moved over to the safe, which was always open, and pulled out two Cokes and an automatic, which he placed on the table. He gestured to Monteverde to help himself to the cigarettes.

"I've got two new messages on the machine," Monteverde said, lighting up a counterfeit Ronson that was a bit too golden and had probably been bought from a street vendor.

Héctor flipped the caps off the two Cokes using the sights of his automatic and handed one to his mysterious informant. He put the gun back in the safe and took a seat. Again he staged the Alec Guinness routine, but this time it was because he didn't know what to say.

"So, where do you get the Cokes in bottles? In my neighborhood all they have is plastic."

"Yeah, well, there's this little kiosk down here and they've had them in stock for years," Héctor answered.

More silence.

Monteverde produced another answering-machine tape and handed it over, shrugging as if apologizing. He blew a mouthful of smoke toward the ceiling and went into his own Alec Guinness.

They spent the next few minutes just sitting there, smoking. The sound of a merengue crept up the walls of the building, entering into an uneasy blend with something vaguely Tex-Mex. The result was awful. Maybe that's why Belascoarán broke the silence.

"Does anyone else know about these messages?"

"No! Of course not! I live alone and I wouldn't dare talk about them at my job . . . They'd think I've flipped. Besides, I don't even know what Alvarado is trying to tell me; I can't figure out what he's talking about."

"And is it Alvarado?"

"Jesús María Alvarado, or whoever it is. Who cares? Maybe it's his ghost. But why me? I mean, we did know each other, but that's about all . . . and it was so long ago."

"So why you?"

Monteverde stood up. He was tall, but he was also a little bent. Tobías the dog got up too and limped over to his master.

"I swear, I've been going over this again and again, and I'll be damned if I know."

"So why me?"

Monteverde looked at him with a startled expression.

"Well, isn't this what you do?"

Is this really *what I do*?

He strolled along Victoria Street looking for a machine

for his office that could play the little tapes from Monteverde. *What I do.* Dead people talking in a country where the living are either not allowed to talk a lot or they talk too much. *What I do.*

When he ran into some vendors with statues of Our Lady of Guadalupe ringed with rose-colored light bulbs, he remembered that December 12 was drawing near. It was about a month to his birthday.

This is a story told by Jesús María Alvarado, and you're really going to like it. One day in Burbank, Juancho, the bin Laden guy, was told he had to stop screwing the actresses in the films they were shooting in the studio next door—actually, the motel next door—for what they said were security reasons. Now, whenever Juancho went next door, he always took off the fake beard they made him wear for the communiqués and dressed up like a professional wrestler, El Horrible, wearing a green mask with little horns and talking in grunts. But his bosses were not happy because the guys in the other motel had offered Juancho a steady job with Lux Cal XXX studios, although they didn't like the fact that he came too fast, and this right in the middle of the Bush election . . . You see? Juancho was always up and down, taking screen tests, borrowing the Kalashnikov and giving it back, drinking tea, getting his eyebrows plucked, but his superiors wanted him full-time and they kept telling him, Mr. Juancho, no more fucky fucky, *and he just grunted, but then he snapped to attention cause they paid cash money, very important for a taco vendor who gave no credit and didn't believe in banks, not even numbered Swiss accounts, because after the Salinas administration, people in Mexico aren't even sure that Switzerland even exists, so he had a suitcase under his bed full of hundreds, which he laid out every night on his bed. In any case, he only* appeared *to be following orders, cause the next morning the agent who was always stationed by his door brought him some hotcakes for breakfast and discovered that Juancho was gone, how do you like that? Bin Laden beat it. But this bin Laden actually thought he was making commercials for turbans and field tents. This was a goddamn bin Laden who didn't even know who bin Laden was. So how do you like that? And he took the mask, the dumb fuck—*

Then a busy signal. Héctor turned off the recorder and ran his fingers through his hair. He had it cut short and some white ones were peeking through. And now he was about to get a whole lot more. He looked out the window and began to laugh softly, as if he didn't dare make any loud sounds. Then he lit up, still chuckling.

Héctor Belascoarán Shayne was Mexican, so absurdity was his daily bread. He was Mexican and had only one eye, so he could see only half of what other people saw, but more clearly. In recent years he had been living on the edge, on the borders between strange territories skirting incoherence, irrationality, and extravagance; this, along with tragedy, cowardice, collective insult, impunity, fear, and ridicule. These were territories that might be called anything but innocent, territories where you might suddenly lose an eye, have a friend die, or run into a shotgun blast as you come out from buying chocolate donuts. These territories were a challenge to rationality, but were full of dark reasons. The country was one big business, a territory being looted by phony, part-narco horsemen of the apocalypse, a supermarket run by a drunken Friedrich Nietzsche, but *really* drunk, where nothing was what it seemed. It was like a Venezuelan soap opera starring the forty thieves, with Ali Baba in a supporting role. But this? This was too much. Juancho–bin Laden was more than he could take. This was a planetary intrusion. It was like all of a sudden Mexico would run off with the World Cup, the Olympics, and the Davis Cup. It was like, without the like, a Mexican taco vendor had taken over CNN.

The second narrative relayed by Alvarado on Monteverde's answering machine seemed a little more within the bounds of reality, but totally disconnected from the stories he had told before.

"*Listen, brother, this is José María Alvarado,*" the gravelly voice said, cutting directly to the chase.

> *Do you know how Morales got rich? He hired himself seven judicial policemen who were out of work because they had tortured the wrong person, a rich merchant related to a PRI member of parliament, and he bought one of those long barricades that rich people use to close off their neighborhoods, and he took it up to a high pass along a country road that was all mud and loose dirt, but used a couple of months a year by the coffee growers to bring their harvests down into town, so he had the barricade and his hired guns, and when the farmers arrived with their sacks, he would stop them and buy their coffee, but at about half the already shitty price they were getting from the middlemen twenty or thirty kilometers downhill. That's what he did for a couple of years—fucking everyone, but nothing crude, no sir, he had himself a steel barricade like the ones rich people use with signs that say* Private. *That's what he did. It was the shittiest of all the neoliberal shit: He privatized the public road, closed a pass, and fucked the poorest of the poor.*

* * *

Héctor slowly dialed the eight numbers.

"Hey, listen, Monteverde, do you really believe all that Juancho–bin Laden stuff?"

"No way! Sounds completely crazy to me."

"Had you ever heard of this Morales character?"

"Never."

"So what do you make of all this?"

"I don't even think about it anymore. I just receive these insanities and pass them on to you . . . You're the one who's supposed to make sense of it. What do *you* think?"

"That if the deceased José María Alvarado wanted to leave us a message, he really picked a bizarre way to do it," Belascoarán said.

"That's true, but if he wanted to get our attention, he has succeeded," Monteverde noted.

"The fact is that reality is getting very strange."

"Come again?"

"No, nothing, just something a writer friend of mine likes to say," the detective answered, then hung up.

He was trying to imagine that road in the mountains—the pass, the steel barricade, the thugs with shotguns. Which mountains? Which state of the republic? Which coffee communities? What year? How did he get the barricade up the—

The telephone interrupted his chain of questions and imagery. It was Fritz.

"Listen, Belas, you want to talk to the Chinaman, to Fuang Chu? That right?"

"The one who was Alvarado's cell mate."

"Okay, if you go to Félix Cuevas's Gayosso funeral parlor, you'll probably find him there in the evening, after 10. He'll be attending Samuel's funeral, most likely, that's what they told me. I'll talk to you tomorrow cause I've got a few things on Alvarado . . ."

"Samuel who?" Belascoarán asked, but Fritz had already hung up.

He ordered tacos at the stand across from his office, but they were too dry and the sauces didn't help much. Back in the office, he proceeded to waste his time looking though the Mexico City telephone directory, trying to find one of the 12,000 Moraleses, as if merely looking at a name, address, or number was going to give him the clue he needed. He asked a friend of his, part-hacker and part–curiosity psychopath (which in the '60s was called a nosy parker), who the Moraleses were with the most hits and who were the strangest, but half an hour later he lost heart when she called back.

"Belascoaráncito, listen, Google had 3,700,000 hits for Morales. Can you be more specific? Poems by Lolo Morales? Cooking recipes by Lola Morales? Morales Undertakers?"

"Could you try *Morales Mexican*?"

"Okay, hold on a minute," Cristina Adler replied, and he could hear her fingers on the keyboard.

"We got it down to 870,000. The Morales Hacienda? Martirio Morales, aunt of someone who gave someone else a drawing."

"Can you tie it in with the year 1971?"

"I can, Belascoruddy. I can . . ."

Silence. Coughing.

"Okay. We're down to 64,000 hits. Is this guy Mexican?"

"Yes!"

"Let me limit this to news reports in Mexico."

Héctor waited, trying not to make any noise that might break Cristina's concentration.

"Great, we're down to 9,510 and heading for a score . . . Hold on, I'm going to exclude a restaurant, the Morales Hacienda, all the Moraleses in lower-case text, auditors . . . Damn, Elba Esther's full name is Elba Esther Gordillo Morales . . . a soccer player who wears the number 7 . . . a printer in Chihuahua—"

"That's no good," Héctor interrupted. He still didn't know what he was looking for.

"Mexico City! Let me narrow it down to Mexico City . . . 815 hits. Now that's a reasonable number . . . Let me get rid of the address on Insurgentes Sur, which appears lots of times. Okay."

"What's okay?"

"671 hits."

"Check the police," Héctor said, growing desperate. Too much information was a lot like—too much like—too little information.

"Okay," Cristina mumbled into the phone, "171. Pretty decent. What did you say you were looking for?"

"I don't know."

"Let me read this to you: veterinary police, a photographer . . . There are a couple of Morales brothers in the Enforcer Brigade of Lucio Cabañas's Party of the Poor. What is that, Belasco-man? I wasn't born yet in '71. Then there's a deputy chief of Traffic Police whose second family name is Morales, a haute couture shop that makes uniforms for the cops . . ."

Héctor sighed so hard he almost damaged his surfer's eardrums.

* * *

"That guy is just dumb, he's a jerk, that's all, and we're condemned to be governed by crooks or idiots, one after another, and right now we have an idiot," lectured Javier Villareal, an engineer also known as the Rooster, an expert in deep drainage and other subterrainities.

"I'm closing on twos," said Gilberto Gómez Letras, plumber by trade, as he slammed a domino tile on the table. "But the worst thing is when they're idiots *and* crooks. I pass, of course."

"Buttocks!" announced Carlos Vargas, illustrious upholsterer, playing the two-four. "Haven't we had two idiots in a row?"

Héctor winked and gestured left with his arm. He passed. Gilberto should have stuck to his twos.

"What's so bad about this idiot?"

"He's always saying we're growing, that the economy is growing, that we did seven percent, five percent, thirteen and a half. Where does he get those figures? They don't jibe with anyone else's. If that asshole were head of the national lottery, nobody would ever win. Whose economy is growing? His, probably, the prick," said the Rooster, who wasn't usually vehement about politics but knew a bit about mathematics.

"We're out of here, buddy," Gilberto told Héctor, and then, turning to his opponents, "Count them up, gents," playing his last two.

The game of dominos is an exact science, just like the Marxism of Engels, Plekhanov, and Bukharin. There are twenty-eight tiles distributed around the table and seven rounds to play them. In theory, if you study the first plays and take into account the tiles in your own hand, it is relatively simple to deduce the tiles in anyone else's hand. That, like Marxism, is the theory. But a social revolution did not take place in nineteenth-century England, despite the fact that it was crawling with horrible little factories and a hard-fighting, beer-drinking proletariat; the dictatorship of the proletariat never actually defended the proletariat, and sometimes quantitative leaps produced qualitative regressions. In dominos, as in life, the chance factor plays a role, sometimes the starring role, and if that isn't enough, there're four morons around a table trying to dupe one another.

That Friday night, just like the past forty-five or fifty, in compliance with a New Year's resolution, the Francisco Villa Club, made up of the four office mates, got together to play dominos and talk politics, the two main factors in the education of any Mexican worthy of the name.

"How're we doing?" the Rooster asked.

"Badly! Didn't you say you can't even trust the numbers anymore?" answered Carlos Vargas. "It's sixty-two to forty-two. Straight-up numbers with no presidential shuffling. We're losing!"

"Stop crying, engineer man, and shuffle the tiles."

Villareal began to move the tiles around the table in slow circular movements.

"The trouble with you is that the free-trade agreement has no impact on plumbers."

"If you say so, but then how come I've been working half-time for the better part of a year? If those assholes out there get a leaky faucet, they don't call a professional, they patch it up themselves with Durex and rubber bands."

"Damn, that's why Bejerano wanted so many rubber bands—to repair his plumbing," Belascoarán commented, referring to a high-profile corruption case where a leader of the PRD had been videotaped stealing thousands of dollars, and was later caught with rubber bands in his briefcase.

* * *

They lost. Furthermore, in the last two games, Carlos and Villareal, the engineer, had murdered them, actually humiliated them. That was why he was almost happy that he had to go out into the chill night air of downtown Mexico City to find his Chinese guy. He caught a taxi to the Colonia del Valle funeral parlor. The sky was gray, the color of lead, and traffic was a bitch. He couldn't really tell if there were more antennas, but he was certain that there were more cars. What the hell did the people of the capital do when they had nothing else to do? *Les go, man, les go see what the traffic is like*, or, as they say on the radio, what the *vehicular congestion* is like.

Héctor tried it out on the taxi driver.

"So tell me, what's the vehicular congestion like?"

"Vehicular congestion, my ass. It's the friggen middle class in this friggen city who don't have any money to go shopping in December, so they just pretend to go shopping. Before they used to go to the movies, but now they just go to the mall parking lot and then sneak back to their houses," the driver replied, demonstrating remarkable sociological insight.

"But they spend money on fuel and parking meters, tips for takecarofits, valet parking, and the keepercomins," added Héctor, showing off his own sociological acumen regarding the new city fauna he had discovered.

The takecarofits had appeared in the last few years. You would park your car on some lonely street and out of nowhere would appear a character with a flannel chamois over his shoulder and a broad smile, saying, *Takecarofit for ya, boss*, with the implicit threat that every malediction in the Talmud and every earthquake in Mexico would befall your car without his protection. Valet parking was not what the word suggests—Bolshoi dancers on strike—but private parking attendants at restaurants. The keepercomins were a lot like the takecarofits, but they were a lot younger and would appear when you started to back into a parking space. The kid, always smiling and wearing a baseball cap backwards, would stand by you and offer guidance: *Keepercomin, chief, cut a little, now keepercomin.*

Héctor was more of a pedestrian and fervent user of public transportation, so he hadn't had many professional dealings with these most recent offspring of Mexico City's endemic economic crisis, but their appearance could not escape his trained eye.

"Instead of the PRI fucking us with the gasoline money from PEMEX financing campaigns for their asshole candidates, I think it's better for the PEMEX staff to steal it," concluded the driver, who had presumably voted for Cuauhtémoc Cárdenas the last few times around.

The Gayosso funeral parlor was relatively empty. It was cold in the early evening. Mexico City is aggravating to bone aches when the sun doesn't shine, Héctor reminded himself. He looked up and found a *Samuel* among the deceased, then walked over to one of the chapels. This Samuel didn't appear to have very many friends, or else it was too early, since there were only half a dozen men and women, all over fifty, around the coffin and the tables littered with ashtrays. He approached the only Chinese person there, an extremely thin man, wrinkled and leathery, wearing a rust-colored suit and a black tie.

"Fuang Chu?" Héctor asked as he neared the man.

"Martínez, everyone calls me by my mother's name. How can I help you?"

"Would you know if José María Alvarado might still be alive?"

Fuang Chu stared hard at Héctor. "And who might you be?"

"Héctor Belascoarán Shayne, independent detective," he answered, and getting his first good look at the man's face, he was instantly sorry he had come.

"You must be breaking my balls," the Chinese man said, drawing the words from deep inside his soul.

CHAPTER 5

SOME PIECES OF THE PUZZLE

There are live ones and dead ones. The dead ones are better than the live ones.

That's what El Sup told me when he was giving me instructions before going into the Monster. He was explaining about the drops, the citizens' drops—cause there's also mountain drops, which is when we do it with medicine, food, weapons, ammo, equipment, books. That's when you don't want to go carrying everything around all at once, so you hide them in different places according to the plan. Mountain drops are very tricky and you have to go around checking them cause the rain or the coons can maybe get into them, spoil them, that is. But it's not the same in the city. They have rain in the city and some say they even have coons, but it's not the same cause in the city the drops are used for leaving and picking up messages. So in the city they have live drops and dead drops, and the dead drops are when there's nobody to take or give the message, and what you do is you leave the message for somebody to pick up and you don't have to have a meeting between the one who drops and the one who picks up. So a dead drop is where there's no people, just places and things, and the live drop is where you have a real person who receives messages or gives them or both. You call it a live drop cause there's a real live person that receives things and holds onto them awhile and then delivers them to another person when that person gives the right password.

Thing is, El Sup went on explaining about how the dead drops were better. And I say he's right.

That was before I went into the Monster, Mexico City. It was real difficult. Getting around in the Monster, that is. The *pesero*, the microbus, that is, kept taking me around and around cause I was gawking at everything stead of looking where I was going, and sometimes I even went around three times cause of staring at a big old street called an avenue cause it was so big and all, what with cars going every which way, and a body can't be diddling around cause you can get deceased out there. Well, in my case I'm already deceased, but maybe the cars didn't know that, so I waited till there was a clearing and then ran like hell to the other side.

In the metro, well, that's different cause the metro runs under the streets and there's no cars . . . yet. As I was saying, I was already in Mexico City, the Monster. I think it was El Sup who said that the ground grows upward, but I think that's because he hadn't walked around there, since the simple truth is that the ground grows down. What I mean is, on the ground there's only cars—well, cars and a shitload of antennas with buildings growing out of their feet.

The Monster has big houses and small ones, tall ones and little bitty ones, fat and skinny, rich and poor. Like people, but without hearts. In the Monster, the most important thing is the houses and the cars, so people get sent underground, to the metro. If people stay up there in car country, well, the cars kind of like get very pissed and try to gore them, like bulls would.

In the city, they don't really know how to speak the language, cause they don't even know the difference between a mare and a stallion; they just call everything a *horse*. Then there's *cool*. When city people don't know how to explain how they feel or when they're angry or when they're happy or anything like that, they just say *cool*. Like the other day, I was on a *pesero*, which is a microbus, and there was a couple of youngsters looking really in love and all, and the youngster boy asks the youngster girl if she really loves him and she says *cool*, but you could tell in her eyes that what she meant was *you matter a lot to me*. And then they kissed and all. But on a different day, the driver all of a sudden had to stomp on the brakes and this little old guy went flying into this big guy who caught him, and the old guy says *I'm so sorry*, and the big guy says *that's cool*, which you could tell in his manner meant *it don't matter none*. So I figger *cool* means a whole lot of things and city folk don't have to learn a lot of words after they learn *cool*. Maybe that's why they have their heads all mixed up like me, Elías Contreras, Investigation Commission, Zapatista National Liberation Army.

Well, like I was saying, the people who get around walking, or how city folk say, by going *pedestrian*—the cars seem to want to run into those pedestrians. So if you don't have a car, you really have to be quick so's they won't make you deceased, so you can take the *pesero*, or just go straight down and take the underground way, which is the metro. So when I got off the second time around from the *pesero* and I was on the street again, I figgered I had to get down there and take that metro. Now, the metro is like a lot of cars tied together with a kind of chain, and the one pulls the others. When the metro finally arrives, the people outside all bunch together real tight and the people inside all bunch the same and some want to get in and others want to get out. The one who pushes the most wins. In the beginning, I thought this was the way city folk did their exercises and I got into the spirit of things, urging them on with, "A people united can never be defeated," but I finally decided it wasn't that, and that they were just like that, pushy, I mean, at least the pedestrian ones, cause the ones in the cars are all different. They just cruise around all the time and holler *blow it out your ass* at each other, or *asshole*, like they was really pissed, but they're not, that's just what they do, blow it out their asses, I guess. The other day, I asked Andrés and Marta what there was more of, cars or people. They said people. So I got to thinking why cars were more important than people, cause you could see plain as day that the city was made for cars and for antennas, but it sure ain't made for people. So since they don't all fit together—cars, people, and antennas—they had to dig a hole under the city, that is, under the ground. And down there you have a lot of people. There's men and women and children and old people, and they even have policemen. They have people of all kinds and sizes same as up top. But what they don't have down there is rich people.

One day I went and took the metro to a station called . . . called . . . Gimme a second here so's I can check the map . . . Got it, it's called Azcapotzalco. After I got there, I went to catch another *pesero* that took a long time, and I finally got to a place that looks like a paddock but ain't one. What they had there is a thing called a *circus,* and I went to see where it was that the giraffes lived. As it turns out, those giraffes are a lot like cows, meaning they have horns and all, but their heads are way up on the end of a real long neck that looks like somebody stretched them too much when they were being born, or maybe they just want to see real far and they stretch their necks far as they can, or maybe they just want to look like the houses in the city. So you might say that giraffes are like cows, but with antennas.

Okay, now, back to the point, cause I didn't really want to see no giraffes, what I had to do was see a comrade who was going to be seeing the giraffes at exactly 7 p.m. and who was going to have blue hair—the comrade, not the giraffes. The guy was a youngster, and you know youngsters don't really mind much if they don't get where they have to be on time, but he finally got there. In the Monster, you know, youngster boys and girls sometimes like to dye their hair different colors. Sometimes they dye it red or yellow or green or lots of colors, and sometimes blue. So the youngster who came late had blue hair. I went right up to him, but not too close cause you never can tell if he ain't the one. Then I says real soft without looking at him, "The giraffes walk like they're rock 'n' roll dancing." And the young man answers without looking at me, "Giraffes united can never be defeated." So I could tell he was the one, and he left his bread bag by the fence and walked away without another word.

Guess you'd like to know how I knew I was sposed to go find the youngster with the blue hair, right? Thing is that the clues, that is, the instructions, came coded in the communiqués about the Broken Pocket, in the greeting to Don Manolo Vázquez Montalbán, and in the communiqué about the giraffes. El Sup had already told me that the communiqués would let me know where I was sposed to pick up or drop messages. Sometimes they would be live drops and other times they would be dead drops. So with the codes I could tell when and where I was going to get a message. I guess I'll let you figger out how the codes went. That last one was easy. The difficult ones were in the communiqué about the *video you must read.* I had to go to this real uppity place called Santa Fe that's real fancy and look behind a latrine, I mean behind the toilet, in a place that sells tamales.

There was a message there from El Sup and I found out I had to pick up another message from El Sup on the 8th and deliver my report on the 15th at that same drop, meaning the latrine in the tamale place. Then there was the time with the communiqué about the *speed of dreams,* when I had to go to the Oceania metro station and find a shoe shop with a number 69 on the door and they gave me a pair of shoes that didn't really fit too good on my left foot, but I looked inside and saw that there was a piece of paper with a message and that's why I couldn't get my foot in, so I read the message. With the Miguel Enríquez communiqué, I wound up right in the middle of the Monster, on a street called República de Chile, looking for a sign that said *For Sale,* and I stuck my report behind it for somebody else to pick up, so this was one of those good dead drops.

All in all I had a real hard time in the beginning, but then later I began to understand city ways and I kinda liked it. El Sup had told me that if you want to know the Monster, you have to walk it. *Walk through it,* he told me, *and you'll see that the city is built on the people who can save it.* So that's what I did, I walked all around that city. And I went everywhere, and everywhere I went I ran into people like us Zapatistas, which means people who are screwed, which means people willing to fight, which means people who don't give up.

Okay, like I was saying, the youngster with the blue hair left a bread bag by the gate where the giraffes are, at the circus called Circo Unión. Then I moved in close and grabbed the bread bag that didn't have no bread, but instead a message from El Sup addressed to me and saying only, *Find Mamá Piedra.*

The Barcelona–La Realidad–Monster Axis

Stay alert, keep moving, trust no one.

That was the general recommendation I gave Elías before he left. With that, I was repeating what Che Guevara said in his book *Revolutionary War Passages*; it was also what each one of us was told when we had to move alone. I spoke to him about Mexico City too, or rather, what I remembered about the capital. And I'm not talking about the generous and caring city that welcomed us for the Indigenous Pride Demonstration. No, I spoke to him about the city I left more than twenty years ago, when I came to the mountains. Though according to what I heard later, that city has nothing to do with the one there now.

Elías's visit had been in the works since Pepe Carvalho brought me some papers written personally by Manuel Vázquez Montalbán. The papers came with a brief note from his son:

> *Subcomandante,*
>
> *When looking through my father's papers shortly after his death, I found these notes which I imagine might make some sense to you.*
>
> *My regards,*
>
> *Daniel*

One of the papers contained a sort of diagram, all interconnected with arrows, lines, circles, and squares, that read as follows:

- BARCELONA. *Hotel Princesa Sofía. Plaza Pio XII, No. 4, Financial Center, Diagonal Avenue; María Cristina metro station. Morales.*

• DIPLOMATIC POUCH MEXICO-MADRID-MEXICO. *Check flights 1994–2000. Morales.*
• DISAPPEARED—DIRTY WAR. *Morales. The White Brigade.*
• ACTEAL. *General Renán Castillo. Morales.*
• MONTES AZULES. *Morales.*
• ZEDILLO-CARABIAS-TELLO. *Morales.*
• BIODIVERSITY—TRANSNATIONALS. *Morales. Checks. Accessories?*
• EL YUNQUE. *Morales. Reactivation of the paramilitary.*
• MURO. *Re-edited?*

Another piece of paper contained a series of questions:

1. What was Morales doing in the suite at the Princesa Sofía? Was he staying there alone? What was he doing in the Financial Center? He went in at 21:00 and left at 22:00. What about the María Cristina metro station? He entered at 22:30 and left at 23:00. The hotel.

2. What was Morales up to with those continuous trips between Mexico and Madrid? Never twice in a row on the same airline. No apparent pattern.

3. What was Morales's role in the Dirty War in Mexico? White Brigade? What about Acteal?

4. What was Morales doing with the Montes Azules materials he carted around in his briefcase?

5. Why was Morales at that dinner with former president Ernesto Zedillo, Julia Carabias, and Carlos Tello Díaz?

6. Who or what was the final destination of the briefcases full of euros that Morales carried from the Financial Center to the María Cristina metro station in Barcelona?

7. What was Morales's specific role in the new structure of EL YUNQUE in Mexico?

The third document wasn't really a document, just a napkin with the following:

Barcelona exhausted. Answers . . . in Mexico? In Chiapas? A Barcelona—La Realidad—Mexico City axis?

Was Manuel Vázquez Montalbán making an investigation or a puzzle? Whatever the case, we had to investigate the pieces. I went to talk to the committee. We thought it over for a while and decided to send Elías into the Monster. After Elías left, I sent other commissions out to gather information on the Montes Azules and I asked Deep Throat to send me anything he had on the current antics of Zedillo and Carabias. I wrote a letter to Alvaro Delgado, a journalist with *Proceso* magazine and an expert researcher on El Yunque and its reactivation under the Fox administration, begging him for information on that ultrarightist group. I wrote one other letter, addressed to the Good Governance Board of Los Altos, asking them to contact the Fray Bartolomé de las Casas Human Rights Center to gather information on the Acteal massacre. As I was compiling information, Elías would be learning how to get around in Mexico City.

When I deduced from Elías's reports that he was ready, I instructed him to find Doña Rosario Ibarra de Piedra. She would know where to find Belascoarán, and perhaps she and the ladies of Eureka might also know something about this Morales and his role in the Dirty War.

A Little Card

Me, I knew right off that Mamá Piedra was the one we call Doña Rosario Ibarra de Piedra, who works with a group of ladies we call the Doñas, and they're organized to locate men and women who were disappeared by the bad government of the PRI, and the other bad governments, which are the PAN and the PRD, cause they just clam up and never admit where they disappeared those people, that is, fighters for justice for the poor, which means that they were on the side of the people who are screwed, which is all of us. The group is called Eureka, which means that they get real happy when they find a disappeared person and reappear them, and then they have a party that they call Eureka.

So I found Doña Rosario. It took awhile cause she wasn't in the Monster. She was in Monterrey. So when she turned up, I went to see her at her little house.

She got real happy when she saw me and she kept hugging me and calling me *my son* and all, and she kept hitting me, but not like she was mad; it was just the way she was, cause she's from the north and that's kind of how northerners behave. And she asked me about El Sup and how he was and if he was sick and about the cold up there, which is where I am now, because *up there* for the city people means *right here* for us, and *out here* is *up there* for the city folk. You can see why people keep saying that I got my head a little mixed up.

So the thing is, I couldn't hardly say nothing, what with all the hugging and questions from Mamá Piedra, as we called her. When she finally got through with her hugging and things, she asked me if I was hungry and I said I was, a bit, and while she was cooking *cuche* with *mole*, or something like that, I explained to her just what it was that I was doing in the Monster and that I was on an Investigation Commission. When I mentioned this Morales, she sorta got real still and quiet, like she was thinking. Then she said the food was ready and we ate and it was real delicious, the *cuche* with *mole*, and really hot and spicy.

When we were having our coffee, Doña Piedra said that the simple truth was she couldn't remember no Morales, but that she was going to ask the other Doñas and visit the museum home of Dr. Margil, which is also in Monterrey. I said that would be good. And then I asked her if she didn't know where abouts I could find a guy called Belascoarán who did the same kind of work I do, only he does it in the city, and El Sup told me she might know about this man and might even know where he lives or where he works. She took another sip of her coffee and answered me.

"He works downtown somewhere. He's got an office on Bucareli Street. I'll get you the exact address right now."

And she began searching in a stack of papers on her table and mumbling something about a little card, and *I know I have it here somewhere, so where the heck did I put it . . .* and it took awhile, but she finally found it and gave it to me, that is, she gave me this little card that said:

Héctor Belascoarán Shayne
Independent Detective
Donato Guerra, near the corner of Bucareli
Mexico, D.F.

Fragments of the Conversation between El Sup and the One They Call Deep Throat ***(intercepted by an EP-3 spy plane***

and transmitted to one of the SIGNIT satellites of the Echelon Network and relayed to the Regional Security Operations Center at Medina Annex, U.S.A., coordinates 98°W, 29°N, NAVSEC-GRU and AIA, under code name "morai"):

"Zedillo and Carabias have business interests in Montes Azules. The NGO run by Carabias is just a front for poaching animal species, which they distribute all over the world through an international black market. Their trade in macaws, tapirs, monkeys, and other animals I can't remember right now is just the first step. They're paving the way for the entry of giant corporations that are going after the wood, the uranium, and the water. Water is going to be as important in this century as oil was in the past. I'm talking about money, a great deal of money. The Fox administration knows all about it, but they're not saying anything. Morales is a kind of sales agent and wandering bag man . . . Well, that's what he's doing now—in the past, he did a lot of other things."

"What about Tello?"

"A pissant climber; that's his whole life. I imagine you already know this, but the book he is alleged to have written about the Zapatista uprising was actually written by the intelligence services of the Federal Army on direct orders from Zedillo. They had asked Pérez Gay, I don't know if it was Rafael or José María, but he refused on ethical grounds. Then Aguilar Camín recommended one of the courtesans, Carlos Tello Díaz. This Morales individual gathered some facts and invented the rest to weave stories about the guerrilla organizations he had fought against or infiltrated in the '60s. It seems Morales was under the orders of Nazar Haro, but he also had his own initiatives. When Nazar and Salomón Tanús tortured prisoners, it was Morales who recorded what the victims said, true or false. He wrote his reports in duplicate. One he turned in, and the other he kept. When Nazar fell out of grace with his superiors, Morales vanished, but with a copy, his own copy, of the secret and unedited files of the Federal Department of Security. The real files, not the ones that were released publicly. Morales vanished for a while and just turned up recently. I'm no expert in the Dirty War, but I can tell you that the people who were in it then are still active now; they were sort of recycled. The government of change is really the government of recycled evil. Where it used to say PRI, it now says PAN. Bottom line: Morales wrote, Tello signed. That appears to be the extent of the relations between those two. Zedillo was so pleased with the book that he brought Tello into his inner circle. While Juan Ramón de la Fuente adopted Nilda Patricia, Zedillo started a, shall we say *intimate*, relationship with Julia Carabias. Tello's previous tourist trips into the Lacandona rain forest coincided with the appearances of Zedillo and Carabias in the region. In their evening get-togethers, Tello Díaz shared more than just dinner with those two. Tello might appear to be something like a bridge between Zedillo-Carabias and the people behind the *Nexos* and *Letras Libres* magazines, but it seems he wasn't. I think he's just playing the gofer for Zedillo, who's got the same sense of humor he displayed during his administration. I don't think Krauze or Aguilar Camín would invest a cent in Tello, not because they have anything against making a buck, but because they see Tello as no more than a disposable napkin—although Tello might turn out to be the theoretician behind the ecological-Disneyland transformation of the Lacandona rain forest. There you have it: pillaging of natural wealth behind the façade of ecological protection, and all of that with intellectual backing . . . the perfect deal."

"Could it be that this Morales had something to do with Acteal?"

"I don't know, but it wouldn't surprise me."

"Did you find out anything about El Yunque?"

"That information is still in the inner sanctum. I haven't been able to get any of that."

"Does Morales have any contacts with the Fox cabinet?"

"Looks like it, but I'm not certain. If he does, they are so insulated that it's difficult to pin them down. There was one meeting where his name was mentioned; everyone looked at Creel and the subject was quickly changed. I think the one who mentioned him was Martín Huerta. You might be interested to know that this Morales has a permanent pass into the American embassy. According to my information, he's been seen dining with Ambassador Tony Garza in a very exclusive restaurant."

"Do you have a picture of this Morales?"

"No, just general descriptions. Between fifty and sixty years old, about my size. Supposedly he looks like a prosperous banker. He likes to dress well and he enjoys fine cuisine."

"Okay. I think I've got enough. Did you have any difficulty getting here?"

"No, none. I thought I should come and tell you personally because I didn't like the idea of sending this in writing. What I can tell you is to take care of yourselves. They're practically hysterical with the coming elections."

"The gringos?"

"No, the gringos don't worry about these things because whoever wins will be eating out of their hands anyway. I'm talking about the domestic turds, what you call the *political class*. There's a lot of money up for grabs. It will be lucrative for anyone who can get his hands in the privatization of the power companies and the oil. Since it's obvious that this won't happen during the current administration, the smart money is betting on the next one. They're going to throw so much shit at each other . . . They're attacking López Obrador, but not because they're afraid of him or because he's a populist or anything like that. In his four years in office, all he's done is suck up to his superiors. They're after his ass because he's in the lead for the top prize. Today he's the target; tomorrow it'll be whoever takes the lead. López is getting hit in waves: First they throw the PGR at him, then Interior, then the Supreme Court of Justice, and then all of them together. Cabinet meetings are not used to plan policy, but to check the polls and plan the next strike. When the dust settles, Martita will be the only one left standing. In the PRI, they're pounding each other with everything, but the press doesn't notice it because of all the other scandals. Carlos was responsible for the Enrique Salinas thing. It's a clear message to Raúl and it says, *Shut up*. In the PRD, they're trying to figure out if it's better to sell López Obrador down the river or to get on the bandwagon. In the auction, Cuauhtémoc is the highest bidder for *Numero Uno's* head. In the end, only the worst will survive: Martita for the PAN, Madrazo for the PRI, and Cárdenas for the PRD."

"I asked you for information, not for a political analysis."

"Yes, I know, but these pricks are turning the country into a syphilitic old whore. Begging the old whore's pardon, but it really gets me mad. Listen. Tell the comrades in the committee to get me out of there. Being a prick might be contagious."

"Wasn't it you who used to say that some birds can cross a swamp without getting soiled?"

"Yeah, but this isn't a swamp, it's a goddamn sewer, and it's about to blow up. We're going to be swimming in shit."

"Come on now, you're sounding like the European Union."

"Hey, don't even joke about that. You know what side I'm on."

"So don't sweat it. What's missing is missing . . ."

Another Card

To tell the truth, I was kinda jealous of that Belascoarán and his card, so I went on down to the print shop in Santo Domingo, down there by the Zócalo, and I had me some of them cards printed up that say . . . that say . . . Gimme a minute, I got one here in my backpack. Yeah, here it is, take a look:

Elías Contreras
Investigation Commission, EZLN
Mountains of S.E. Mexico, near Guatemala
Chiapas, Mexico

Now my problem is that I have to get some more cards made up for Tzeltal, Tzotzil, Chol, and Tojolabal. That'll be the next time I go into the Monster. Okay, so I couldn't just go and find that Belascoarán feller, cause first I had to figger out whether or not I was even sposed to find him yet. So I wrote my report and I sent it to El Sup asking if I should go talk to Belascoarán and all, or if I should wait. Then I got the answer:

Do not find the soda man yet. Wait for some papers I will be sending you. When you have them, then go find him. Do not meet with him at any of his regular places. Meet someplace you already checked out before. Make sure he hasn't got a tail on him. If he's clean, make contact. From there on, it's up to you. If you think he's okay, then give him the papers and tell him we want to work together. If it looks to you like something's not right, then just tell him I send my regards and that's that. It's up to you to judge. Report when it's done. That's all. Regards.

From the mountains of Southeast Mexico,
Insurgent Subcomandante Marcos
December 2004

CHAPTER 6

ONCE YOU'VE GIVEN UP YOUR SOUL . . .

Héctor Belascoarán Shayne was in love with a ghost woman. A woman who had disappeared. This was nothing new to him. Not that he kept falling in love with ghosts, but that women with whom he had been in love, on and off, for more or less long periods of time, would suddenly disappear.

According to the mysterious agenda of the girl with the ponytail, who wasn't a girl anymore and who hadn't worn a ponytail in the longest time and instead had a lock covering one eye (Veronica Lake–style), a few marvelous and elegant white hairs, a doctoral degree in philosophy, and the ability to kick back tequila *caballitos* . . . well, according to her own weird perspective, she was nowhere. And she hadn't even taken the trouble to say goodbye, which she never did anyway. She had simply vanished. She failed to turn up for work, the university was on break, she didn't answer her telephone, even the answering machine had gone deaf and dumb, and the door to her apartment was becoming a wasteland of junk mail, electricity bills, bank statements, and issues of *La Jornada* and *Proceso*.

Sometimes Héctor would accept these disappearances as

a kind of mandatory recess from a relationship that couldn't quite be defined: intermittent but regular lovers? Unstable couple with sidereal escapes? Maori-style marriage? The lovers from *A Man and a Woman*, but twenty-five years later? A *de facto* couple with an *ex post facto* pacto?

But this time she should not have disappeared like that, because without knowing it she had left Héctor sad, depressed, feeling like he had been gypped by a pirate *pesero* . . . and a little bit older than usual. When had he fallen so crazy in love with this woman that he was ready to slit his wrists for her? This was the source of his sudden anxieties, those absolutely adolescent pangs that pursued him, those cinematographic appearances of her face when he was shaving, eating tacos, or listening to Mahler.

Mahler? What the hell did this ex girl with the former ponytail have to do with that marvelous bedeviled Jew of the dawn of the twentieth century? He had discovered Mahler many years *after* the girl with the ponytail. She was there before. And what linked the girl and the composer was not the adagietto of the *5th Symphony* (it was months later that he found out an adagietto is just a wilting adagio that never perks up, and that an adagio is a piece played slowly), the one that most people remember in connection with the movie *Death in Venice* based on the work by Thomas Mann and much improved by Visconti. That rise and fall of passions cresting and crashing like waves in the sea, and there isn't a sonovabitch alive who can recover them. No, it was not *that* Mahler that he associated with the ponytailed girl and her appearances and disappearances. Curiously enough, it was instead this tremendous piece of music he had discovered when the Mexico City Symphony had asked him to help recover a truckload of instruments. One afternoon, when they were halfway through their rehearsal, in the middle of that empty theater populated solely by a handful of musicians and a universe of sound, Héctor had caught himself drenched in tears because of music that was seizing and overwhelming him. That was why he ended up spending more time in the rehearsals than in the actual investigation. It was Mahler's *8th*. It was a paean to the greatness of humanity that Héctor interpreted on a very personal level amid the miseries of Mexico City. It was *this* Mahler that he associated with the girl. And let no one ask Héctor Belascoarán Shayne, the solitary detective in the craziest and most upside-down city on the planet, why. Let no one ask, because he would not be able to answer.

So, with a feminine and Mahlerian yearning, he sat on the side of the bed, the one he had not made in a fortnight and needed a change of linen, and played Mahler's *8th* on his stereo, instructing the machine to play it *ad nauseam*. And while it was playing, he reviewed his conversation with Fuang Chu Martínez and chain-smoked till the room was a cloud of haze.

"You have got to be breaking my balls," the Chinese man said, drawing the words from deep inside his soul.

Héctor did not feel obliged to explain why he was working as a detective in Mexico City, so he stared right back at this Chinaman who was refusing to take him seriously. Showdown: Chinese man against one-eyed man.

It was the latter who won, perhaps because all of his energy was concentrated into a single eye.

"Why are you asking about Jesús María Alvarado?"

"Because the person who hired me has been receiving voice messages from him on his answering machine."

The Chinese guy took another long look at Héctor before answering. "Alvarado is dead. I wasn't at his funeral because I was in prison, but he's dead. He died in '71, a shitload of years ago . . . So you say you're an independent cop? Which department of the Ministry of the Interior?"

Belascoarán lit a cigarette. You were still allowed to smoke in funeral parlors. For some strange reason, they had been spared from the wave of anti-tobacco Puritanism rolling down from the United Stated and sweeping across middle-class Mexico.

How could he explain the last thirty years to Fuang Chu Martínez? How could he explain his tortuous relations with the authorities? He decided to follow the method of using his scars as signposts, *the way of the scar*, his Cheyenne friends called it.

"You see this eye I'm missing? It was blown out by a former member of the Judicial Police . . . now deceased. You know why I got one leg longer than the other? From a shotgun blast fired by the same people who organized the *halcones*. I spent seven months and three days in a prison cell in Tabasco for proving an election fraud was committed by the PRI some years ago. I was beaten by a mob led by a priest in Tlaxcala who was trying to exorcize the Pokémons, and it was me who gathered the evidence to put Luisreta, the banker, in prison."

"You've got my attention," the Chinese man said.

"I'm a decent sort, some say. But about Alvarado—the only thing I know is that you two were cellmates after '68."

"So why would anyone want to know more?"

Héctor handed him a copy of the five messages the dead man had left on Monteverde's machine.

"Shit! How about that Alvarado? Sonovabitch coming

back from the dead!" Fuang Chu said with a smile out of the silent movies, only half of his face moving.

"Do you know who killed him?"

"I'll be damned. Sending messages from the beyond—that was some character, Alvarado was," the Chinaman answered, avoiding an answer, "and he brought Morales with him."

"What do you know about Morales?" Héctor snapped, swearing to himself that it would be the last question he was going to ask Fuang Chu. He would just let him say what he felt like saying.

"Me, I got this," Fuang Chu said, pulling a wrinkled piece of thermal fax paper from his pocket.

Héctor took the paper and read aloud:

He's not a dog, but he bites;
He's not Speedy Gonzales, but in pictures he's a blur;
He's not an ostrich, but he has quills;
He's not poison, but he kills;
Like me, he returns from the dead.
Who is it?

Your old cellmate,
Jesús María Alvarado

It's a shitty riddle, Héctor thought, but even so he added it to the other materials, without Fuang Chu trying to stop him.

"Do you have an answering machine?"

"No," the Chinaman said, "I'm premodern: no TV, no gas . . ."

"That's why he sent a fax."

"But he didn't send it to me, he sent it to the public baths where I work, in Guadalajara."

Héctor conjured up Alec Guinness again and prayed to le Carré for it to work. It did. The Chinese man took a long breath and began his story.

"You know how traitors develop? People don't rot overnight. They don't go to bed one night as guerrilla fighters and wake up agents of the Ministry of the Interior. They just grow weak. They betray out of exhaustion, out of boredom, out of inertia. It's as if they take so much abuse that the flesh they're made of begins to get flaccid and mushy; as if the spaces in their muscle tissue get clogged with tiny particles of shit and the remnants of old tumors. And the entire process requires ongoing justification, a growing mountain of self-pity, a dense cloud of self-deception.

"Do you know what Morales did on his twenty-fifth birthday? He turned his ex-wife in to the political police and she wound up getting tortured in the cellars of their facilities facing the Monument to the Revolution. Can you imagine what Morales did to justify that treason? He said he was saving her from certain death. Do you know what Morales dreamed about? He dreamed about his ex-wife walking barefoot on the sands of a beach in Veracruz. In the meantime, she was being raped three times and getting half her teeth kicked in."

"How do you know this?"

"Because in a two-by-three-meter cell with two other prisoners, we can hear each other's dreams, even without words. Not even our fucking dreams are private. Because Alvarado had big *cojones*, and since we'd heard all about Morales and knew he was a traitor, a plant put there to see what they could get out of us, Alvarado decided the piece of shit didn't exist and never even acknowledged his presence. And me, since I'm Chinese, I went into the most Oriental of all silences and convinced myself as well that Morales did not exist. There we were, three of us in a cell acting as if we were only two. If Morales spoke, we wouldn't answer; if he handed us a spoon, we let it drop; if we bumped into him, we didn't apologize, we just walked through him."

Héctor had kept silent, but Fuang Chu was getting lost in the past.

"Was Morales his real name?"

"Go figure. That was the name he brought with him and that's the one we know."

"Did he have a first name or only Morales?"

"Morales, only Morales. He left a lot sooner than Alvarado, and a whole lot sooner than me. I got out three months *after* Jesús María."

"Do you believe that Morales killed Jesús María Alvarado?"

"I do! Don't ask me why, but I do. Jesús left prison anxious to rebuild the network he had set up when they arrested him near the end of '68, and he was ready for anything. He said that the time for words was over; that demonstrations only served to provide the Army with target practice. He was very ready to act. Five days after he got out, they killed him. A bullet in the back of his head."

"How do you tie that to Morales?"

"I can't. I just know it! I remember the look on his face."

Héctor thought that over. It was as good an argument as any.

"I went off to Guadalajara, but it was a long time before I stopped checking the shadows and walking with my back to the wall—just to keep from making it too easy for them."

"Did you ever see or hear of Morales again?"

"Never! But when the fax arrived, I remembered something I think I read in a Henry Miller book about how once you've given up your soul, the rest follows with absolute certainty."

It was a good picture of Morales . . .

"And if Alvarado is back for vengeance, he has every right to it, and so do we, and I hope he fucks him," the Chinaman said, turning back into the funeral parlor and putting an end to the conversation.

Héctor had vague recollections of Henry Miller. The *Tropics* were anything but tropical; they were women's underwear in the air, flying ejaculations, and the puritanical capacity for astonishment of a nineteen-year-old engineering student, the spawn of a Mexican middle class capable of producing an Irish folk singer and a Basque sailor exiled in Mexico City. When had the dead man met Morales . . . or Henry Miller? Why drag him out of the past? Héctor didn't think that people like Henry Miller, or the Marquis de Sade for that matter, were subversive at all . . . just whoring pains in the ass. But in the deepest recesses of his heart, there where he never discussed literature with anyone for fear that his own loves and hates might be deemed sinful, politically incorrect, or simply unconventional, Héctor probably thought that Henry Miller was just some gringo who must have one of his balls much bigger than the other. And yet, the part about giving up your soul was familiar. Amazingly familiar for an atheist who didn't believe in souls, except as in *heels and soles*. Images from the narratives of Henry Miller began to overlap with those he conjured of the ordeal suffered by Morales's ex-wife, and it made him sick. He gave an involuntary gesture of disgust and felt a chill run up his spine. With that chill fresh in his mind, he fell asleep huddled in a corner of his bed, as if he wanted to leave room for the ghosts and the dead.

Fritz walked a few yards ahead of Héctor and crossed into what used to be cellblock 7, using his authorization to take a look, just a little peek, at each cell. There was nothing to see. Boxes and papers. All traces had disappeared. The historical archives had devoured the historical memory, the simple memory.

"Is there any way to dig up the prison records of 1968?" Héctor asked.

"Easy! Let's go up to the reading room. There's a guy there doing research on 1968 and Lucumberri."

They approached a man with Coke-bottle glasses practically hidden behind a stack of boxes, documents, and folios.

"My friend Belascoarán needs to know something about the prisoners of 1968."

The super-nearsighted researcher looked up with a smile as Héctor spoke.

"Jesús María Alvarado and Fuang Chu Martínez shared a cell here in '68. I need to know if there was anyone else in that cell. Was there another temporary occupant?"

"Crujía?"

"*The* C," Fritz said without hesitation.

The researcher brushed away a shock of hair that was threatening to block his vision and began searching through what appeared to be his own notes. He soon found a list that he traced from top to bottom with an index finger.

"Alvarado Estrada, Jesús María; Chu Martínez, Fuang."

"What about the third man?"

"There was none. According to the prison records, there

was never anyone else. You see, the lists show the changes, the newcomers. And when there were temporary inmates, they appear in brackets . . . And this is the official list of prisoners for the year 1968, the one the prison director had on his desk."

"Is there anyone at all on the list by the name of Morales . . . just Morales?" Belascoarán asked anxiously, as the man's fingers ran down the whole list again in alphabetical order.

"No Morales was ever imprisoned because of the 1968 movement," the efficient nearsighted researcher averred.

Héctor drummed on the table, eliciting a scorching glare from another researcher.

"Show him the pictures," Fritz suggested.

"What pictures?" Belascoarán demanded.

"These," and about a dozen photographs appeared out of the magic folders.

Héctor studied them intently. They were the prisoners of '68; he recognized Pepe Revueltas and the most famous ones: Cabeza de Vaca, Salvador Martínez, and Luis González de Alba. They were standing in a chaotic pose in front of a fountain.

"There are three of them I haven't been able to identify, but I know who all the others are," the researcher said, not without a hint of pride, as he pulled out a pencil trace of the photograph with a number in each of the silhouettes corresponding to a list of names.

"Which one is Jesús María Alvarado?"

"This one," said the researcher with complete certainty, pointing to a powerfully built young man with a strong mustache and curly hair.

"And the guy beside him is Fuang Chu, right?"

"Yeah, that one was easy."

"How about this other one?" Héctor asked, pointing an index finger. "He's probably one of the three you haven't identified."

"How did you know?"

"My friend here is a detective," Fritz explained proudly, as all three of them studied the blurry half-profile of a very skinny young man with a sharp nose and glasses, no more than twenty-five years old. Just an ordinary young man.

Hours later, back in Belascoarán's office, his friend Cristina Adler told him that there were no males with Morales as a paternal last name in the public-service directory of the first level of the federal government; there was, however, a female Morales who worked with Creel in the Ministry of the Interior baking animal crackers for the minister's official presents.

Héctor went out into the streets to see if the cold of the night would focus his intelligence. The foggier this Morales got, the more real he seemed to be. He flagged down the first taxi that passed his office and gave the driver the address for the Pachuca supermarket in La Condesa. He wanted to buy himself a half-pound of Spanish *chorizo de cantimpalo* and some provolone for dinner.

Fifteen minutes later, the driver pulled into one of the many dead-end streets around Mazatlán Avenue, stopped the car in a dark spot, and twisted around, brandishing a large kitchen knife. Héctor, who had been trying to imagine Morales thirty years older, just gawked.

"Give me all your cash and credit cards . . . That's today, asshole!" commanded the driver-turned-mugger.

"Just look at this bad eye I have here, young man," Héctor said, pointing to his patch. As the surprised ex–taxi driver shifted his focus to the patch, still waving the knife about two inches from his face, Héctor slapped the weapon hand aside and whipped out his .45 from his shoulder holster, sticking it between the man's eyes as he pulled back the hammer.

"Hey, what's up, amigo?"

"What's up is you're going to die, moron. Now, real slowly, drop the fucking knife, because in about a second I'm going to blow your brains out."

The guy dropped the knife, but Héctor had a hard time not firing because adrenalin is a bitch once it gets going. Like so many Mexicans, he was thoroughly fed up with the gratuitous violence that made it almost impossible for a guy to simply finish an honest day's work and come home to some *chorizo* and provolone for dinner.

"Whose taxi is this? Is it yours or did you steal it?"

"It belongs to my cousin, he lends it to me."

The thief had the look of a wild animal. His eyes kept darting from the muzzle of the .45 to his own weapon lying on the floor, yet his face was not one of defeat, but of rage.

"So now your cousin is fucked too for lending you his cab to pull this kind of shit."

Héctor hit him in the middle of the face with the gun, but you see, when they do that in the movies, the guy goes out like a light, nice and easy, but here the driver began screaming as if *he* were the victim, and bleeding out of his head like a stuck pig, so Héctor had to hand him a couple more whacks before he finally went still. Then he dragged him by the feet out of the cab and tied him to a tree with a chain and padlock he found in the trunk for securing the spare tire from thieves. He was inclined to believe that it was a real taxi, and that it was lent and not stolen, because the rear license plate was covered with mud.

Héctor decided to take the taxi. You know what they say

about thieves who steal from thieves . . . His hand was bleeding from a cut extending from under his pinky all the way to his wrist. It wasn't deep but it bled like hell. Furthermore, his shirt was drenched with blood from the assailant-driver's head. He drove the taxi to a nearby drugstore and had the pharmacist patch him up in the back of the store.

"That's an ugly cut there; how'd you get it?"

"My mother did it by accident when she was cooking," Héctor said. He loved innocent lies.

He drove the cab all the way back to the neighborhood and, taking advantage of the darkness on Mexicali Street, decided to abandon it in obscure anonymity. He checked the papers in the glove compartment, half wishing the owner's name would be Morales, but it wasn't. Unfortunately, the title was registered in the name of one Casimiro Alegre, who had nothing to do with Morales Motors or Morales Used Cars or anything of the sort. His dinner had been nicely screwed. He wasn't about to go to the supermarket at this time of night covered with blood to buy *chorizo* and provolone. He left the car with the door ajar and the keys in one of the folds of the front seat cover. If someone stole it, that would be too bad. Thieves who steal from thieves who steal from thieves . . .

Walking up to his doorway, he found Monteverde and the limping dog there waiting for him.

"What happened to your hand?"

"I cut myself on a chain saw trying to save a kid from drowning," he lied nonchalantly, though the dog seemed to look at him askance.

The street was filled with people having fun. The restaurants on all four corners were jammed, the car watchers happy as hell, and the bikers, an Aztec version of *Born to*

Lose, were behaving themselves and sucking on lemon-strawberry popsicles in front of a mini-mart.

Monteverde wondered if he should ask about Héctor's state of health, or make some stupid comment about how dangerous the streets are, but since Héctor didn't seem to care much either way, he decided to let the whole thing slide.

"I got another message from Alvarado. In your office they told me I could find you here, so seeing as how we're neighbors . . ."

"Come on up; let's hear what he has to say," Héctor replied. "I have an old turkey pot pie for your dog."

"Tobías loves pot pies."

The answering machine began its tale:

> *This is installment number twenty-seven of the history of modern Mexico, supplied free of charge by Jesús María Alvarado. It starts with the victory in the last election when the outgoing PRI administration and the incoming PAN administration signed a pact. It was a very odd pact because it was never put in writing. This secret pact had to do with an amnesty.* If you let me govern, everything in the past will be forgiven, *said the pact that was never written. Nothing had to be spelled out. Everything was said with winks, grunts, suggestions, allusions, uncertain certainties. If any of them had sworn to anything specific, the whole understanding would have collapsed; if there's one thing those bastards know for sure, it's that a sworn oath is always a lie, even if you swear to Our Lady of Guadalupe and the Mexican National Soccer Selection. But a pact was a pact. A few days later, the ex-president of the republic turned up on the board of directors of two major corporations, Proctor & Gamble and one of the gringo railroad companies, as a full*

member, leather armchair rights and all. Curiously enough, both companies had received sizable benefits from his administration: bargain-basement railroads, cheap, tax-free real estate.

The amnesty was in place. The fact that the incoming president did not say a word, did not even seem to notice that his predecessor had acquired stock options juicy enough to buy him a seat on those illustrious boards, confirmed that the fix was on. The executor of the whole thing may have been Foreign Minister Jorge Castañeda, who had said on a number of occasions that there would be no change of government without an amnesty. But that was just one deal. The last thirty years have witnessed a great many dirty deals, many suspicious overnight fortunes, many murders, many unexplained affinities, a whole lot of shit that had to be swept under the doormat.

But sometimes the pressures are just too much and a pact develops cracks. Could it be that poor old Morales was going to be left holding the stick? Naah, who could even imagine that . . . !!! To be continued—

Then silence followed by a busy signal.

When Monteverde and his dog left, Héctor tried to replace the provolone and *chorizo de cantimpalo* with an omelet of smoked oysters from Japan, and as he cooked he listened to Mahler.

He was beginning to like this dead guy. He had a certain historical perspective that living people never have—that and a strange sense of humor.

The telephone rang at the crack of dawn. In the dim rays of early day, the interior of his room was barely lit. As he moved toward the door, he stumbled into a twenty-four-pack of Cokes wrapped in plastic. With half his big toe jammed in the twenty-four-pack, Héctor hobbled on one leg, the bad one, cursing ridiculously as he made it over to the table by the chair of his dreams, just when the answering machine cut on.

> *Listen up, old buddy, this is Jesús María Alvarado.* [Coughing spell] *I know that Monteverde and his dog put you on the case. What are you going to do? Prove that I'm dead? Then what? In the meantime, let me give you a present. Do you know where Juancho is? Do you know who has him? Do you know where the taco vendor bin Laden from Juárez City is? Morales has him. If you need more data . . . Juancho, carrying his briefcase stuffed with hundreds, decided that he liked that fucky-fucky stuff and the taco stands, and he immediately thought of Mexico City, where there's a shitload of both. Great, but—*

Belascoarán smiled at the machine that was now playing a busy signal. The thought of picking up the receiver had never even crossed his mind. Rules were rules. So one was looking for him while the other left him messages. That was the game and that was how it had to be played. How had this person gotten his telephone number?

It was true enough that there were many taco vendors in Mexico City, but the part about easy sex, well, that was just a malicious rumor, a delusion of grandeur generated in the recesses of the nether regions of the biggest city in the world. It's us goddamn *chilangos* who are always going around bragging. And to judge from these latest developments, the mythical, metaphysical, and probably metaphorical Juancho–bin Laden, the taco vendor, the nonexistent Osama, the evil genius, had completely swallowed the story spread around by the defective natives that in Mexico City there's a whole lot of fucking going on.

CHAPTER 7

AND PANCHO VILLA WAS NOT A WITNESS

They can't come to me with that crock of shit that globalization is modernity." The Russian wasn't angry, that was just the way he talked. And without stopping his talking, he went on making tortillas. "What the hell modernity are they talking about? Go ahead, you tell me. That's old as the hills. They been trying to globalize us for bout 500 years. First the fuckin Spanish, then the fuckin gringos, then the fuckin French. And now they're all gettin together to gang up on us . . . even the fuckin Japanese."

The Russian is a Purépecha Indian, so go figure why he turned out tall and blond. I mean real blond, not peroxide blond. He's originally from Michoacán, but he has a "saved tortilla" stand in Guadalajara, over by the Cathedral, and its name is The Pearl of the West. Anyone who wants to understand that thing about saved tortillas would have to go the stand and check it out with the owner. The Russian works in an apron that says *Lifeguard* and he has a poster of Pamela Anderson from *Baywatch* and a large sign that says, *Our tortillas are not drowned. We save them in time. Say NO to fast food,* and further down there's another sign: *This stand is true through and through and we don't accept propaganda for America or any other religion.* Other than being blond, the

Russian is called the Russian because in '68 he went to the Olympic Village in Mexico City to find the sports delegation from the U.S.S.R. to rally their support for the political prisoners of the student movement. They sent him packing, and he started shouting that they were all fucking CIA agents and that he, the Russian, was more Soviet than any of them, because he, the Russian, had sold tacos to Leon Trotsky in Coyoacán. The Russian spent three days in Lecumberri for "lack of Olympic spirit and brotherhood among nations," the judge said. They sent him up because he was a pain in the ass, and they released him for the same reason. They couldn't deal with him. During those days in prison, the Russian met the Chinaman Fuang Chu during a political argument. The Russian might be very Russian, but he's a Maoist, and the Chinaman might be very Chinese, but he's a Trotskyite.

They spent two days and nights arguing about the essence of the Mexican Revolution—one might be very Russian and the other very Chinese, but they were both very Mexican. They wound up the best of friends thanks to Adolfo Gilly, a tenant in Lecumberri since 1966, who intervened with a presentation that later became part of his book, *The Interrupted Revolution*. The Russian got released because he had beaten up one of the guards. It had taken another six guards to get him under control. Lecumberri did not have all that many guards, so it was easier to turn him loose than keep him. The Russian and the Chinaman met again at the National Democratic Convention held in August of 1994 in Zapatista territory. On that occasion, after the downpour, they argued again. The Russian insisted that the Zapatistas were Maoists and the Chinaman insisted that they were Trotskyites. On the night of August 10, 1994, they talked to

Insurgent Major Moses and Comandante Tacho and they both became official Zapatista supporters. They've worked together in different Zapatista initiatives and they both live in Guadalajara, Jalisco, in the western part of the Mexican Republic.

At this point in time, the Russian has before him Elías Contreras, Investigation Commission of the EZLN. Elías is not talking; he's just eating his tortilla.

"Them fuckin gringos, they stole half our country in a war and then they persecuted Pancho Villa but couldn't catch him, and now they're tryin to steal the other half of the country with their fuckin transgenic hamburgers and hot dogs and radioactive waste."

The Russian went on preparing tortillas and Elías eating his.

"Then the fuckin French deposed Don Juarito Juárez, who had really big *cojones*, not like this little prick who has his photo taken with Don Juarito's picture behind him. But Don Juarito went into the resistance and he fucked the fuckin frogs. Then came the fuckin Japanese with their goddamn peanuts and their *takechi* and *koyi* and all their sweet food."

A bite by Elías into his tortilla.

"Nothing doin, my friend. What did you say your name was on this mission? . . . Well, okay, Elías, Elías Contreras. El Sup probably gave you that last name. I used to know a guy called Contreras back in 1969, a bastard who cheated at dominos. He carried a marker and made spots on the tiles, and it was a mess because then you'd get two or three rounds and no wins."

Another bite out of Elías's tortilla.

"No, the Chinaman went to Mexico City. I think a relative of his died, I don't rightly know. Goddamn Chinese. First they screw us with their Bruce Lee movies, then with their strange food, and now with their tools, which break at the first squeeze."

Next-to-last bite out of Elías's tortilla.

"So if you want to wait, be my guest. The Chechen will be coming in a while because she's going to take these tortillas to the those Altermundista kids they've got in prison. They want to break them and castrate them and bring them into El Yunque, but with these tortillas I'm sending them, full of vitamins and minerals and hydrocarbons and all, they'll be able to resist and nobody'll be able to break them. Here comes the Chechen . . . So what's happening, my beautiful Chechen? Mr. Elías here is looking for that goddamn Chinaman, cause he's got a message from El Sup. I already told him the Chinaman isn't around."

The girl the Russian called "the Chechen" to Elías: "Don't you believe this goddamn Purépecha Indian Russian, my name is Azucena. He calls me the Chechen because he's trying to start something with me and he figures it'll be easier with a bit of geographic determinism, but he hasn't got a chance. The Chinaman just returned from the capital and I'm off to see him right now. If you like, I can give you a lift."

The tortilla finished disappearing into Elías's mouth, the napkin no more than a piece of greasy nostalgia.

The Russian to Elías: "The thing is, this Chechen wants to get it on with an intellectual, and I keep telling her that I AM . . . but that I'm an organic intellectual and not a transgenic one."

The Russian to Azucena: "Don't go getting lost again in the Glorieta de Minerva . . . and don't eat the tortillas . . . and don't give any to that goddamn Chinaman!"

The Russian to Elías: "And if you run into El Sup, tell him to quit screwing around with his stories and his novel and just plain tell us outright how it all ends."

Azucena, with her bag of saved tortillas, and Elías Contreras got lost in the Glorieta de Minerva.

"Watch your hands!" the Chechen said, irritated about being lost. Elías sneaked a peek at his hands and wiped them on his pants. It took them an hour to find their way out. They parked two blocks away from La Mutualista. "Just in case we're being followed," Azucena said. "I'll go in first," she added.

Elías waited in the car. A while later Azucena returned. "He's there. He'll be waiting for you at the lockers," she said. Elías didn't know what *lockers* were. Azucena explained. "They're like gray steel boxes with locks on them. There's a mess of them in several rows. That's where the Chinaman will be."

They said goodbye and Elías entered the public baths. Sitting on one of the benches facing the *gray steel boxes with locks* was Fuang Chu.

The Chinese man said hello and asked how everyone was doing. Elías said okay, that he was on an Investigation Commission, and handed over the envelope. Fuang Chu opened it up, checked the documents, and noticed a picture.

"So you guys are looking for this Morales too? Sounds like an epidemic. In Mexico City, I ran into a guy calling himself a detective who was also looking for him. I got a fax from some comrade who's already dead. I met a guy named Morales when I was in prison. A real prick, he was. But he didn't look like the one in the picture. I'll write this all down for you."

While Fuang Chu wrote, Elías strolled down the aisles of lockers as if he were looking for something. On one of the lockers, behind an old poster announcing an event in honor of Manuel Vázquez Montalbán at the International Book Fair, there was a little piece of paper stuck on the metal. Elías read it and lit a cigarette, then returned to where Fuang Chu had finished writing.

The Chinese man gave Elías the papers and the picture, shook his hand in farewell, and said, "You give my best to Moy. And if you run into El Sup, tell him to quit screwing around with his stories and novel and just plain tell us outright how it all ends."

A Hacker in the American Union

Paris, Texas, U.S.A., December 2004. Natalia Reyes Colás, 100% Ñahñu Indian, wetbacked it over to the other side in 1944 when the Second World War was still going on. At the age of twenty, she married some meatball who she soon sent packing because he beat her. She recently turned seventy-five and has been an Internet junkie and ham operator for the last fifteen years. With a lot of reading and practice she became a skillful and respected web hacker, signing herself *NatKingCole*. Cruising the ether very late one night, she broke into a satellite electronic surveillance system known as Echelon, one she had been following for years. *NatKingCole* downloaded and decoded a message. Running it over in her mind, she thought: *Damn Zapatistas, they just won't keep still. Let's give them a little hand and screw the hawks* and *the doves!* She keyed in her own encoded message and attached a little present. A few more strokes and the Echelon transmission was amended. At the Medina Annex earth station, they received a nonsense message: *Over in the fountain/the spout was in the middle/the stream first got real big/and then it got real little.* The disconcerted operator ran the tape over and over again. The virus that would come to be known as Bitter Pozol slowly infiltrated the operating system and spread throughout the entire Echelon network. It took the experts three weeks to sweep the system clean of the complete works of Francisco Gabilondo Soler, alias Cri-Cri, whose ideological persuasion was not on file with the Central Intelligence Agency. To correct the "accident," Bush had to reorganize his intelligence services, and the State Department issued a press release accusing Al Qaeda and Osama bin Laden of cybernetic terrorism.

NatKingCole, better known to the former migrant workers of Tlaxcala as Doña Natalia, turned off her computer, caressed her cat Eulalia, and said, "Well, what do you think? Have we earned some warm milk and cookies?"

"Meow," Eulalia answered.

"Me too," said Natalia Reyes Colás, neo-Zapatista of Paris, Texas, U.S.A., as she opened her refrigerator door.

La Magdalena

Sometimes even God makes mistakes. The other day, I was roaming around the Monument to the Revolution—that is, I was exploring the terrain, cause you gotta know which way to run when the thing (or the *case*) gets nasty. So I had spent some time in a little park called San Fernando, which is right there by the cemetery. And I stayed awhile facing the statue of General Vicente Guerrero, the one where they have the motto of the Zapatista National Liberation Army: *Live for your country or die for freedom.*

Then it got a little late and I walked off down the street called Puente de Alvarado, and right there the police got me—that is, the *Judiciales.* They asked who am I and what am I doing and said that I should fork over what I had and a lot of other strange things, cause those *Judiciales* talk real strange. So they were trying to push me into the police car, and then a girl comes over with a really, really short skirt and a tiny blouse—that is, she was practically naked even though it was cold. Then she talked to the *Judiciales* and they sort of let me go. And then she came over to where I was and we talked and she said her name was Magdalena and she asked where I was from cause I talked real different and, seeing as how she must be a good person cause she shooed the *Judiciales* away, I told her I was from Chiapas, so she asked me if I was one of those Zapatistas and I said I didn't know what Zapatistas are, and she said I must be one cause real Zapatistas don't go around saying they're Zapatistas. So then she told me she had been in the Zapatista National Liberation Front, the FZLN, but she hardly didn't have time to go to meetings and all, and then she started to explain how she wasn't a she, but a he, and there I was not understanding much, and she picks up her skirt and I see plain as day that there was something under her bloomers making a big bump. So I asked how it was that she was a he but dressed like a she, and he/she explained that she's really a woman but got born in the body of a man. And then she said that since there was no clients around that we could go up to her room, and when we were there he/she told me the whole story about how she needed to save money to have the operation to make her a woman's body and that's why she was street-walking, and I said I walked a lot of streets and she explained how street-walking was a kind of job to save money, and then she fell asleep. So I made myself as comfortable as I could in a corner with my jacket and a blanket Magdalena loaned me. But I didn't hardly sleep at all cause I got to thinking how God makes mistakes, cause

Magdalena, who is a woman, got put in the body of a man.

The next day we had some coffee, but almost at noon cause Magdalena didn't get up. And I started talking about the Zapatista struggle and about how we're organized in the resistance towns, and she was real happy listening. But I didn't say I was on an Investigation Commission or nothing, and she didn't ask what I was doing in the Monster, that is, Mexico City. And I looked at her and thought she was a good woman, cause she was discreet and didn't go around asking what a body was doing. And she said that if I had to, I could stay in her room however long I needed. So then I thanked her and I went out and bought her a bouquet of red roses and gave them to her, and I said that as soon as we win the war we were going to set up a hospital to put right everything that God got wrong. Well, right there she started crying, maybe cause nobody ever gave her flowers, and she went on crying for a while. And later she went out to do her street-walking and I went out to find that there place Belascoarán works at.

Fragments of a Letter from Álvaro Delgado (*reporter for the Mexican magazine* Proceso), Addressed to Sup Marcos, Late 2004:

> *There is definitely a connection between El Yunque in Mexico and at least one fascist organization in Spain known as* Ciudad Católica. *This organization remains loyal to the Franco program and is a hardline detractor of democracy.*
>
> *The founder of El Yunque, Ramón Plata Moreno (assassinated in 1979, allegedly due to the work of an inside informer), venerated José Antonio Primo de Rivera, leader of the Spanish phalanx. Aside from Spain, El Yunque maintains relations with ultrarightist organizations in France, Argentina,*

Brazil, and Peru. Everything about El Yunque smells of the obscurantism of the Middle Ages and the persecution of ideas.

The Fox cabinet is packed with Yunque members. For example, Emilio Goicochea Luna (alias Jenofonte), private secretary to Fox (and national leader of the Boy Scouts); Guillermo Velasco Arzac, ideologue for Fox and Marta Sahagún; Ramón Muñoz Gutiérrez (alias Julio Vértiz), head of the President's Office for Government Renovation, and along with Marta Sahagún, the real power behind the throne; Enrique Aranda Pedrosa, director of Notimex; Martín Huerta, federal secretary of Public Security; Alfredo Ling Altamirano (alias Daniel Austin), Institute of Access to Information; Luis Pazos, general director of Banobras and notorious for having misdirected federal funds to Jorge Serrano Limón's Provida, a "pro-life" group.

And the PAN is not far behind: Luis Felipe Bravo Mena (national president), Jorge Adame (senator), Manuel Espino Barrientos (general secretary), and Juan Romero Hicks (alias Agustín de Iturbide, present governor of Guanajuato), among others.

It is not only MURO (University Movement for Renovation Orientation) that serves as a front for El Yunque. There are also organizations such as the Nationalist Integration Vanguard (VIN), Anticommunist University Front (FUA), Christian Movement Yes, National Council of Students (CNE), Comprehensive Human Development and Citizens Action (DHIAC), National Civic Women's Association (ANCIFEM), National Pro-life Committee, Testimony and Hope Movement, Mexican Human Rights Commission, National Morality Alliance, In Favor of the Best, Citizens Coordination, Iberian-American Unifying Guard (GUIA)—just to mention a few. Father Maciel's Legionnaires of Christ appeared at almost the same time, so there's probably some connection.

Although the right, like the left, is not a single, indivisible monolith (there are differences and even confrontations), the ultraright has real power in Mexico and is working to infiltrate every aspect of society—social, political, and cultural.

I don't know if there is any Morales in their structure, but the one thing you can be certain of is that El Yunque, also known as the Army of God, has a paramilitary structure and their indoctrination meetings are run with military discipline. One of their branches is called Crusaders of Christ the King. El Yunque has done everything possible to get close to the Army, though I don't have any data linking them to the organization of paramilitary groups.

I'm sending you my book, The Army of God: New Revelations on the Extreme Right in Mexico, *published by Plaza y Janes. In it you will find thoroughly chilling facts.*

Piece of Cake

You cannot live
with a death inside
you have to choose:
hurl it far away
like rotten fruit
or be infected
and die.

That was how the deceased Digna Ochoa and the deceased Pável González began their communiqué. It was part of a poem by a lady who defended all of us screwed people, and her name was Alaide Foppa. The poem was called

"Misfortune" and I knew that the communiqué was going to be released on January 6. Cause the thing is, one day I ran into this comrade Alakazam, who's a magician—that is, he makes things appear and disappear and he knows what people are thinking. So this Alakazam gave me the message that I should go find the Chinaman, over where I already knew, and he gave me some papers so I'd show them to the Chinaman and he should tell me what he thought about them—that is, the Chinaman should tell me his thinking on it. So then I left for Guadalajara, but I didn't go directly to where I knew the Chinaman was. No sir! I went first to find the Russian. So there I was, eating tortillas with the Russian, when this woman from Guadalajara comes up, I mean the female comrade named Azucena, the one who took me to see the Chinaman. Then I talked to the Chinaman and I showed him the papers and a picture El Sup sent me with Alakazam. And when the Chinaman was busy writing his thinking, I took a walk around to find something that had to do with Don Manolo— that is, Manuel Vázquez Montalbán—and I found a poster with his name on it, Don Manolo's, I mean. So I felt around behind it and I found this piece of paper that said, *The thing by the deceased appears on the epiphany; when you get the papers, go see the soda man.* Now it was clear that on January 6 I was sposed to find the papers for the investigation that we were gonna do with the Belascoarán feller, although at that time I didn't rightly know if he was gonna come in on it or if he was gonna shrivel up like a flower that can't take the heat. So when I got back from Guadalajara, I went looking for his workplace—his office, I mean—over where that little card said, the one I got from Mamá Piedra, Doña Rosario Ibarra de Piedra, that is. I already had some kind of idea what this Belascoarán was like, cause the

Chinaman told me about him, so I went to that street called Donato Guerra and I played the dummy awhile to check if Belascoarán was being watched and to see if he even showed up. It was real late when this feller went into one of the buildings, all loaded down with Coca-Cola bottles. Now I knew right away it was Belascoarán, cause he only had one eye, and besides that, he had a leg that didn't work too good either. But I stood around awhile cause I says to myself, what if there's a few one-eyed gimps on Donato Guerra Street, near the corner of Bucareli, over in the Monster. Finally, I figgered there was only one of them and that it had to be that Belascoarán, cause he had one eye and a limp and that's the way the Chinaman said he was. Besides that, he was loaded with Cokes and that musta been why El Sup called him *the soda man*. So let me tell you that this Belascoarán was about as old as me—as old as me, that is, before I was deceased, which means that he must be around fifty years old going on sixty. Then I got to thinking how what with being crippled in the eye and in the leg, he was real easy to peg. And then I thought that I had to see him in someplace with a lot of people, cause with so many people maybe he wouldn't stand out so much. So I figger he sleeps there—in the office, I mean—cause I left there real late and he never came out.

Then the next day I was on him at the crack of dawn, and I had to wait till about noon before he came out so's I could slip into the building. Inside, I climbed the stairs looking to find the workplace and ran across a door with a sign that said:

Héctor Belascoarán Shayne, Detective
Gilberto Gómez Letras, Plumber
Carlos Vargas, Upholsterer
Javier Villareal, Engineer Whatever

So I stuck my ear against the door. I heard somebody singing that old one about *A bed of stones to lie on/a stony mattress to feel/If ever some woman loves me/she'll have to love me for real*, and then he screwed it up on the *ay, ay, ay* part. So I knocked on the door. And I left this message for Belascoarán, I left it with a feller called Carlos Vargas who tears the stuffing out of chairs all day. Okay, so I put the message and my card in this envelope and it said, *I'll meet you at Villa's tomb. On the Epiphany. At 23:00 hours, Southeastern Combat Front time.* So that's what I did, cause at the Monument to the Revolution there's always a shitload of people walking around with their families and eating *garnachas* and all them fried things city people like so much and I already tried them and, yeah, they're tasty enough. Then, what with so many people milling around and eating *garnachas* and all, nobody was going to notice just this single one-eyed gimp. So on January 6, I bought the newspaper called *La Jornada* and I saw that there was no communiqué, and that's when I went looking for Andrés and Marta to see if they knew something about it, and that's when I started to get a little bit really worried, cause if no communiqué came out, then I wouldn't know where to go for the papers that I was sposed to take to this Belascoarán, and that would mean I would be really screwing up if I got to see him without the papers. But then Andrés and Marta got to pecking on this computer thing they got, and at about 4 in the afternoon, Fox time, he says that in Germany they already received the communiqué. So I asked where that Germany was and Marta showed me on a map, and I saw how Germany was really far away. And then I got to thinking whether El Sup had gone to Germany. But Andrés and Marta explained that the communiqué gets sent out from the Zapatista Information Center and it goes to the whole world, and they probably already have it in *La Jornada*, but it wouldn't get published until the next day. Well, right there I thought I was in deep shit, but then Andrés and Marta got to pecking again on that computer thing, and all at once they said, "We got it." And then they did a little more pecking and it got printed, the communiqué did. So I got a whole lot happier cause I had the communiqué, but I still had to go about figgering where I had to pick up the papers. My job then was to read the communiqué very carefully, cause it was in there that El Sup would tell me where to go to find a message.

I read through the communiqué word by word and I understood that I had to go to the UNAM library (that was over at the university, right in the Monster) and I had to find a book by a lady named Foppa and then the exact place where the poem is, and that's where the message from El Sup was going to be. Then I took a metro to get to that university campus real quick, the *UC* they call it. But the thing is, the metro doesn't take me right where I want to go, it just leaves me on the edge of that campus, and that's when I wound up walking a stretch. Now, even though it was 6 p.m., Fox time, there was young guys and young girls all over the place with books and knapsacks, and I figgered that this campus must be a real happy place.

So I finally got to a building they call "Philosophy and Letters," where there's lots of people milling around and guys selling CD movies real cheap. But that wasn't where the library was, according to this young girl with very dark skin who was asking about a movie called *Alice in the Subway* or something like that, and they didn't have it, the movie, but the dark-skinned girl did manage to tell me where the library was, which was right nearby, and I went in and asked if they had books by Alaide Foppa and they told me how they had one called *Poetry*. And so I looked in there and found a poem called "Misfortune" that's a little long and all, about a lady who's really in love and her husband dies and she's all sad cause she loved him so much.

So that poem starts on page 87 and when I got to page 110, I found the part that El Sup put in the communiqué about the deceased Digna and Pável, and right there on that page there was a little key and a note that only said, *North Bus Depot*. So I could tell that I had to go to that there place and pick up the papers I needed for my job as Investigation Commission. And I took off real fast cause it was already 7 in the evening, Fox time, that is, 20:00 hours Southeastern Combat Front time. By that time, I was a little bit worried cause there was only three hours before I had to see the Belascoarán feller, so I took the metro again with a bunch of people and I got to the North Bus Depot about 21:30 Southeastern Combat Front time, which was 8:30 Fox time. Well, soon's I got there I started wondering exactly where I was sposed to start looking for the papers, and just then I remembered those steel boxes over where the Chinaman works and I figgered that the little key must be to open one of them. Well, I finally found them but I noticed that there was a lot and that they was all the same, so I thought, how am I gonna find the right one, cause if I start looking over them too much they're going to think I'm fixing to rob something, so I sat on one of those benches and started rereading the communiqué all over again, and that's when I noticed that the first poem had seven lines to it. I figgered I just had to find the box with the seven on it, and I found it and opened it, and sure enough, there was a envelope all bunched up cause it had so much stuff in it.

Well, that's when I got really glad and rushed to the metro station called Hidalgo to go meet Belascoarán, and what do you know, I did make it on time for the meeting with him. So by the end of it all, I asked myself, was that a piece of cake or what?

A Hat

I got myself a hat, but not one of those *sombreros* we use up in our part of the country. Nope, this was a city hat, one where the visor is soft all the way around and it's made out of real nice material, warm like. El Sup it was who gave it to me, and he told me his daddy had given it to him a bunch of years ago, when he was still city folk—I mean, when El Sup was city folk. *It's going to come in handy*, El Sup said, and sure enough it did, cause it's cold in the Monster. So me and El Sup's hat went to the Monument to the Revolution. There was a lot of people, families, that is, all in the fair and having their pictures taken with the three Magi Kings and all. With so much noise and hubbub going on, I followed Belascoarán awhile till he stopped to light a cigarette in front of that hoity-toity hotel called the Meliá. Now, I could tell right off he was checking his back to see if he had a tail on him, but I knew he didn't.

So this Belascoarán gets stuck in the crowd that was all balled up in front of the ISSSTE house, and I decided to cut around and wait for him in front of Pancho Villa's tomb. When he got there, I looked straight into his bum eye and said, "That Pancho Villa had real *cojones*, that's why they deceased him," and I lit one of my cigarettes, the ones we call Scorpions.

Then he took out one of his own and I could see it was one of those called Delicados, and he lit it and said, "It wasn't his *cojones* got him killed; they killed him because he sided with those who get screwed."

Then we hung around awhile, just smoking and looking at each other. I figgered this Belascoarán was on the up and up, so I give him my card saying, *Elías Contreras, Investigation Commission.*

He stuck out his hand and gave me his card saying, *Héctor Belascoarán Shayne, Independent Detective.*

Then he started going on about how the deceased Pancho Villa wasn't really buried where they said he was, but that the aforementioned . . . that's when I found out that *aforementioned* is the word you say when you already mentioned somebody and you don't want to have to come back and say the name all over again, so in this case (or *thing*), the person is *Pancho Villa*, so when I say the *aforementioned*, what I'm saying is actually Pancho Villa, but not all the time, it depends on when you use it—in any case, it's all mixed up, but since it's a new word I learned, I'm using it all I can, but not too much cause I already have my head all mixed up anyway. So he went on about how the aforementioned—that is, Pancho Villa—wasn't in that tomb, cause there was this lady where he was sposed to be and he was someplace else, least that was what Belascoarán was saying.

After a while of talking, I said, "I'm out looking for the Bad and the Evil, so there you have it, now you tell me if you want in," and gave him the pack of papers El Sup sent me.

Then Belascoarán looked at the papers real quick and flicked his cigarette and said real clear, "I'm in."

I was glad about that, cause he coulda said he didn't want in and then I woulda made the whole trip to the Monster for nothing. We decided to meet again the next day, after he looked at the papers real slow like, so we could agree how we was going to work in coordination, which means together, the both of us, him and me, then we said goodbye, but before leaving, he asked me if I needed anything, and I said, "Yeah, I do. I don't know where I can get some *pozol* here in the Monster—in Mexico City, I mean—and I also need to find a grape flavor soda called Chaparritas El Naranjo."

"Let me check it out," he said, "and I'll let you know tomorrow."

So we left and the noise went on. Back in Magdalena's room I wrote a small report to El Sup, and a couple days later he answered:

> *Copy meeting with soda man. See him again to coordinate investigation. Over here everything normal. We're having some laughs with the crap Fox said on his visit over here. In case you haven't heard about it in the news, he's repeating the same nonsense we heard from Hernán Cortéz, Agustín de Iturbide, Antonio López de Santa Anna, Maximilian of Hapsburg, the gringos Polk, Taylor, Pershing, and Eisenhower, and Porfirio Díaz, Gustavo Díaz Ordaz, Salinas de Gortari, and Ernesto Zedillo: He said that we were long gone. Later, when I finish laughing, I'll send you some more information I received. Regards and Happy New Year.*
>
> *From the mountains of Southeast Mexico,*
> *Insurgente Subcomandante Marcos*
> *January 2005*

CHAPTER 8

A NIGHT WITH MORALES

Three things would stick in Héctor Belascoarán Shayne's mind from his encounter with the Zapatista investigator, Elías Contreras: the super pandemonium of the monument to a lost revolution, now populated by hawkers and vendors; the expression on envoy Elías Contreras's face when he began to talk about the comparative virtues of Pancho Villa and Emiliano Zapata; and the "Morales file" sent to him by the Zapatistas. All three things took root in his soul.

The Monument to the Revolution in Mexico City was born like some monstrosity to the greater glory of the Porfirio Díaz administration; the Revolution of 1910 left it half-built, and that's the way it stayed until the mid-'30s, when it was recycled as a grandiloquent mausoleum for the obsolete armed struggle. Somewhere under its columns lie the remains of Venustiano Carranza, Plutarco Elías Calles, Lázaro Cárdenas, and, allegedly, Pancho Villa: personalities who often fought on opposing sides and lay in the same plot thanks only to the pragmatic magic employed by the PRI to turn history into consumable material and a legitimizer of its own power.

They've somehow forgotten that Villa fought against Carranza, that Calles participated in the assassination of both, and that Cárdenas ordered the expulsion of Calles from Mexico. Regardless, there they are, all together. The people of Mexico City are convinced it's because of these uncomfortable graves that the city is afflicted by so many killer earthquakes.

At this time of year, the monument was crawling with carousels, taco vendors, *bolita* bookies, metal-horse races, handicraft hawkers, and hundreds of Magi Kings, complete with stalls and photographers, representing the only monarchy Mexican believers in the republic will allow. The night was alive with music—*cumbias*, crap from the north, and the *chuca-chuca* of the crumbiest tropics—played at hundreds of decibels and seasoned by the aroma of candied apples and cotton candy.

The center of the monument had not been overrun by the revelers of the Epiphany, and under the shadows Belascoarán made his way toward the person with the gray hat at the foot of the Pancho Villa Mausoleum with whom he was supposed to, curiously enough, identify himself by means of a business card.

"Did you know that Pancho Villa is not buried where they say he is?" Belascoarán asked, pointing to the ultra-official tomb.

"So who did they put in place of the aforementioned?" Elías Contreras asked.

"Well, it's somewhat complicated, but funny. You see, in November of 1976, President Echeverría decided to stick another feather in his cap and ordered that the remains of Villa be taken from Parral and brought for burial with military honors under this corner of the monument. But somebody had already rifled through Villa's tomb in 1926 to steal the head, which never turned up, and one of the widows—"

"You mean he had more'n one?"

"Officially, three. In reality, about twenty-five. So one of the widows, wanting to prevent the further disappearance of pieces of the general, took the rest of him out of the tomb and moved them about 120 meters further down in Parral Cemetery. Then, as luck would have it, this widow, who was making trips to the United States for cancer treatment, died, and the locals figured they might as well bury her in Villa's old grave. That's why, when they opened the grave in '76, under the direct supervision of an anthropologist, somebody told the Army that the deceased had the head and pelvic curve of a woman. The soldiers in charge told him to fuck off, cause they had a mission to fulfill and nobody gave a rat's ass if he had a head, and the woman's pelvis be damned. So in an open caisson, escorted by cadets of the Military Academy in full dress formals, they brought the lady and buried her with high military honors, and every year the honors are repeated, complete with bugles and trumpets. Most people figure she deserves it for going and dying in Parral."

"How bout Villa?"

"No! Villa gave them the slip . . . once again."

The amazing character with the antediluvian hat perched on his stiff hair just stood and stared at Belascoarán.

"You probably believe that Emiliano Zapata had bigger balls than Pancho Villa, right?" Belascoarán said, trying to break the ice with the Zapatista comrade.

Elías Contreras not only thought it, he knew it, and he couldn't imagine how anyone with half a brain could even doubt it. So he just stared at Belascoarán, asking himself what kind of *nauyaca* had bitten him and liquefied his brain.

He had to keep this fellow from saying that Villa was better than Zapata, or else the whole relationship would go to pot, cause El Sup had told him that if this Belascoarán was even a little bit chickenshit, he should forget about him. So he just handed him the envelope.

Héctor took the package and read the capital block letters on the cover: *MORALES.* There were several folders, a number of files on a certain Morales. The surprise almost bowled Belascoarán over. He didn't know whether to shit or go blind. Next, the bin Laden–Juancho thing would be real as well. Could the Zapatistas be after Morales too?

"Do you believe in coincidence?"

"That's the only thing I *don't* believe in."

"Do you believe in chance?"

"Only when there ain't none."

The Zapatista Elías Contreras then said very seriously, "I'm looking for the Bad and the Evil. Now *you* decide if you come in on this or what."

"Of course I'm in," said Belascoarán, without giving it a second thought.

Now, Héctor Belascoarán Shayne did not believe in plots; he had experienced too many to wind up believing in them. He was a Mexican, subject to the Mexican definition of paranoid: *a guy who believes that he's being followed by a couple of guys who are following him.* But he didn't have a simplistic attitude either. His brother, Carlos, the family's eternal militant, used to say that Héctor, the existential Martian, was one of those guys who paradoxically believe that the social being is the vehicle of the social conscience, that Ali Baba ran around with the forty thieves so much that he became one and joined the PRI. Héctor believed that if you were a chair for too long you'd ultimately enjoy having somebody's ass on you all the time. But he did not believe in the innate evil of politicians; he believed that if you become one for too long you end up turning into a prick, and that having power too long creates an obsession with power, and when your political power is over you're left with money, which is another kind of power, and that's why there are so many open drawers to stick your hand into, so many abuses; and to keep the country the way they wanted it, Mexico's leaders in recent years had established a kind of supreme law of the land (one that was never made public and was kept in the supreme closet of the supreme leader), which dictated things like: *The only principle of survival is the principle of authority. When your principles are in the gutter, the best thing to be is a rat. The Revolution will do us justice. Finders keepers, losers weepers. You scratch my back and I'll scratch yours. The law of the budget is to take your fill; if you don't steal it, someone else will.* Héctor was convinced that in earlier times Mexico had been essentially unfair, ruled by abuse of power, arbitrariness, and violence against the underprivileged; and more recently by mediocrity, phony religiosity, spite, and bad taste.

But when he glanced over the Morales file, he thought his mouth would never close again, and his cigarette almost burned his fingers. This was too much; this was the Ken and Barbie album of power abuse. It justified the very idea that the system had bribed the devil.

The package contained the documents of Manuel Vázquez Montalbán, a mysterious photograph, a typed page entitled *The Earthquake Deal*, the White Brigade's black book, a few communiqués from Zapatista headquarters, an excerpt of a conversation between a certain Marcos and somebody known as Deep Throat, and a short note from the subcomandante:

Greetings to you from all of us here, and from me personally. A few weeks ago we received a collection of notes by a writer named Manuel Vázquez Montalbán that his son found among his papers after his death, and which contained very interesting information about a character he calls "Morales." We do not know the outcome of the investigation in Barcelona that produced these notes. We do not know whether they were notes for a future novel, or if they are something much more alarming, or both. Since they look like some sort of detective puzzle, it occurred to me that you might be interested in helping us figure it out. I don't think I need to warn you that if this character exists, he is extremely dangerous. If you agree to collaborate in the investigation, Comrade Elías will be your permanent liaison with us. If you do not, we urge you to be extremely discreet.

Best regards from the mountains of Southeast Mexico,
Insurgent Subcomandante Marcos

Of all the possible times and places to study the materials, he had chosen his office in the middle of the night, perhaps because if he was going to spread them all out, he would need his own desk, the one belonging to the Rooster Villarreal, Gómez Letras's plumbing table, and the broken chairs awaiting plastic surgery from Carlos Vargas. He tried to place them in some kind of order and complement them with his own findings, to see if he could get the whole hodgepodge into perspective; *perspective*, that grand lady whose favor it would seem he had lost.

Toward the end of 1968, a former guerrilla fighter of about twenty-five years of age betrayed his comrades and his wife and became an ally? informant? agent? for the Mexican government's Secret Service (according to the talking corpse). This man shared a cell with Jesús María Alvarado and Fuang Chu Martínez (according to the Chinese man).

He went by the name of Morales, but there was no trace of him in the prison records, just a picture of a very skinny young man with a pointy nose and the glasses of the terminally nearsighted. He couldn't have been more than twenty-five.

This individual murdered Jesús María Alvarado when he, Alvarado, was freed from prison in 1971 (according to the Chinese man.)

In later years, he joined (may have joined) the White Brigade (according to the Vázquez Montalbán papers) in the period known as the Dirty War. The notebook entitled *The Black Book of the White Brigade* contained eight pages of an anonymous text run off an ancient mimeograph machine and bound with a pale blue cover. It was an overwhelming catalogue of horrors connected to that police-military organization that arose in 1974 during the presidency of Luis Echeverría. A cross-ministerial organization involving the Army and the Ministry of the Interior and dedicated to the eradication of the incipient urban guerrilla, whatever the means, whatever the cost. They did everything, above and beyond all legality: kidnapping, murder, torture. It was headed by a certain Nazar Haro. A tiny account in the booklet, telling of some of the operations of the White Brigade, seemed to attest to the presence of Morales in it. It was underlined in red pencil and said, *Among the torturers were Morales, agent Urteaga, and a "minder" by the name of Canseco,* and that was all.

Deep Throat's papers made another mention: When the brigade tortured someone,

that Morales was one of those taking notes (. . .) When Nazar fell from the grace of his bosses, Morales disappeared, but he took with him an uncensored copy of the records of the Federal Department of Security—the real records, not the ones they released publicly.

Belascoarán jotted down 1983 as the probable date when Morales dropped out of sight. That date was more or less clear. Then came a brief gap. After that, you could insert the data from the mimeographed sheet, which appeared to be a fragment of the transcript of a recording, which read:

—what Gustavo Arce told me, who was a member of one of the brigades organized by the anthropology students to stop the pricks, because after the earthquake they were trying to take advantage of the cracked walls and sinkholes, particularly in the center, to pull down the homes and evict the people so they could build whatever they fucking well pleased. Then the grenadiers would come with eviction notices, supposedly for the people's protection, right? And the brigades of students from the school of anthropology would mark the buildings with notices saying, Building catalogued as a national monument, *right? Then nobody could tear it down without the authorization of the Anthropology Institute. So, together with the community, they would stop them. It was a real bitch . . . a few pricks speculating with the misfortune of the people, and the one coordinating the operation with the police and the building owners was a certain Morales, Señor Morales. Gustavo, who had a few altercations with him, a few shouting matches actually, says he was a toad, a freaking cynic about fifty years old who had a limp and wore rings with red stones on his pinky and ring finger of his left hand. Later, I got curious about that Morales person, because he didn't work for the Mexico City govern-*

ment. When everything had quieted down, he was no longer seen in the historic city center. I asked about him and no one could tell me anything, but he ran squads for the Ministry of Public Works of the Mexico City government, and bossed around officers of the grenadiers like he was their damn father. When I tried to write about this, he was no longer around, but Laura, the one from the Union of Earthquake Victims, remembered him and told me he had a mustache and white hair on his temples. Not a lot, but . . .

So Morales could be placed in Mexico City in 1985 at the time of the earthquake that registered 8.1 on the Richter scale . . . except that this Morales was "about fifty years old" and the White Brigade Morales mentioned by Alvarado would not be more than thirty-five to thirty-eight. Could it be the same time-worn Morales? Maybe. People were usually rotten at guessing ages. Just ask María Félix: She celebrated her fiftieth birthday three times and people either didn't notice or didn't care enough to notice.

Then there was a quantum leap.

Another piece of paper with a note: *Beginning of the Zapatista uprising in Chiapas. January 1994.* Belascoarán picked up the phone and dialed Luis Hernández, an anthropologist and journalist who wrote about the Zapatista movement, had the only knapsack that kept beers cold, and answered the telephone at the paper any time of night.

"This is Belascoarán. What does the name Morales tell you?"

"At this time of night, it tells me everything and nothing. Can't you give me something more to go on?"

"The Zapatistas, for example?"

"Right on! There's the Morales that betrayed them. A

guy called Daniel, if memory serves me, but there's an article on the web by Gilberto López Rivas. Morales was the one who gave Tello all the information about the Zapatista movement for the book he wrote called *Las Cañadas.*"

"I owe you one, buddy."

"What are you onto? Something I can write about?"

Belascoarán's grunts and groans were open to a number of interpretations.

"Yeah! Okay! Right!"

Belascoarán dialed again, this time it was his web surfer, Cristina Adler. He knew he wasn't running any risk of waking her up because she did her best work at night, translating mystery novels.

"Listen, sweetheart, there's an article in who knows what newspaper published who knows when by one López Rivas about a certain Daniel. Can you find out what the hell is up with this Daniel guy? I'm still at the office."

"You thank God I'm such a genius. Back to you in a flash, Belascoroni."

Héctor took the opportunity to step out into the hallway and use the shared facilities for a perfunctory leak. He had to cut down on sodas, though the first thing he did when he got back in the office was make a beeline for the safe, where he found a Coke that was miraculously still cold. And just then the phone rang.

"Yes, there is a Morales, Salvador Morales Garibay, a.k.a., Daniel. That's why there was so much confusion with the names. Comandante Daniel. He was one of the military leaders of the Zapatista Army, but right before the insurrection, in October of '93, he left the forest under the pretext of hooking up with a contact for a load of weapons coming from Central America, and he never returned. He resurfaced at the entrance to the Presidential Staff Headquarters, right there in Molino del Rey, offering his services as an informant to the Mexican Army. He gave them information about the leadership of the Zapatista Army and their first clear picture of what was going on—according to this article."

"Any idea why he deserted?"

"It seems he was officer-in-charge at a camp that was discovered by the Army and he really screwed things up, almost squelching the Zapatista uprising. So he got punished or something. Yet he wound up as a mole 'with the rank of Captain, Second-in-Command in Quartermaster Administration, with specific functions in the second section of National Defense General Headquarters,'" Cristina concluded.

"Does it say what he looked like?"

"Not in this article, but it does in a different one. I'm way ahead of you, Belascoreeno, and I quote: 'five-foot-eight, forty-two years old'—forty-five now. Go figure when exactly they're talking about, but it can't be more than a couple of years ago—'black hair with advanced baldness, dark brown eyes, thin lips, white skin, and slim. He was christened *The Finger* by the lower ranks; others called him *Chava*.'"

"You got anything else, genius?"

"There's an interview with him by Maité Rico and La Grange in *Letras Libres*."

"I don't read *Letras Libres*."

"So you're screwed, cause I don't read it either. I used to run the Angela Davis cell of the Communist Youth in the '80s, and something must have rubbed off."

Héctor returned to the Zapatista papers. The noise in the street was waning; only the low roar of traffic remained. He lit a cigarette, only to discover that he already had two lit ones sitting in the ashtray.

According to the notes by Manolo Vázquez Montalbán, between 1994 and 2000, Morales had access to the diplomatic pouch of the Mexican embassy in Madrid. What would he use that for? Who would he contact? What business did he have in Spain? Who was he negotiating for?

But his day job was as snitch for the Army, and he also had access to the archives of the Federal Department of Security, plus he was involved in the greatest real estate fraud in the history of Mexico following the earthquake. And he had . . . *Hold on, Héctor, first organize, then ask.* He returned to the second timeline and pulled out a piece of paper that read in capital letters: ACTEAL.

11:20 a.m., December 22, 1997. The Acteal slaughter. The Vázquez Montalbán papers linked Morales with the massacre and asked, *How does this tie in with General Renán Castillo?* According to an EZLN communiqué, a paramilitary group organized by the PRI and financed and equipped by the Army had murdered forty-five Tzotzils while they were praying in a church. The Tzotzils belonged to a neutral faction that had no ties with the Zapatistas. The communiqué was very precise: The paramilitary was

> *supported, trained, and financed by official agencies and elements of the Mexican Army. Among the military personnel who participated were: Brigadier General (Ret.) César Santiago Díaz; Private Mariano Arias Pérez of the 38th Infantry Battalion; Pablo Hernández Pérez, a former member of the Army who led the massacre; and Sergeant Mariano Pérez Ruiz.*

The name Morales did not appear in the report. Had he been there? Was the organization of paramilitary groups part of the strategy?

Then another quantum leap to 2002. Vázquez Montalbán's notes go into an urban geography: *Hotel Princesa Sofía, Plaza Pio XII, Financial Center (in the hotel?).*

"Me again, little one. What can you tell me about a hotel called the Princesa Sofía in Barcelona?"

"Then what? Market quotes? The price of corn on the open market? Wait a second; don't even think of hanging up the Belascophone. You should have a flying machine and someday get lost in the magical mystery land of the web. Bingo! Three hundred and ninety euros a night, one hundred and thirty four with the special rate, hair dryer in every room, located on Diagonal Avenue, close to the Museum of Decorative Arts. A big old barn of a grand old hotel with good old-fashioned luxury on Pius XII Plaza . . ."

"I owe you," Héctor said.

What was going on over there? Quoth Manolo:

> *Morales lived alone in a suite at the Reina Sofía. He used to visit the Financial Center. He entered at 21:00 hours and left at 22:00. He would go into the María Cristina metro at 22:30 and emerge at 23:00, and from there to the hotel.*

According to Montalbán's notes, the briefcase he carried into the María Cristina metro was stuffed with bills, euros. Another call.

"When was it that the euro began to circulate in Spain, kid?"

"Don't even need the web, sir. What is it you're doing? Crossword puzzles for retards? January 2002."

He had other materials in his briefcase as well. (How did Manolo know that? What materials?) About Montes Azules. (What the fuck was Montes Azules?)

Another call to Adler.

"You're lucky I'm translating a rather crappy horror novel and these surfing missions are keeping me alert. A hotel in Barcelona, a mysterious traitor called Daniel, circulation of the euro, an ecological preserve. Are you becoming a tree-hugger, Belascoboy?"

"Nah, screw the dolphins!"

Ten minutes later his phone rang.

"Here you go, Belascus Belascorum, but the truth is, your interests are getting hairier and hairier. You sound like a detective out of *The Century of Lights*. Between 16 degrees 4 minutes and 16 degrees 57 minutes North Latitude, and from 90 degrees 45 minutes to 91 degrees 30 minutes West Longitude, in Chiapas, to the east of the state. Ocosingo and Las Margaritas municipalities . . . Sonovabitch, that's Zapatista territory . . . They're calling it a Reserve of the Biosphere, and it comprises 331,200 hectares. On December 8, 1977, it was declared a Reserve of the Biosphere; the decree was not published until January 12, 1978, in the *Diario Oficial* of the Federation. And this next one is solid gold. Just look at their substantiation, my dear Belascus: 'On the other hand, given the natural beauties of the region, the Reserve had a considerable tourist potential complemented by the presence of archeological remains in and around the area.' A whole lot of *eco-deals* were pulled off in the late '90s in the Reserve. Then it goes on about butterflies and bacterial samples and birds, and what do I know? I don't really understand this stuff. Will that be all, your Belasconess?"

Héctor hung up and continued running all this through his brain. So the federal government promotes interest in an ecological reserve during the Zedillo administration, right in the middle of the conflict area, years after the Zapatista uprising and amidst high military tension. An ecological reserve to protect the buzzards and make sure the natives don't piss in the water and the tourists don't leave Coke cans on a Mayan pyramid.

Someone in the *Federales* had been smoking low-grade weed.

There was a photograph in one of the Zapatista files and on the back, in pencil, a cryptic reference:

Morales, President, Legazpi, Ramos de Miguel
Hotel Reina Sofía, Barcelona, 2002

The one identified as *Morales* appeared to be just over fifty, prematurely bald, mustache, penetrating eyes; the one identified as *President* had his back turned. (President or ex-president? Ernesto Zedillo? Had he been in Spain?) Héctor could not recognize the other two characters in the picture.

What came after that?

October 13, 2004. One of the documents sent by the Zapatistas was a communiqué from Marcos on the Montes Azules communities:

Due to the harassment of paramilitary groups and the intolerance stirred up in some communities by the PRI, dozens of indigenous Zapatista families were forced to leave and form small settlements in the region known as "Montes Azules Biosphere." The whole time they have been in that terrible situation, estranged from their original lands, the displaced Zapatistas have complied with our laws providing for the protection of the forests. The federal government, however, in collusion with the transnationals that have been trying to sieze the wealth of the Lacandona rain forest, have repeatedly threat-

> *ened to forcibly evict all the settlers in the region, including the Zapatistas. The comrades in a number of threatened communities decided to resist as long as the government failed to fulfill the so-called "San Andres Agreements." Their decision is respected and supported by the Zapatista National Liberation Army. We announced this at the time and we reiterate it now: If any one of our communities is evicted forcibly, we will, all of us, respond in kind.*

Zedillo, Carabias, and Tello. Morales, Manolo's notes read. There's a reference to a dinner. Okay. Montes Azules, the ex-president, the ex–Secretary of Ecology, the author of the book on the Zapatistas, written by order of Zedillo himself and with the collaboration of Captain Morales. Business? Big business? Eco-business?

And that brought Héctor to the end of 2004. And to this character in the riddle sent by the Corpse Who Talks: *has quills* (a writer?); *faster than Speedy González; returns from the dead; kills and bites*. And to the present.

In the present there are relations with El Yunque, the ultrarightwing secret society that metastasized throughout the Vicente Fox administration. And also in the present, according to the phone calls from the Talking Corpse: Morales kidnapped a taco vendor called Juancho from Juárez, a man the CIA was using as a double for Osama bin Laden.

Héctor leaned out the window to let the air wash over his face.

If Morales was all of these Moraleses, he'd had a very lively existence—but there was something that didn't fit, aside from the age differences and the contradictions between the two photos, which weren't all that significant because people change a lot over thirty years. No, it wasn't that. But this murderer-cum-spy turned into a torturer, then became a traitor captain a second time, then a transnational financier, then a paramilitary commander, made strange deals in Barcelona, then became a *super* transnational financier, a liaison with the ultraright, and finally the kidnapper of a taco vendor.

Could there be three Moraleses? A single shape-shifting mutant Morales? Five of them? Fifty? A trio? The Moraleses? No, those were some other guys. A father and son? What was the deal with the Montes Azules? Had they closed it? Who had taken over Alvarado's voice to rake this all up again? Was it the script for a novel set in Mexico by Vázquez Montalbán and Carvalho? Could it be just that . . . and a stack of coincidences?

He wrote up a summary of the Talking Corpse's recordings and a note for Contreras. He caught himself yawning and closed the window to keep the night breeze from blowing the papers that covered pretty much the whole room. Then, suddenly, he remembered something important.

"Cristina, I need you to find out where they sell Chaparritas El Naranjo, grape flavor."

"Are you serious? You've got to be pulling my chain; it must be 3 o'clock in the morning . . . Yeah, of course you're serious. You're like an astronaut dog, Belascola . . . I'll call you back."

A few minutes later the telephone rang.

"It seems they no longer sell it in Mexico City. The plant that produced it, a certain *Alimentaria de Refrescos*, has a website, but I can't get it to open. They do have it in Guadalajara though, and in Tuxtla Gutiérrez they bring it right to your door. 'From us to you, twenty-four bottles of tangerine, pineapple, or grape for only sixty-five pesos.' But I think that was some time ago, because I haven't been able to access the offer and buy you some. People say they merged with Coca-Cola. There's a guy with a website dedicated to what you might call *redneck compliments*, including one that says, 'Hey, Ms. Citrus, I wish I could peel your tangerines.' And another one that goes, 'Oh, mama, I wish I was the nail that punctured your tire.' Should I go on?"

"Nope! Leave it right there."

CHAPTER 9

THE BAD AND THE EVIL

. . . which relates what Magdalena and Elías talked about in a Chinese café; explains how the geography of evil is crooked and the world is full of windows and doors; reveals how the Zapatista comandantes put together the puzzle sent by the deceased Don Manolo; and details what happened when Elías went to Belascoarán's workplace, the questions they asked each other and the answers they gave, the agreement they reached, and how a dominos match with an uncertain future got started. All this, plus some ideas (or definitions) of the Bad and the Evil, given by involuntary guests in this novel.

That would be like a very big daddy, like the daddy of all daddies, like the city people say.

That's what I said, me, Elías Contreras, Investigation Commission of the Zapatista National Liberation Army, EZLN, as we say. And that's when Magdalena started laughing like she might bust a gut. She laughed and laughed like she just couldn't stop, not till she had to go for a pit stop, like they say, cause with all the laughing and all, she really had to pee. And everybody was staring at us cause of all the laughing Magdalena was doing . . . Course, the fact that she had on a really small dress where you could see pretty much everything she had—I mean, that Magdalena, she was kinda naked—that didn't help much either. So then we were drinking coffee in a Chinese café on Alvarado Bridge Street, and it was late at night cause Magdalena had gone by her room in the Guerrero section of the Monster—Mexico City, that is—to pick me up. And the fact is, I was really suffering a little cause they cut Magdalena's water, so we had to carry the water up the stairs in buckets, and the bucket had a hole in it and a lot of water dripped out, so I had to make a bunch of trips, and what with the dripping and all, there was a slippery mess, and I slipped on it and fell. So then I was washing my clothes and I accidentally poured bleach on my pants and it got all pale, like it had some disease or something, and the shirt, which was white, isn't white anymore; it's kinda spotty cause I stuck it in the same basin with my pants. So like I was saying, I was really suffering cause those were my Sunday best—I mean, the best I got and that I took with me on my Investigation Commission in the Monster. Well, just then Magdalena came in saying that there was too much street-walking competition right then and the only thing you could catch out there's a cold, so that's when she said we should go out for some coffee on her treat. And without changing clothes or nothing, or not actually changing but putting on more, cause she hardly didn't have none on at all, we went out to the Chinese café. Between drinking coffee and all, I asked Magdalena what it was that she told the *Judiciales*—that is, the police, the ones that wanted to arrest me the other night. I mean, what did she tell them to keep them from taking me away in their car? And that's when Magdalena said she had told the *Judiciales* that I was her *pimp-daddy*, and did I know what a *pimp-daddy* was. Well, I said I surely did, and then she, or maybe he, asked me what it was, and then me, I told her what I already said I said about "a very big daddy, like the daddy of all daddies," and that's when she started laughing and went on for a while. And she was just about to finish laughing when I told her that it made her like my daughter, or son, or something, and then she went from laughing to hysterical.

So I was thinking that Magdalena must have her mind in a muddle, cause she went right over from laughing and laughing to crying and screaming. So what I did was I passed him/her my coffee, since she/he had already drunk hers. I guess the coffee did the trick cause she calmed down, but still with a little bit of crying. I told her she shouldn't have a sad heart. And then she said how she/he didn't and how she was crying cause he was happy.

And that's when I knew Magdalena really did have a muddle in her mind.

Then I said that as soon as we beat the Bad and the Evil, she/he would be able to have whatever was wrong fixed, and then she would be able to find herself a husband and get married and all. And I was going to be the best man and we would get a Mariachi band and have dancing, and serve *pozol* and sweet toast, and who knows, maybe we might even slaughter a pig, soon as we start getting paid, that is, and have some soup. And Magdalena just kept saying, "Oh Elías, oh Elías," and went on laughing and screeching, and all in all it was a real good time. And then he, or rather she, said she wished we—the Zapatistas, that is—would really win the war, cause we were fighting for the little people, the ones that are always getting screwed. Then he/she said it didn't really matter if he/she got to see the day, or the night, when we win, but that she would be with us all the way since a cause like this one—that is, the Zapatista cause—deserves the support of the best, and the best is always down at the bottom of the heap, the little people. After that, Magdalena asked where it was you could find the Bad and the Evil so she/he could go right over and stomp them right then and there. So I explained that that there was exactly what I was investigating—that is, where can we find, or where can we begin to trace, the Bad and the Evil.

THE BAD AND THE EVIL ACCORDING TO FEDERICO GARCÍA LORCA, SPANIARD, POET, SHOT BY THE FALANGISTS OF FRANCISCO FRANCO, CHARGED WITH BEING A HOMOSEXUAL, AN INTELLECTUAL, A CRITIC OF THE CHURCH, AND AN ENEMY OF CONSERVATISM.

Black is the color of their horses' hides,
shod in the blackest steel they ride.
Spots of ink and streaks of wax
stain their solemn capes of black.
And they shed tears
for their bones of lead.
Galloping down the high road pass
their leather souls agleam.
So twisted in the ashen night,
they animate and then impose
the silence of darkest rubber first
and then the fear of finest sand.
If they wish to pass, they do their will,
bringing hidden within their minds
the vaguest pale astronomy
Of menacing pistols undefined.
—Excerpt from "Romance de la Guardia Civil Española,"
Romancero Gitano, 1924–1927

THE BAD AND THE EVIL ACCORDING TO MAGDALENA. Look here, Elías, you can probably understand me because being an Indian, you know what it feels like to deal with discrimination and racism. I don't know, it's like there's this hatred for anything that's different. And that hatred doesn't just stop with looking at you askance, making fun of you, joking about you, or humiliating and insulting you. No! That hatred goes as far as murder. Some of us guys, or rather girls, have been killed. Sometimes you hear about it and sometimes you don't. And I'm not talking about being murdered in the course of a kidnapping or a robbery. No! They murder us for no other reason than hating that we're different. And when something bad does happen, the first thing they think is that it was one of us, because they believe that our difference is not anything natural, that it's some kind of perversion, some kind of evil. As if our sexual preference is the result of a criminal mind, a personality trait of delinquents . . . or of animals—one bishop said that we were like roaches. It's no wonder that whenever anything bad happens, it's always one of us, someone who is gay, or lesbian, or a tranny, or a sex worker—one of us is always the first suspect, the first one accused of anything bad. So then, one has to hide his or her difference or bury it in some dark street. And why should we hide what we are? Don't we work like everyone else? Don't we love and hate like anyone else? Don't we dream like anyone else? Don't we have defects and virtues like everyone? We're the same but different. But no, to them we're just animals, horrible degenerate creatures that have to be exterminated. And don't ask me who I mean when I say "they," because I wouldn't know what to say. It's just they, them, all of them, even the ones who call themselves progressive, democratic, leftist. You see what they said about Digna

Ochoa and Pável González? The authorities said she was a lesbian and he was a homosexual, as if that were reason to preclude justice. And since they *were* that way, well, they got depressed, and the best thing they could do was commit suicide. It's disgusting! Screw the city of hope! Yes! Because if anything happens to one of us, male, female, or otherwise, the best they can come up with is "he/she had it coming," "they probably know why," and that kind of garbage. Besides, isn't the condition of homosexuality itself an insult? Don't we call people we dislike "queer," "faggot," "fruit," "sissy"? But why should I be telling you all this when "Indian" is still an insult in this country, which was built and is still being built on the backs of the indigenous population. Who are "they," you ask? All of them! Or none of them. It's like a certain state of mind. Like it's in the air. And to top it all off, they're hypocrites. By day they insult us, but as soon as they have the cover of night, they come to us "to find out what it's like," or to have their bodies confess what their minds deny: that they're just like us. They say we're aggressive. True! But that's the only way we can defend ourselves. If someone is always trying to screw you, it's only logical that you should feel that people are trying to screw you. And I wish I were talking about sex—no, I'm saying they're trying to fuck you over. So we use the same rejection we suffer to defend ourselves. But why does it have to be like that? I wish it could be like you said. I wish I could get my operation and have my body match what I am and get married and have children. But I wouldn't want to lie to my kids about who I am. I wouldn't want them to be ashamed of me. Yes, I know there have been changes. Homosexuality and lesbianism are not as persecuted as they once were, but that's mostly in the upper classes, among people who have money or prestige, who can defend them. Now, down here, well, that's another matter altogether. Down here, it's still the same shit. Evil is this inability of people to understand differences, because when we understand, we respect. And people persecute what they don't understand. Evil, Daddy Elías . . . if I may call you Daddy Elías, it sounds much better than pimp-daddy . . . Evil, Daddy Elías, is incomprehension, discrimination, and intolerance. It's everywhere . . . or nowhere.

THE BAD AND THE EVIL ACCORDING TO DON QUIXOTE DE LA MANCHA AND SANCHO PANZA, HIS SQUIRE. ANCIENT RIGHTERS OF WRONGS. (SOON TO BE 400 YEARS OLD.)

Then they discovered thirty or forty windmills there in that field, and as soon as Don Quixote saw them, he said to his squire, "Good fortune would seem to be guiding our affairs far better than we dared hope, for look there, friend Sancho Panza, where we may see some thirty or more desperate giants with whom I intend to do battle and deprive them of their lives, as their spoils enrich ours, for this is the good war, and it is a great service to God to rid the face of the earth of such bad seeds."

"What giants?" Sancho Panza asked.

"Those that yonder stand," answered his master, "those of the long arms, many of which are up to two leagues in length."

"I beg your lordship to notice," Sancho answered, "that those that over yonder stand are not giants, but windmills, and what appear to be arms are the blades that are turned by the wind to move the millstone."

"Clearly, it would seem," answered Don Quixote, "that you are not at all versed in matters of adventure: Those are

giants, and if you fear them, move out of the way and go to prayer while I engage them in fierce and unequal combat."
—Miguel de Cervantes Saavedra, *Don Quixote of La Mancha, Vol. 1*, 1605

THE BAD AND THE EVIL ACCORDING TO DOÑA SOCORRITO. Maybe she's walking down by the beach that, perhaps, is deserted at this time. And maybe she stops once in a while to pick up a seashell. Maybe she's about to be seventy-one years old. Maybe in March. Maybe she has one of her granddaughters with her. Maybe the child is less than five years old. Maybe they're both singing, *May you always be with us/as we are with you/in the same pocket of those pants* . . . And maybe the little girl sings the last syllable out of key.

Maybe Doña Socorrito is saying right now that the world can be like a big house, or like a little prison; that the world is full of windows and doors; that the world is a great puzzle full of rooms, some dark and others lit; that the world is full of distinct (and sometimes contradictory) realities; that in this world, each reality has but two doors, and that one of them is the door of certain Bad and the other of uncertain Good; that sometimes you can choose the room you want to live in, and other times you cannot, and evil and life pursue you everywhere; that if you want to choose, it has to be twice: if you can, first, you have to choose where you want to be, and second, you have to choose your way in; that the job of adults is to show the children as many windows as possible so they can look into as many rooms as possible; that the job of adults is to wage a permanent struggle so that children may always have the freedom to choose the room of the world where they want to be, and the freedom and responsibility to choose the door by which they are going to enter that room;

that everyone can then be whatever they are and wherever they are, but they all have to choose between good or bad.

Maybe Doña Socorrito is saying that evil is fighting to deprive everyone of the right and the freedom to choose their room and their door; that the men and women who fight against the Bad are fighting for children, no matter the color of their skin, their last name, age, nationality, race, or language; that a new world is pointless if we don't fight to change the one we have; that the Bad presents itself to children as an excuse where evil is a manifest destiny; that those who fight against evil want childhood to be, very simply, a time of wonder.

Maybe Doña Socorrito is saying this as she walks along the eastern sea. Maybe the child is listening.

THE BAD AND THE EVIL ACCORDING TO PEDRO MIGUEL, JOURNALIST WITH THE MEXICAN DAILY LA JORNADA.

But the present occupant of the White Heouse (George Walker Bush, President of the United States) talks so much about the Lord that you have to ask yourself the relevance of brushing the dust off theology and using it as an instrument with which to analyze today's world . . . George Walker . . . appears to be honestly convinced that he and God (in that order) make up an impressive team. Of course, the president is convinced that divine assistance is the primary asset of the traditional earthly alliances of the United States (France, Germany, Spain, Canada) . . . Yes, the Celestial Empire is part of that alliance, and so what if a couple of no-account countries abandon it? What possible need could there be to define evil, when it is so obvious that evil is anything that antagonizes the Lord, Who, it would seem, has turned out to

be a brilliant strategist, a clairvoyant economist, and a sharp and precise (re)election advocate.
—"Bush and God," *La Jornada*, January 25, 2005

THE BAD AND THE EVIL ACCORDING TO LA CHAPIS.
La Chapis is a nun, a sister, a woman consecrated to God, or whatever you choose to call her. We cannot say that she "took the habit," because she dresses in normal street clothes, although there is a certain austerity and simplicity in her dress that gives her away.

The religious congregation to which La Chapis belongs is, as the Zapatistas would say, very different. Instead of locking themselves away to pray or to flatter the powerful with promises of indulgences, the members are devoted to the very Christian calling known as "option for the poor." So, as some say, they work for the little people who are screwed. Aside from being a nun, La Chapis is small. So small, in fact, that the nickname *Chaparrita* was too big for her and people called her La Chapis. So that actually, even her nickname is small. La Chapis chose *Lucrecia* as her fighting name, because the enemy would never think that a Lucrecia could be a nun, but it was to no avail because everyone kept on calling her Chapis.

At this point, Chapis Lucrecia is chatting with Elías Contreras in a takeout food joint somewhere around San Pedro de los Pinos, in Mexico City. Elías holds her in the highest esteem, because although she knows that he is dead, she's not afraid of him and talks to him, so Elías is quite happy eating, for twenty-five Mexican pesos, a cup of chicken broth, rice, liver with onions, rice pudding, and *horchata* water *ad libitum*. La Chapis is talking and Elías is listening.

"The problem with the Bad and the Evil is geographical.

The geography of evil was turned around, set upside down. So when they tell the story of creation, the rich turn everything around. According to them, heaven, or God, goodness, is up in the heights, while the Bad and the Evil, the Devil, are down below. But it really isn't like that. God is not up in the heights. To correct that mistake, God sent his Son, Christ, to earth—to prove that goodness, heaven, is not up in the heights, far away from what happens on earth. The powerful of those times convinced everyone that the earth was organized like heaven, that the Good were up high, the rulers, the ones in charge, and down under were the ones who obeyed, the Bad. So heaven was equivalent to the government, and God was equivalent to the ruler. And that's the way they used to justify, and continue to justify, the dictate that you have to obey the rulers. So you get Bush, who drags God up whenever he feels like it—he uses God to justify his every wrongdoing.

Christ was crucified because he came to question all this. And him being the Son of God, instead of meeting with the rulers, dining in their palaces, organizing a political party, and becoming their advisor, what did he do? Well, he went and got born in a manger, surrounded by animals; he grew up in a carpenter's shop and created an organization with the poorest of the poor. Now then, would God go where the Evil is? Of course not. He stayed with those at the bottom, and this tells us that goodness is not up in the heights—he would have been born in the home of that bastard Salinas de Gortari or that damned Bill Gates, but he wasn't. So heaven is not up there and neither is goodness. Evil is up there, on the right, with the rich, with those who govern badly, with the opressors of the people. So where is goodness? We don't know. We'll have to find it.

I don't know, maybe goodness is down on the left, it

might be the best place to start looking. That's why I look down when I pray; I'm praying to God, who is with the underdog. That's why I don't agree with the damn bishops and priests who are always siding with the rich and then become just like them, even in the way they dress. So my advice to you, if you're looking for the Bad and the Evil: Start searching upward and to the right. That's probably where they live.

Hey, listen, Elías, don't go telling El Sup that I use swear words. And if you're not going to eat your rice pudding, I'll take it."

THE BAD AND THE EVIL ACCORDING TO LEONARD PELTIER, NATIVE AMERICAN, ARTIST, WRITER, HUMAN RIGHTS ACTIVIST, ILLEGALLY AND UNFAIRLY IMPRISONED.

> *The government, under the pretext of security and progress, liberated us from our land, resources, culture, dignity, and future. They violated every treaty they ever made with us. I use the word "liberated" loosely and sarcastically, in the same vein that I view their use of the words "collateral damage" when they kill innocent men, women, and children. They describe people defending their homeland as terrorists, savages, and hostiles, and accuse us of being aggressors . . . My words reach out to the non-Indian: Look now before it's far too late—see what is being done to others in your name and see what destruction you sanction when you say nothing. Your own treaty, the one between yourselves and the government, is being violated daily; this treaty is commonly known as the Constitution.*
>
> —Leavenworth Penitentiary, Kansas, January 2004

THE BAD AND THE EVIL ACCORDING TO A CERTAIN MORALES. I don't want you to get the idea that I'm a cynic. I'm just a realist, and reality shows that he who fucks not gets fucked. I certainly make deals, and don't come to me now with this foolishness about ethics and fairness, because all business is dirty; it's always a matter of buying low and selling high. Otherwise, how do you think the high and mighty of Mexico and the world made their great fortunes? Everything is for sale and anything can be bought: your land, your body, your conscience, your country. Okay, so maybe I didn't always buy—I took, I pillaged—but if it hadn't been me, it would have been someone else. There are people who are born to be screwed. It's like they have it tattooed on their foreheads: *Screw me*.

Betrayal, you say? Well, that's all a matter of how you look at it. As I see it, all I did was go through a change of paradigm, and everyone in the world does that, only they call it "maturity," "realism," "good sense."

I killed? Well . . . yes! But the fact is, you can't get up there without getting your hands a little dirty.

No, I never killed face-to-face. But it wasn't a question of cowardice, no, it's just that I felt sorry staring into the eyes of the future corpse. Besides, they were going to die anyway. All I did was expedite their departure. Okay, yes, sometimes I was afraid to kill face-to-face, but that was when the corpse-to-be was a real tough bastard.

Why do you say I cheated? I didn't cheat any more than any politician or businessman. Well, yes, there are degrees. In this matter of doing evil, there are amateurs and professionals; me, I'm a pro, but I started as an amateur. I still hope to get into the big leagues, into politics, and who knows, I might even have a shot at president of the republic. Others have done it, so why not me? You have to understand, evil has its levels: There are those who screw the screwed, and there are those who screw the screwers of the screwed. You might say that I'm somewhere in the middle. Let me explain. When one of the guys with real power and money wants to get something done but doesn't want anyone to know about it or doesn't want to have to deal with the tiny difficulties that arise along the way, that's where I come in. I'm a kind of intermediary, but a lot more effective because I not only inspect what has to be bought, I prepare it and clean it and deliver it pressed and folded. The client never has to get blood on his hands and never has to deal with all the red tape and formalities. Well, of course I get my commission. You might say that I am an intermediary of evil. Let me explain something. Would you like to know the secret to success in all this evil business? You have to know how to land on your feet and keep running; you have to know how to play on any court, with any racket; you have to be in good with God *and* the Devil, you have to fuck the prick who's being fucked by the biggest prick, suck up and piss down. You see, it's all contemporary politics. So there you have it. When you're in the evil business, timing is of the essence.

What did you say? Look at myself in the mirror? Why should I do that? Besides, don't you know that everyone with money and power looks beautiful? Aspirations? Hopes? Well, of course. I hope to live to a ripe old age without a care in the world, and I aspire to having a mattress stuffed with credit cards and wads of millions in foreign banks. You heard me, just like old Pinochet. You don't understand; little old men inspire pity. It doesn't matter how many scams they pulled or how many people they murdered.

The trick to being good at evil is to make it to old age.

Name one murdering old thief who ever got punished. My political affiliations? Well, that's a matter of convenience. Political affiliations are like underwear: You change them when you have to. Yes, any political party will accept you if you make yourself attractive enough. Money? Yes, that's what they are after; that's what we're all after, and I know where the money is and what has to be done to get it. Afraid of the law? Come on, get serious. Haven't you understood yet that we *are* the law?

THE BAD AND THE EVIL ACCORDING TO ANGELA Y. DAVIS, ACTIVIST AGAINST RACISM AND POLITICAL REPRESSIONS, SENT TO PRISON ILLEGALLY AND UNFAIRLY.

> *The announced function of the police, "to protect and serve the people," becomes the grotesque caricature of protecting and preserving the interests of our oppressors and serving us nothing but injustice . . . Fascism is a process, its growth and development are cancerous in nature. While today, the threat of fascism may be primarily restricted to the use of the law-enforcement-judicial-penal apparatus to arrest the overt and latent revolutionary trends among nationally oppressed people, tomorrow it may attack the working class en masse and eventually even moderate democrats.*
>
> —Marin County Jail, California, May 1971

THE BAD AND THE EVIL ACCORDING TO THE RUSSIAN. Betraying the memory of our honored dead. Denying what we are. Losing our memory. Selling our dignity. Feeling shame for being Indian, or black, or Chicano, or Muslim, or yellow, or white, or red, or gay, or lesbian, or transexual, or skinny, or fat, or tall, or short. Forgetting our history. Forgetting ourselves. Accepting what the powerful stuff down our throats. Giving up. Not fighting. Making believe we don't see that the fuckin fascists are taking over everything. Assuming a permissive attitude in our lives and letting the powerful do as they please, and putting up with every fuck-job they do on us. Letting ourselves be fooled by the mass media. Fighting with our own brothers in the struggle. Fighting against people who are as screwed as we are. Letting them take our lands and poison them with their fucking transgenics.

Not protesting against the wars of conquest. Voting for Bush. Shopping at Wal-Mart. Lying to ourselves and lying to our own.

Letting them abuse, kill, pillage, hoodwink, and ultimately get away with everything. That is evil. That and a whole lot of other things that I can't think of right now because I'm so pissed already. So take your fuckin tortilla.

THE BAD AND THE EVIL ACCORDING TO GENERAL VICENTE ROJO, CHIEF OF STAFF OF THE PEOPLE'S REPUBLICAN ARMY, WHO FOUGHT AGAINST THE FALANGISTS IN DEFENSE OF THE SPANISH REPUBLIC.

> *Nonintervention weighed down like a tombstone on the Republic; and while an atmosphere of isolation developed around it, we received reliable reports about the weapons and war matériel of all sorts that were being unloaded in the ports of the Cantabrian coast and in the south; we could see how, banking on the total frustration and defeat of the Republic, expected in the month of April, treaties were already being signed with the countries that were invading our soil; we witnessed the incessant growth in the number of Italian and German technicians that swelled the Gambara Divisions, and*

we could see in the air above us wave after wave of new models of Italian and German aircraft, borne of the experience of our war and sent to conduct new experiments on Spanish soil and Spanish flesh. What horrible crime could have been committed by a republic that was merely defending its constitution and its laws for it to be subjected to international physical and moral suffocation, condemning it to witness the sterility of its efforts?

—From *España Heroica,* 1942

THE BAD AND THE EVIL ACCORDING TO THE CHINESE MAN. There is a kind of internationale on the right. Yes, just as there was once an internationale on the left—although later all hell broke loose and it disappeared. You can see how they killed Leon Trotsky and persecuted us for as long as the Socialist camp existed. That's what proletarian internationalism was good for—for the left to give itself an internationalist fuck-job. There you have it. The internationale of the left was not wiped out by imperialism or by the CIA . . . We did it . . . We hit it right between the eyes, and lickety-split it was gone, the internationale was *kaput*. The internationale of the right, however, kept going, and it's now reorganizing. That's what neoliberal globalization is: the reorgnization of the internationale of the right. You see, the right learned what we did not—the old left, I mean, not the current left, which hardly makes it to the center. The right has an open element and a clandestine element. And it learned how to infiltrate. It infiltrated the Church, the political parties, the mass media, the universities, big business, the unions, the Army, the police, the judges, the representatives and senators, and even the soccer teams. But don't let me give you the idea that the right is all model behavior and discipline.

Not so! They have their divisions and their internecine struggles. For example, there is the ideological right and the business right. The latter are in it for the scratch, the dough, the gelt, the mazuma . . . the money. The ideological right is in charge of doctrine and they don't have a very good opinion of the business right. So the right does have its internal contradictions. The idealogues are the real fanatics, and they're dangerous because they are capable of starting wars for no practical reason, like the Cristeros did.

The business right, they're more practical. They assign a price to everything, including their "prudent patience." A high position, a medium position, or a lowly position will do, for the time being. Haven't you seen how the PAN members hop from one party to another at the drop of a hat? Okay, it's not only the PAN. They all do it.

But you see, the PAN is an excellent example of a local branch of the fascist right. The Internationale of Evil, that's what globalization is. So that'll be forty-five pesos for the shower, with shampoo, soap, and towel. Yeah, we have a special going cause it's too cold and nobody's taking baths. A squirt of deodorant is all they do. And sometimes not even that.

THE BAD AND THE EVIL ACCORDING TO MUMIA ABU-JAMAL, JOURNALIST AND ACTIVIST AGAINST RACISM, ILLEGALLY AND UNFAIRLY CONDEMNED TO DEATH IN THE U.S. (REFERRING HERE TO THE DEVASTATION CAUSED BY THE RECENT TSUNAMIS ON THE COASTS OF ASIA).

Yet there is another watery war that is being waged, that may affect the lives of millions . . . Yet all across the globe, in Africa, Asia, and Latin America—and even here in North America—people are living under the very real threat of the corporatization

of water and water systems. The waters of the earth, which have been, since the dawn of human civilization, for the collective usage of the community, is fast becoming just another commodity—something to sell. If you can afford it, cool. If not, tough . . . In short, there's money in water, and where money is, there too are corporations, trying to get paid. That's the dark, unforeseen, and treacherous side of the globalization movement among western governments and corporations. That's also what privatization really means—taking the common inheritance of nature, and making it into someone else's private property.
—Death Row, Pennsylvania, December 30, 2004

THE BAD AND THE EVIL ACCORDING TO COMANDANTE ESTHER AND COMANDANTE DAVID (ESTHER AND DAVID EXPLAIN TO EL SUP THE PROBABLE ORIGIN OF THE NOTES LEFT BY MANUEL VÁZQUEZ MONTALBÁN).

"I think what happened is that Don Manolo was preparing an article on the right in the government of Spain," David began, looking over his own notes.

"Yes," Esther added, "he was explaining how the Franco program was being reorganized—"

"That's right," David interrupted, pointing to a world map. "He was investigating that fascist Spanish organization known as Ciudad Católica and noticed that it had relationships with other extreme-right organizations in other countries."

"In Mexico, for instance, with the organization that's called El Yunque," Esther explained, holding up a book with the same name, by Álvaro Delgado. "In Mexico, as I was saying, we find that in 1998 an entity called the International Civil Commission for the Observation of Human Rights (ICCOHR) began visiting Chiapas. It is, or was, made up of people from countries around the world, mainly from Europe, who were concerned about violations of the human rights of the indigenous communities, as well as the militarization and paramilitarization processes. The commission made its first visit after the Acteal massacre, right in the middle of the attack by Zedillo and Croquetas Albores on the autonomous municipalities. To keep them from seeing the shit they were pulling, the government expelled a number of those people from Mexico, especially the Italians."

David picked up the line of reasoning: "One of the members of the commission was, or is, Daniel, a son of Don Manolo, who, among other things, is a video buff. So during the work of the commission, Daniel Vázquez Montalbán shot videos of the military posts and the meetings with the representatives of the bad Zedillo government. Once they were back in Barcelona, Don Manolo, along with Pepe Carvalho, was able to watch the videos that his son made in Chiapas."

David checked his notes again, then continued his narrative: "Pepe Carvalho was, or is, a detective, and he was helping Don Manolo with his research into the resurrection of the Franco agenda in the Spanish state. While they were watching the videos, Mr. Carvalho replayed the parts with the representatives of Zedillo's bad government and the shots of the military posts. Neither Don Manolo nor his son understood why then, but they soon did. At one point in the rerun, Mr. Calvalho identified someone and snapped, 'That's Morales.' The person had appeared beside General Renán Castillo who, as you know, organized the paramilitary in Altos de Chiapas and, together with Zedillo, helped plan the Acteal massacre of December 22, 1997."

"Then Mr. Carvalho explained to Don Manolo that in his research on the Spanish right, he had run across this character on a number of occasions—the guy had a close relationship with the José María Aznar administration, who knew him simply as 'Morales,' with no other identifying information," explained Esther. "Then Don Manolo asked Carvalho to get more information on this Morales."

"Yes, as we say over here," David added, "he wanted Morales *tailed*."

"That's it," Esther agreed, "they put a tail on this Morales person and found out about the hotel, the metro station, the Financial Center, the Mexican embassy, and, with a little creative investigation, they found out about the briefcase full of papers and euros."

David continued: "Following up on the investigation, he discovered the links set up between the Aznar government and the intelligence services of the Mexican government to harass the Basque citizens residing in our country and accuse them of belonging to ETA. As you know, many Basques were kidnapped, tortured, and later turned over to the courts, using the same techniques developed by the White Brigade in what came to be known as the Dirty War. Carvalho discovered that in Mexico, not only is there a conspiracy of silence among the powerful to suppress the truth about the Dirty War, but that El Yunque was reactivating paramilitary groups through one of its organizations known as MURO. Then Carvalho found—"

"The Morales person," Esther interrupted.

"And what about the Montes Azules, biodiversity, and the transnationals?" El Sup asked.

Esther answered, "According to the Deep Throat report you sent us, this Morales individual was supposed to be trafficking in endangered species in the Lacandona forest, aside from working closely with Julia Carabias and Ernesto Zedillo on the machinations to sell tracts of land in the Montes Azules to the transnationals. Don Manolo might have found out about this through something Mr. Carvalho ran across in that briefcase carted around by Morales, and because he had learned of the meeting Morales had in Spain with Zedillo, Carabias, and Tello."

"Hmm. The pieces are beginning to fall into place," El Sup commented, lighting his pipe.

"Where's Elías?" David asked.

"He's in the Monster. He already met up with the detective, Belascoarán, who agreed to cooperate with us in the investigation. Elías is going to see him again very soon to exchange information and decide what to do from here on out," El Sup answered.

"I think it's time to bring him back in," Esther said.

"Yes," David agreed, "according to the reports from the Good Governance Board in La Realidad, this Morales person was part of the Fox group that recently visited the Lacandona forest and had a secret meeting with some unidentified characters. That's why Fox stayed overnight. The entire Fox party returned, all except one—"

"The Morales person," Esther again interrupted.

"The area of Chiapas that Fox visited is full of fine hardwoods, oil, bountiful animal and plant life, uranium . . . and water. If there's any one place where you can find the Bad and the Evil together, it's there!" David exclaimed, jabbing his finger into a corner of the Chiapas map labeled, *Montes Azules Biosphere Reserve*.

THE BAD AND THE EVIL ACCORDING TO JOSÉ REVUELTAS, MEXICAN WRITER AND RADICAL LEFTIST MILITANT, WHO WAS, AMONG OTHER THINGS, A POLITICAL PRISONER.

The PAN represents the economic sectors whose endeavors are less "fruitful and creative" in the life of the nation: banking capital, commercial and real estate capital, and the capital that thrives in the so-called comprador *economy. Their physical incarnation is the Licenciado, whose historical debut on the national scene dates back to the colonial period and the Pontifical University . . . Now then, the fondest wish of the PAN and its Licenciados is to set Mexico up as an open field for the growth and development of foreign capital, without whose momentum (as avowed by the PAN) our economy would be doomed to have its entrails devoured by vultures for rebelling against the gods, who, in our case, would be the big interests of North American imperialist capital.*

—*Mexico: A Barbaric Democracy*, October–November 1957

THE BAD AND THE EVIL ACCORDING TO PABLO NERUDA, CHILEAN POET AND LEFTIST MILITANT.

I have seen the Bad and the Evil, but not in their lairs.
It is a tale of evil in caverns . . .

I found evil sitting on tribunals
in the Senate I found it dressed
and prim, diverting debates
and ideas into pockets.
The Bad and Evil
had just emerged from their baths: They
were framed in satisfactions
and were perfect in their softness
of their false decorum.

—Excerpt from "Se Reúne el Acero" (1945), in *Canto General*

PORTIONS OF THE REPORT ON THE WORK OF ELÍAS IN THE MONSTER SENT BY EL SUP TO THE INDIGENOUS CLANDESTINE REVOLUTIONARY COMMITTEE AT THE GENERAL HEADQUARTERS OF THE ZAPATISTA NATIONAL LIBERATION ARMY IN EARLY 2005.

According to this report, Elías was a waiter at the Champs-Élysées restaurant in Polanco, and he brought about one of the most intense attacks of rage ever suffered by Diego Fernández de Cevallos, senator from the PAN (National Action Party), lawyer of criminals, consort of drug traffickers, and architect of the campaign to elect Santiago Creel, current Secretary of the Interior, to the presidency of Mexico on the PAN ticket.

As it happens, La Coyota, which is what they call Fernández de Cevallos, was eating in a restaurant with his friends Jesús Ortega (a corrupt politician from the PRD, notorious for his misappropriation of party funds and his bid to become governor of Mexico City after the López Obrador fiasco), Manuel Bartlett (member of the PRI, linked to drug trafficking and looking to hook up with one of the narco groups vying for power along with the PRI nominees for president of the republic), and Enrique Jackson (also a member of the PRI, also a nominee, owner of a number of rackets in Mexico City, and, according to reports by the U.S. Drug Enforcement Agency, also tied in with one of the drug cartels).

Elías was supposed to serve them. Mr. Fernández de Cevallos yelled at him, "Hey, barefoot Indian trash, bring us the menu!" and turning to receive the approval of his guests, he added, "Let's see if this lazy Indian falls asleep along the way," as the others flattered him with chuckles and applause.

When Elías brought the menu, Fernández de Cevallos said, "Listen, you, don't pay any attention to those Zapatistas; you Indians are here to serve us; that's what we conquered you for."

More laughter and applause from the narco-legislators.

Elías waited for them to finish their orders, pretending he was writing them down. Then he left, and after a while he returned, not with the orders, but holding an antacid bottle with a pom-pom on top and a note that said, *For La Coyota and her pups*. Fernández de Cevallos turned every color of the rainbow; he could hardly speak. All he could do (according to Elías) was open his eyes really wide, like when he gets angry with reporters. The captain came to the table to see what was happening and Fernández de Cevallos pointed at Elías as his three little pigs pounded him on the back and fanned him with napkins. They called an ambulance. As they lifted him into the vehicle, Fernández de Cevallos mumbled, "Rat-shit Indians." Maybe they fired Elías, but he didn't hang around to find out. Diego Fernández de Cevallos was admitted to a hospital, so he said, "to have some lab analyses done and rule out cancer." The fact is, he had such a severe bile attack that it turned his beard green. A very exclusive beauty parlor charged a fortune to dye it back, with white hairs and all. The Senate of the Republic picked up the tab.

. . . Before the incident with La Coyota Fernández de Cevallos, Elías worked as a room steward at the Oxford Hotel, over in the Tabacalera district. While he was working for them, Elías slipped a ski mask over the head of the Che Guevara bust in the park behind the San Carlos Museum, in that same district. That happened just last year, on October 8, 2004, but no one ever found out because just before first light, before anyone could see it, the personnel of the

Cuauhtémoc Station tore off the ski mask, along with a sign that read, *He shall return, and they shall be millions.*

THE BAD AND THE EVIL ACCORDING TO MANUEL VÁZQUEZ MONTALBÁN, CATALONIAN WRITER AND FIERCE CRITIC OF THE RIGHT (AS WELL AS THE LEFT).

> *No. There are no single truths, nor are there final struggles, but we can still find our way by siding with the possible truths against the evident non-truths and fighting. One can see part of the truth and not recognize it. But it is impossible to look upon evil and fail to recognize it. Good does not exist, but evil, I think, or I fear, does.*
> —In "Panfleto desde el Planeta de los Simios," late 1994

THE BAD AND THE EVIL ACCORDING TO HÉCTOR BELASCOARÁN AND ELÍAS CONTRERAS.

So I went to see this Belascoarán over where he works, which is his office. I left when it was getting on in the afternoon, which was almost like the evening. That morning, I had been reading in this newspaper called *La Jornada* about what a guy says who knows a whole lot of things and his name is . . . his name is . . . Gimme a second . . . That's it, Miguel León Portilla. And I copied down what this Mr. León Portilla said, which was:

> *A person's word must neither be bought nor sold, says an old adage (pre-Hispanic) that a mother shared with her daughter. Beautiful, isn't it? Such a contrast with what so many contemporary politicians do and think.*

That's what the man said in that newspaper called *La*

Jornada. Well, I just stood there thinking about what that wise man said, but not too long, cause I had to go and find that Belascoarán feller.

I reckon it musta been a Sunday, can't really tell now, but what I do know is that I crossed in front of that big old building where they have that newspaper called *El Universal,* and I noticed that it was 6 p.m., Fox time, which is 19:00 hours Southeastern Combat Front time. I can tell that was the time, cause just as I was walking in front of the building, I heard the music of the National Anthem of Mexico, and so I snapped to, which means I came to attention and I brought my left arm real stiff to the side of my head, which is how us Zapatistas salute the anthem and the flag of our country, which is called Mexico. So there I was, all by myself cause there was no one else around at that time, standing there at attention and all, and twisting my eyes every which way to figger where it was coming from, the music to that anthem that says, *Mexicans, at the call to war/your steel and your bridle prepare* . . . and I couldn't find where, till finally it finished and I turned and saw that it was coming from the big old clock on top of that newspaper. The thing is, that street is called Bucareli, and right around the corner is where that Belascoarán works, where he has his office, on the street that's called Artículo 123 on the one side and Donato Guerra on the other.

I was just getting there when this Belascoarán walked up with some drinking glasses and a loaf of bread and we said hello and went up where he works with those other three Christians who seem right enough and make a lot of noise. Belascoarán introduced me to the others and said something like, "Let me introduce Elías Contreras, he comes from Chiapas." And they all applauded and asked what I did and all, and since I could see that Belascoarán trusted them, I said that I was an Investigation Commission. Belascoarán told them that I was a detective, but that in my own territory, which is the rebel territory for humanity and against neoliberalism, that's what they call us: Investigation Commission. So then I told Belascoarán that we should go see that thing about that Morales. And he said that was what we were going to do—that is, that we were going to see the thing, or the case, depending, on that Morales. And that's when Belascoarán explained that you don't say *thing*; you have to say *case*. And I said, right, whatever, let's go see the thing, or the case, depending, on that Morales. Then Belascoarán brought out the file I gave him the other day— actually, the other night—and there was the papers El Sup sent with the reports we had on that there Morales. But now Belascoarán had them all fixed together with some of his own reports and investigations, and it was kinda messy.

Thing is, Belascoarán organized it all to get some order and perspective. So I asked what that *perspective* thing is, and he explained that perspective is when you look at things, or cases, depending, from all sides at the same time and kinda from a little far away, so's you can see how it all fits together. Then I figgered that this perspective thing is to look at things, or cases, in a group, cause you can tell that one person alone can't look from all sides at the one thing (case?) all at once, but with a group you could. That's when the gentleman called Gilberto Gómez Letras butted in.

"Don't be a pain in the ass, boss, just tell him what it is so it's clear, or Mr. Elías here is going to repeat what you told him and people over there are going to think we're ignorant."

Then the furniture gutter, that Carlos Vargas, spoke up:

"You ever seen a goddamn plumber who knows what perspective is?"

And then the one who was sposed to be a goddamn plumber piped up, "Pay attention, Mr. Wilson, and you'll find out why my second last name is Letras."

So he went over to this really fat book called the *Dictionary of Modern Spanish* and started looking, till he found it, and what it means is, just a minute, what it means is . . . Let me look in my pad, cause I have it right here next to *aforementioned* . . . Here it is:

> *Perspective: The art of representing volumes and spatial relations on a flat surface; a work of art employing this technique; the aspect of an object seen by an observer from far away; a fallacious and apparent representation of things; a foreseeable contingency in a business deal.*

Well, that's what I wrote down in my pad about what it said in that book that Gómez Letras checked. Then the sofa gutter, Vargas, said, "Sonovabitch, if the cure ain't worse than the disease."

Belascoarán said that it would be better to stick to his, Belascoarán's, definition of the word. So I asked if it was to see everything all together at once, and Belascoarán said that, yeah, it was something like that, and I got to thinking that my head was all mixed up, but with perspective, cause I always see everything at once all together. So Belascoarán's thinking is in "ordered perspective," and mine's in "mixed-up perspective," but then he's a city detective and I'm a Zapatista Investigation Commission, so I think that's the difference, and my kind of thinking is not his kind of thinking—Belascoarán's, that is. Then he started explaining that you had to arrange investigations according to the way you see them, and figger out where they happened and how they happened so you could tell if they had anything to do with each other, or if they just happened and that's all, and when you got that down, then you can see where you are in the investigation and where you're going, or maybe you're just staring into a hole in the ground. Anyway, Belascoarán told the others that they should hurry up and eat their donuts. Now, you see, donuts are like a roll with a hole in them—that is, they have part of them missing, but they charge you the same as if they were whole . . . I mean, without a hole.

So like I said, Belascoarán told them to hurry up with their donuts and coffees, and then either they could shut up or he, Belascoarán, would shut up. He said they had their own choice in "free democratic discipline," that's what he said. So they figgered that shutting up themselves was better and just sat there listening while Belascoarán and me looked over the thing, or the case, depends, about this Morales, but with perspective, Belascoarán's ordered perspective together with my mixed-up perspective, cause we were working together on the investigation of the Bad and the Evil, in a collective, you see. Belascoarán, he layed out all the papers he had, plus the ones we gave him, and it took awhile and most of the flat spaces in the room, including on top of the Mr. Villareal's coffee cup and on the gutted easy chairs, yeah, there was papers practically everywhere. When he had them all laid out, he began explaining how since we didn't have people to talk to—that is, to ask questions at—then we had to ask the papers what we wanted to know. And how there was big questions and little questions, and I knew right off that it wasn't that the papers were going to talk, but that it was what was written on the papers that was going to give us the answers, or maybe not, depends. Then the big questions would give big answers, and it was from the big answers that we would know what the little questions had to be.

About that time I was feeling real happy, cause this Belascoarán feller had his thinking all mixed up like mine and we were both starting to understand real well, and the others were just sitting there all hushed up, but I didn't know if it was cause of free democratic discipline or cause they didn't understand anything. So Belascoarán said it was time to ask the big questions, and I pulled out my pad and wrote everything down, cause you always have to be ready to learn things . . . Who knows, they might come in handy for the struggle, someday.

The first big question Belascoarán asked was, "Is there any connection between all these pieces of information?" Which means, if all those pieces of paper had anything to do with each other. But the thing is, Belascoarán just stood there waiting and the rest of them were still silent from before, and I got the idea that he was waiting for somebody to say something, so I said that they were, that all those little pieces of paper were connected. Well, Belascoarán leaned back and lit a cigarette and stared at me as he asked me why I said that, what connection I saw between all the papers.

And that's when I said: "The dead."

Well, everybody just kept real quiet, and not on account of free democratic discipline neither, but cause they were expecting me to go on explaining. So I started explaining that the investigations were being done cause the dead had started them. I mean, I didn't tell them that I was already deceased or passed away or dead or nothing, cause I didn't want none of them getting upset about it and maybe chucking up their coffee and hole-breads. Like I said, I explained how the deceased Manuel Vázquez Montalbán was the one who began the Zapatista investigation, and the investigation done by Belascoarán was started by the deceased Jesús María Alvarado, and how one of them wrote and the other talked on the telephone, but they were both deceased, which is dead. But they were dead people who weren't just hanging around waiting for All Souls' Day to come on out and have some coffee and *tamales* and *atole* made with *pozol*—no sir, they were speaking up, or out.

Belascoarán smiled and stared out the window. "Yes, they are . . . because they're our uncomfortable dead." And just when I was about to write the word *uncomfortable* in my pad, he turned around and said, "Very good, Elías Contreras."

But he explained that it was not just the uncomfortable dead that were the connection between all those papers, no, it was that those papers were like the big fat book the plumber feller had—that is, the dictionary—cause those papers were like a dictionary of the shit, piss, and corruption in the system, which made them like a *perspective* of all the ways the system of the powerful fucked everybody else to benefit the rich and the bad governments. Then he said there was a little of everything: There was repression, murder, prison, persecution, disappearances, fraud, robbery, land grabbing, the sale of national sovereignty, high treason, corruption.

"In sum," he said, "those at the top screw those at the bottom."

Then I thought it over, lit one of my cigarettes, smiled, and said, "The Evil."

I could tell that Belascoarán got a little happy, cause he went and got some sodas and opened them with the sights on his gun and gave one to each person.

Then the man called Villareal raised his hand and said,

"May I take the floor?" But he didn't wait for anyone to give him the floor, he just started right out talking, which isn't really "free democratic discipline." If this Villareal feller did that in one of the assemblies in my town, truth is, everybody would have stared him down, but this Villareal wasn't in an assembly in my town, so he just asked, "What about this Morales person?"

Belascoarán and I looked at each other, we both did, that is, and we saw how we both at the same time were thinking the same thing, and that's how we both said together: "The Bad."

Then Belascoarán got to explaining again with the scramble of pieces of paper and the pictures of the alleged Morales that he had glued on a wall beside a lady that was real naked—I mean, she didn't have no veils or flowers or hankies or nothing. And then he said: "What we have on this Morales doesn't match: not the dates, not the places, not the ages, and," pointing to the wall, "not the photos."

Then Belascoarán could tell we was all looking at the lady on the wall with nothing on instead of the Morales feller. So that's when he said how we shouldn't be such dummies and how he was talking about the Bad, about Morales, not the lady, who was really pretty. Then he turns to me and asks: "Is there one Morales or are there several?"

We all started thinking, and finally I said, "The Evil is really big, so there have to be several Bad guys."

Then we got to checking out how many Morales people there could be, whether there were several. And we decided that yes, there could be several Moraleses. And so Belascoarán said that we couldn't investigate and grab them all, cause we were just a few, he said, and I said that what we had to do was we had to pick ourselves just one or two of them, cause we weren't gonna be able to grab them all, not cause we didn't want to, but cause we was shorthanded. Then Belascoarán said how one line of investigation was in the Monster, and that there was another line of investigation that led directly to Chiapas. So we could get together and both of us start off for Chiapas and grab the sonovabitch that was screwing people over there, which is over here, or we could both team up in Mexico City, the Monster, to grab the bastard that was doing his dirty business here, or over there. The other way was that each could take off in his own direction and operate in his own territory—that would be Belascoarán in the Monster and me in Chiapas—but helping each other with constant information exchanges.

So that's what we agreed—that is, each one to his own thing—that is, Belascoarán in the Monster and me, Elías Contreras, in the mountains of Southeastern Mexico. Belascoarán gave me all the information he had that could help me in my investigation work up here in Chiapas, and I gave him all the information I had that could help him with his detectivating in the Monster. Well, right then we were all real happy and we did a lot of laughing with the jokes about the lady with no clothes.

I told Belascoarán how El Sup had asked me if there was enough time to ask him, Belascoarán, to teach me how to play the thing called dominos. And Belascoarán said, "The time is now," which meant that he was going to teach me right there and then. Course, I don't hardly remember the class or the game. Probably Belascoarán could tell you about it, but what *I* can tell you is that I have a felt marker in my backpack, just in case I need it, cause I remembered what the Russian told me about how you could put dots on the tiles if you needed to.

I got to saying how we were all on the same boat, and then Belascoarán said how you can't say *on* the same boat but *in* the same boat, and I says how none of the boats I ever saw had anywhere to get *in* them and you couldn't even hardly get *on* them. They all asked me why I was saying that, and I explained that the way I saw it, we did the kind of job where if you did it right, nobody noticed cause everything went smooth, but if we did it wrong, then we were sunk cause it would be a tragedy, and when you were sunk it didn't matter if you were *in* or *on* the boat.

Then I said how since Mr. Gómez Letras was a plumber, he has to see to it that the water comes out where it ought to. If he does his job right—if the hot water comes out of the hot faucet and the cold out of the cold—then no one notices anything, and if you pull the lever and all the poop and pee goes south, then no one notices. But if Mr. Gómez Letras does his job wrong, well sir, then there's all hell to pay, cause if someone turns on the faucet and he gets piss instead of hot water, well now, and even if he only gets hot water where there should be cold, people aren't gonna be very happy and everybody's gonna say, *Damn Gómez Letras didn't do his job right.*

Then I went on about Mr. Vargas, the upholsterer, the one who guts and fixes chairs and sofas so none of the stuffing shows and so nobody gets a loose spring into his privates, and so's they'll be soft and pretty. If he does his job right, nobody says anything cause they're there real comfortable having some coffee or watching the game or something. But if he does it wrong, well, you can just imagine the feller sitting there and the home team is about to score, and all of a sudden, *boing*, old needle-dick pokes your boo-tocks, or you hear a *riiiip*, and they can't get you out of there even with a plowhorse, or it's so hard that after a few minutes you start looking to confess something, and then everybody says, *Damn Vargas didn't do his job right*.

Then there's Mr. Villareal. He's a drainage engineer and it's his job to make certain all the shit and piss in the city goes where it's sposed to go. So when he does his job right, people walking down the street don't go, *Hey, isn't this great, no shit in the streets*. They don't do that cause all the Villareals do their job right, mostly, but if he goes and gets it wrong and some of them drainage things get clogged up, well, then one fine morning the people of the city might wake up to a shit-and-piss tsunami and then they won't care if they live up on the fourth floor and there's no elevator, cause the people downstairs will be swimming in shit, and you know what they'll say: *Damn Villareal didn't do his job right*.

Then I said how Belascoarán and me, we were Investigation Commissions, detectives, which means that we search around for the Bad and the Evil and we see to it that they face up to their evildoings. If we do our job right, then no one notices cause the bad guys are where they have to be—that is, where they're not out fucking with the good people who just want to do their work and live their lives. But if Belascoarán and me do our jobs wrong, well, it's a problem, cause the Bad and the Evil will be out and about doing bad and evil things, and then everybody says, *Damn Belascoarán and damn Elías didn't do their jobs right*.

Then everybody sat there silent, thinking about if it's true that we were all *on* the same boat or what. But real soon they brought out those little tiles they use for dominos and started talking about everything else until the dominos were over and we all said goodbye to each other and Belascoarán and me hugged each other like brothers and I left, and I think they all left too cause it was getting kinda late.

After that I sent my report to El Sup and I told him how our plenary had gone—that is, the meeting in Belascoarán's workplace—and about the agreements we reached all together.

Then I remember how the moon was real full, just hanging there over the Monster, right there in the middle of the night over Mexico City, when I got a return message from El Sup:

Copy agreements reached. According to our reports, this Morales is somewhere up here, so you come back. When we talk, you can give me all the details and we can make plans. Be careful and make sure you don't have a tail on you. I'll be expecting you because what's missing is missing. Until then, best regards.

From the mountains of Southeast Mexico,
Insurgent Subcomandante Marcos
January 2005

CHAPTER 10

THE PRESENT DISAPPEARS

"He doesn't call me anymore. Jesús María Alvarado doesn't call me anymore," said the progressive official, with a certain sadness. The dog seemed to confirm it, but with an even sadder countenance.

"No. Now he's calling *me*," Belascoarán said, handing the tape over to him.

The guy had turned up in the wee hours of the night with the lame excuse of, "I saw your light on and decided to come up," completely oblivious to the fact that he had roused the detective from the deepest sleep he'd had in weeks. Now the official and the dog were polishing off the last of the Cokes while sitting on Héctor Belascoarán's living room floor, even though Héctor had offered them the easy chair.

"It makes me kind of sad; I was enjoying this thing about being caught up in a secret affair, an investigation. I admit that it's a little bit morbid . . . it's just that my life gets kind of boring sometimes," Monteverde said.

"Well, I *like* it when my life gets kinda boring; I sleep a lot . . . hours and hours, days and days even; I read all the books I never have time to read and I watch movies by Stan Laurel and Oliver Hardy," Héctor said.

The dog appeared to like the idea because he suddenly

took on Ollie's expression when Stan didn't understand what he was saying, and proceeded to eat up the rest of an old sausage Héctor had given him.

"You know, I'm happy that Alvarado is still talking, even if it's only to you. Are you any closer to finding out anything about that Morales person?"

"Found out there's more than one," Héctor said cryptically, like the parish priest explaining the Holy Trinity.

"Well, even if he doesn't send me any more messages, I'll still be financing your investigation," Monteverde declared with convincing resolve, as he rose to his feet and handed Héctor an envelope.

"And what is it I'm supposed to investigate? Who is this Alvarado that's been calling us? Or who and where is this Morales that once murdered him?"

"You tell me. You're the detective."

"The second. I mean, I couldn't accept your money if I had to devote all my time to finding out who this new Alvarado is."

"Me, I couldn't care less . . . although, actually, I was beginning to think of him as a friend trying to tell us things . . . Yeah, sure, okay . . . keep me in the loop."

The dog limped over to Héctor and started licking his naked feet. Héctor took it as a sign of solidarity and lit a cigarette.

He opened an eye, *the* eye, and said out loud, "The dog's name is Tobías."

He didn't know why he always spoke out loud in the morning. Maybe because he needed to hear something, even if it was his own pasty voice, to convince himself that he had to stay awake. Glorious winter sunshine was streaming in through the windows and flashing off the white walls of his room. He lit a cigarette and jumped out of the bed, tripping over a stack of thick, hardcover, historical novels that promised days of interesting reading.

On the way to the bathroom he asked himself, again out loud, "Which one is my Morales? Who is my goddamn Morales?"

Then, limping more than ever, Héctor Belascoarán Shayne, independent Mexican detective, looked at his reflection in the mirror and told himself that the time had come to move from planning to action. But what action? He decided that things might clear up a bit if he splashed his face with really cold water.

Héctor stared down the enormous cellblock. This had been one of the medical sections of the prison, but now there was a counter with cells behind it. He was standing by some tables. A couple of students lifted their eyes from their dusty tomes to check him out. They must not have been very impressed with the one-eyed dick because they were back in their books in no time.

Fritz signaled to follow him into a little atrium on one side of the cellblock. There were a couple of sad-looking trees, a fountain with no water, and a pair of those mutant birds, the ones that Mexico City pollution had turned extremely intelligent.

"Nicotine pause," he said, offering Héctor one of his filtered Delicados.

Belascoarán rattled off everything he had so far, which he had put together on the way to the prison-turned-archive.

"I think I can tie the man who was Alvarado's cellmate and later his murderer to the White Brigade, but I'm drawing a blank after 1980. If the guy had gone for a career with one of the political police agencies in this country, you would have to have heard of him. Morales. These are the kind of people who move up in the world. One Morales, the one in the photo with the sharp nose, very skinny, and with thick glasses, well, if this Morales was about twenty-five in 1971, then he would be just shy of sixty today. Does this character exist publicly now? Does the name tell you anything at all?"

"No," Fritz said, "and I swear I've been through my notes and my photo albums a hundred times and I've talked to a hundred people and I've shown them the picture we saw the other day. Nothing! Now you see him, now you don't. Disappeared! But that's nothing new in the chronicles of the Dirty War. There are all sorts of characters who turn up out of nowhere, do their shit, strike it rich, pull off some big job, do somebody a big favor, and then go up in smoke. They have to be around somewhere: a prosperous furniture-chain owner in San Antonio, Texas; maybe a drug trafficker killed anonymously in Ecuador, thought to be Mexican; an upright president of the PTA at a Catholic school . . ."

"You've got something," Belascoarán said.

"How can you tell?"

"Because you're from Puebla, and when Puebla people have a secret, they do like the people from Pénjamo—they smile and rock from side to side," the detective said.

"Yeah, I do have something. Jesús María Alvarado had a son. Remember what I told you the first time? About that kid I recalled seeing with an older lady? Well, the older lady was Alvarado's mother and the kid was his son."

"How old would he be now?"

"About my age, maybe a couple of years younger, something like that."

Over forty, Héctor made a mental note.

"His name is Ángel Alvarado Alvarado."

"Why the double last name?"

"Go figure! Maybe Alvarado was a single father."

One Alvarado speaking for the first Alvarado, for his father? Could he have dug up his father's voice from the past because he discovered his killer in the present? The Morales he remembers from when he was a child? Héctor threw out the cigarette he was smoking and lit another.

"And he's got a telephone, so you can call him . . ."

Héctor took the slip of paper from the hand of the smiling Fritz.

"And he's got a job you're going to love. He does the voice dubbing for monsters and things in the cartoons on TV. He does bears, dragons, reindeer. He's the voice of Scooby-Doo and Barney.

"Barney?"

"According to my nieces, Barney's a purple dinosaur."

"Sounds like he could be a minister in the present administration.

"Probably is. We've seen stranger things lately."

In the office, Gilberto Gómez Letras and Carlos Vargas were looking very busy. Héctor walked in, grunted something like hello, and went directly to his desk to phone Alvarado's son. He let the home phone ring about six times, then the office phone, and finally the lunch place. Nothing. He went back to his stack of papers in a green folder entitled *Morales* and set himself the task of individualizing the different Morales characters, or at least the three distinct Moraleses who had taken some sort of shape after the conversations he'd had with Elías Contreras. Alvarado's murderer, the Zapatista traitor, and the hand behind the killing and dealing in Chiapas. Once he turned them back into distinct entities, he could begin to pick up the separate threads and work his way in any direction he chose. There is always a trail, so there's always a thread to be followed.

It was a matter of coherence: You had to follow the *right* thread. Was it coherent for a turncoat guerrilla fighter to become a mole, infiltrate Lecumberri to pump information out of political prisoners, and then wait to kill Alvarado on the *outside?* Yes, it was coherent! It was also coherent for this same character to have been a member of the White Brigade and one of its torturers; that would make him the one who absconded with the records in '83. Now he could rule out the one involved in the dirty dealings in connection with the earthquake—that one had a different physical description and might just be the Chiapas Morales who was now the responsibility of Elías Contreras. And this led to a connection between that other Morales—the one who ceased to exist for twenty years—and the madness of the Juancho–bin Laden Morales who was brought into the story by the voice of the talking corpse.

That was his Morales. To the accompaniment of Carlos's hammering and Gómez Letras's cursing as he whacked a rusty fitting with an old pipe, Héctor tried to change his perspective. He decided that he would take anything that looked obvious and consider it to be true: Many, many years after the events, a child discovers (runs into, accidentally finds, remembers) his father's murderer, and not knowing what to do with the information, begins to make phone calls.

Héctor's look of certainty did not get past his office mates, who had been watching him on the sly for hours.

"So, are you very cultured?" Gómez Letras blurted out of the clear blue sky.

"Who me?" Belascoarán answered, caught off guard.

"Yes, you!"

"Naah, I'm an engineer. For all the really important stuff, I have to rely on my own efforts by listening, watching, walking around, and, particularly, reading. But the most important things are what I've learned from you guys."

"I told you, popular wisdom is what it is," Gómez Letras said as he tossed a nut at Carlos Vargas, who caught it on the back of his head.

"You want to play games, you dumb bastard?" Vargas growled as he advanced on the plumber, rubbing his head and holding his upholsterer's hammer in the attack position. "Popular wisdom, my ass! You spend half your life with your nose in those books of yours. It's all that damn reading you do."

Gómez Letras ran for cover behind Héctor's desk. "Save me, chief, the man's possessed by a homicidal rage."

"Doctor Vargas, if you intend to kill him, please do it cleanly; do not spoil my work with the blood of this pipe-sucking plumber," Héctor said, holding his arms in the air to protect himself from the imminent Attack of the Mad Plumber.

"You stupid sonovabitch, I'll give you some *homicidal rage*, you moron. But I'll forgive *your* nut attack if you scratch *my* nuts."

Just then, the phone stepped in to save the day. Carlos Vargas left his hammer aside, picked up the phone with his right hand, and continued rubbing his head with his left. He listened for a second, then said, "Some guy name Blitz or Spritz says he has an important message for Detective Belascoarán."

Héctor took a deep breath, lit up, and took the phone.

"You want to talk to one of them? He set conditions," Fritz said.

"*One* of them?"

"One of them."

"What are the conditions?"

"I can't say who he is and you can't ask. It's not to talk about him, only about your Morales. And you can't record the conversation."

"Why would one of them want to talk to me?"

"Those of us who are working on the history of the Dirty War keep receiving notes, real siren songs: Could we spare some time? Could we talk some things over? Now that it's all coming out, they want to talk, but without talking. They want to tell their part of the affair, they want to invent their own stories. They spent all that time in the shadows; they never appeared in the photos; they never got any medals. They believe it was the *others* who sent them up the creek; it was the *others* who gave the orders. If there's anything they hate worse than the leftists, it's the presidents whose orders they followed. They're all schizos and psychopaths who want to be somebody else and they all have different stories to tell."

"Of course," Héctor said, "nobody wants to be the Wicked Witch of the West. So, are you going to accept the conditions set by one of these creeps?"

"For now, I need to. If later you find that you have to send him up, we'll talk. He'll be waiting for you in half an hour at La Habana Café. It's twenty meters from your office. He's about sixty years old and he'll be carrying a copy of the Constitution so you can recognize him."

"The Constitution? You've got to be kidding."

"That's what he said."

* * *

For years, La Habana Café was a kind of no-man's land. Back in the '60s, the journalists of the Communist Party could coexist there with officials of the nearby Ministry of the Interior, and if you listened carefully you might get the impression that these were people who actually knew something. Then the waitresses grew old, or their coffee got too cold, or it just tasted different. In any case, Héctor never liked coffee, and these days, if you listened carefully you might hear strains of narco-ranchera music, or, if you cared to look closely, you might glimpse some retired narco-rancheros. Nostalgia didn't quite mend the imperfections.

The man sitting there alone with a copy of the Political Constitution of the United States of Mexico looked to Belascoarán like something out of a boring Disney fairy tale remake (like where the Wicked Witch of the West is actually a deep-cover good guy). This character didn't really have a face. He was something like what people call *elderly*, with the nondescript features they love to have on polls or in commercials for the National Lottery. He had a medium-dark complexion with an ordinary white-streaked mustache, black hair that wasn't too black, and a rat-gray suit. The only thing that stood out on this gentleman was his tie, a brilliant garnet red that matched the garnet ring on his left ring finger . . . the right was for shooting and it wouldn't do to interfere with his trigger finger.

Héctor tried to hide his limp, as he always did when meeting the enemy. He tried to take on a fierce look in his eye, the good one, and he hoped the patch would make it even fiercer. He sat down across from the guy and waited.

Suddenly, the character just started in: "There was a war. There was a bunch of sleaze-bag assholes who thought they were the granddaddies of Che Guevara and went around shooting Mexican Army soldiers in the back of the head. What were we supposed to do, just let them?"

No, they didn't *just let them*. They persecuted them and their families; they murdered them, they tortured them, and they killed their children; they raped their women before their eyes; they hid the bodies . . . and they lied to the mothers of the disappeared.

Héctor had known a few of them: the torturers and the tortured. He had heard stories that had kept him awake for months. And worse, he heard about all these things ten years *after* they happened. Because he had been living on Mars; he had been too busy being a happy little engineer while it was all happening.

"What is it with them? Don't they understand that we are the law?"

Héctor did understand, of course, but what he did not understand was this scumbag's use of the third-person *they*, the *them*, the *we*, and the *you*.

"You can't let them give you their bullshit stories now. We all know that if they'd won, they would've lined us up in front of a firing squad against the gates of Chapultepec and shot us. *Up against the wall*, just like in Cuba when Fidel took over."

"Did you know Jesús María Alvarado?"

"I heard about him, but I never met him," Mr. Anonymous said, fiddling with his ring.

"Did you ever meet a certain Morales?"

"A dumb jerk. He was one of *them* . . . but he punked out. We never trusted the little prick . . . and we were right not to. The asshole ended up stealing things. He stole from *us*, no less." The guy tried to produce a sly smile, but it didn't work. "Just imagine, he stole some papers from us to try and cover his ass, but he didn't have the balls—he never even attempted to pull off his faggoty little blackmail."

"When did he quit your team?"

"He wasn't in my team."

"You talk about *them* and *us*; who are you talking about when you say *us*?"

Anonymous let that one go and took a long sip from his coffee.

"When did you see him last?"

"Back around '83. I don't know if they gave him a job in the provinces. Maybe he just pulled a disappearing act, you know, *Going for cigarettes, back in a second* . . . and punked out again . . . Once a punk, always a punk."

"You know anything about his private life? A wife? A day job? An address? Any friends?"

"He was a loner. What do you expect? He had fucked over his wife and friends. For a job, he sold furniture." Anon let out an inappropriate little chuckle. "Yeah, he sold old furniture . . . and he lived in the Santa María district. But what makes this dumb Morales prick so interesting to you?"

Now it was Héctor's turn to clam up. He signaled to a passing waitress to bring him one of the sodas she had on her tray. He and Anonymous just looked at each other.

"Morales wasn't his name; it was just a cover. What was his real name? Do you know it?"

"I know everything," Mr. Anon said, smiling.

Héctor did not return the smile. He lit a cigarette.

"His name was Juvencio. I remember because it was the stupidest name in the whole fucking world. And I can't remember his last name right now, but I'll give you a lead, a pisser of a lead. One time somebody told him that his last name was the same as one of Juárez's ministers."

"Which Juárez?"

"Now you're going to tell me you leftists don't know who Juárez was . . . Don Benito, asshole."

"Oh, that one."

Conjuring up the specter of the liberal president Benito Juárez must have triggered some gut reaction in Anonymous, because he started off again without any further prompting.

"You know what? Instead of busting our balls with all those papers they keep digging up, what they should do is build us a monument, a fucking monument on the Alameda, one with—"

Suddenly he just stopped. He didn't even finish his sentence. He got up from his chair and . . . the conversation was over. He reached his hand out to the detective. Héctor ignored it and picked up the tab for the soda and coffee. He wasn't going to let this trash pay for his soda.

"It's paid," Anonymous said, as he walked slowly toward the door.

With a little bit of luck, the terrible midday traffic on Bucareli Street would be a vehicle of divine justice and some microbus would run him over. But there is no God in heaven, because Anonymous moved in his tired shuffle right into the traffic, simply sidestepping the cars and ignoring the honks from the ones he forced to brake.

Héctor had a couple of threads to follow, but first he had to get rid of the rotten aftertaste from the interview with Anonymous, so he left La Habana Café and took a taxi to Chapultepec.

A chill breeze was sweeping the terraces of Chapultepec Castle. When the sun doesn't come out in the morning in Mexico City, it's a bad omen. The locals, who are like lizards but won't admit it, start to get nervous and all the talk shifts to polar air masses and other things that may happen in Gothenburg or in Siberia, but never around here.

When he got to the courtyard with the carriages, there was a guide finishing up a mini-harangue, all quiet like, but with emphasis: ". . . and it's shameful that they've got Maximillian's carriages here. Oh, they're beautiful and luxurious, but they have no business sitting alongside the carriage that carried Juárez and the dignity of our country."

As the group moved away, Héctor stayed awhile, pacing around Juárez's carriage. He remembered a book he had read about how this carriage carried the itinerant republic, with the French armies chasing it, over a distance of 4,000 kilometers. A carriage holding the authority of the republic protected by a guard of barefoot soldiers because the president did not have the money to pay for their boots, or even his own salary. From Mexico City, Juárez headed to a place called Paso del Norte in the vicinity of Chihuahua, which is now understandably known as Juárez City. As long as the carriage kept rolling on sovereign territory, the republic was alive. It was a beautiful story.

Héctor approached the carriage slowly, watching for some lapse in the guard's attention that would allow him to touch one of the wheels, then stretched his arm over the red protection cord. The wheel was shiny, as if a great many hands had rubbed it over the years.

He decided to eat at home. He went by the Michoacán market to pick up some *chistorras* to have with his Teacher's, along with some avocados, potatoes, tomatoes, and fruit from the greengrocer. He thought about it for a moment and decided to buy a Chinese melon, a little beat up but perfectly ripe.

As he walked through his door, he noticed the light on his answering machine blinking. He took his time, put the potatoes on to boil, sliced the tomatoes so they could breathe, sprinkled salt on the slices, and only then opened a Coke and took his position in the easy chair of destiny. He pushed the button.

> *Don Héctor, this is Jesús María Alvarado. The idea just popped into my head. I didn't have anything else to do, so I said to myself,* Why not call the detective? *It reminds me of the joke about the guy who goes to the doctor one Saturday and tells the doctor that he's very worried because he has three balls. The doctor gives him a thorough scrotum examination and comes to the conclusion that there is no problem, and he tells the man that he has nothing to worry about because he only has two balls. Then the man says that he wasn't really worried. It was just that being Saturday and all, he didn't have anything better to do, so he decided to drop by and have the doctor fondle his balls.*
>
> *Well, that's it. That, and to let you know that years ago I went after Morales, but he found me first and stuck a gun to the back of my neck and killed me, and that—*

The voice cut off; his anwering-machine tape only recorded short messages.

Once he had cleaned the melon stains off his shirt, Héctor called Fritz and took a walk to La Torre de Lulio, a used bookstore a few blocks from his home on Nuevo León Street, and he got a deal on the fifteen-volume complete works, letters, speeches, notes, and essays of Benito Juárez. Finding the books was no problem, haggling the price down was no problem, but lugging the three plastic grocery bags back home almost killed him. Then, as if he had returned to his worst days as a college student, he began skimming through every single one of the horrible orange volumes from top to bottom, trying to find the names of all of Juárez's ministers. It was dark outside when he finally abandoned his quest, absolutely certain that he had overlooked something, that there must have been some change of minister here or there in one of the cabinets.

He dialed the number of Alvarado's son, the line that no one ever answered, and listened to the standard number of rings.

Suddenly he remembered something, a poem he had jotted down. Whose was it? Where had he stashed it? In a book! Which book? What was he reading when he had copied the poem? He was reading *Robin Hood*. He searched the bookcases along the hall till he found the tattered Thor edition that was shedding its yellow binding. He shook the book and the piece of paper glided to the floor.

The poem by the forgotten author read:

If I disappear from the present
And
Live in the past
It is certain
That one day I will be
Real

The two little girls raced around his easy chair. They must have thought that a house without furniture was really cool, because they cavorted happily through the hallways and frolicked into the living room, almost crashing into the chair as they sped around it. These well-mannered children had taken off their shoes and left them in a tidy bundle next to the door.

"What do you need my nieces for? I hope you realize what it took. You just call and ask me to bring them, and here they are, but their mother was something else. You can't just go around saying, *Lend me your daughters and I'll bring then right back as soon as I see this detective*," Fritz said.

"Listen to this, girls, I want you to hear something."

They must have been around six, no more than seven, but very disciplined, so they slammed on their brakes and turned all their attention to the nice man with one eye.

"I want you to close your eyes and listen to a voice, then tell me who it belongs to."

The girls nodded and closed their eyes. Belascoarán pushed *PLAY* on the answering machine.

"*Listen, man, this is Jesús María Alvarado. I hope you've got a long tape, cause I have to tell you what happened to me. It's a really rat-shit story, crazy. There I was in Juárez, in a bar, and since all the tables were taken . . .*"

"It's Barney, it's Barney, and he said a bad word, he said *rat-shit!*" one of the girls screamed, as the other one smirked and opened her eyes wide.

CHAPTER 11

THE TIME OF NOBODY

The trick is to get them to look the other way.

That's what the city comrade told me, the one called Alakazam cause he's a magician, which means he does magic. The thing is, I had to go say goodbye cause I already had to come back here. So we were there eating some of those tacos they call *de suadero*. Well, *we* weren't eating, *he* was eating, cause the other day I ate one of those tacos and spent the next day in the latrine, which is the outhouse. So this Alakazam was explaining how he does his magic, those things he makes appear and disappear and where he reads people's minds and all, and I wasn't understanding very much, but what he said was that you had to get people to look at one hand and then do the switch with the other. So I asked if it was like politicians do when they get people to busy themselves with some tomfoolery while on the other side they're doing their underhanded stuff. And Alakazam said that it was something like that, except that he was a magician who entertained people and politicians were pricks who fucked people; that's what he said, now. And then Alakazam began to explain that, like, for example, there are two agendas, and I asked what was an *agenda,* and he said . . . Hold on a minute, I got it right here . . . it's just that my pad is about as mixed up as my head . . . Here it is, right after *perspective,* it says that an *agenda* is a kind of pad where you jot down what you intend to do, and how, and when, and who you intend to do it with, and it also means the program for the day and what's more important and all that. So he was explaining that there's two agendas, the agenda of the powerful and the agenda of the screwed. So for them it's the agenda of the powerful that's the most important, cause they want to keep getting more powerful and richer. On the other hand, the agenda of the screwed is what's most important for us, which is the fight for liberation. And then Alakazam explained that the powerful—that is, the rich and the bad government leaders—are trying to convince everyone that their agenda, the agenda of the powerful, is the only good one for everybody, even for the screwed. So they are constantly telling us about the concerns of the powerful and convincing us that it's all that's important and it's what we have to be concerned about. So you see, they have us looking one way while they're stealing everything and selling the country down the river, and our natural resources, like our water, oil, electric power, and even our people. And when we finally see what's going on, then it'll be too late, cause there won't be anything left when we get through looking the other way. And the worse thing is not that we're looking off where there's nothing to see, no sir, the worse thing is that they get us to think that their concerns, the concerns of the rich, are *our* concerns, and we take them like our own. So then, according to modern politics, Alakazam says, Democracy is for the majority, the screwed, to be all concerned over the well-being of the minority, the powerful. And the other thing is for all of us that are screwed to look the other way while they steal our lands, our jobs, our memories, our dignity. And on top of it all, the powerful want us to applaud them and give them our votes. And that's when Alakazam said how there's black magic, which is the one you do with demons, and there's white magic, which is the one that Alakazam and other magicians do, and then there's dirty magic, which is the one politicians do.

So Alakazam told me all this before we said goodbye. I had already said goodbye to all the other city friends before that. Well, not exactly all of them, cause the fact is, I didn't come back alone. See, I brought Magdalena back with me, cause she, or he, said they both wanted to get to see the Zapatista territories and at the same time help me find the Bad and the Evil. So I explained that what they gave me for the trip didn't amount to enough for the both of us, and then he/she said that it didn't matter none cause there was the money she had saved for the operation. So I got to thinking that it was a good thing for Magdalena to come along and see the struggle of the Zapatista communities for herself. So here we are: We did part of the trip with the Muciño feller and the rest by bus.

Elías's Return Trip

My name doesn't matter now, but they call me Muciño. Yeah, like the soccer player. But that Muciño was known as *El Centavo Muciño* and I think he played for Cruz Azul. Besides, I don't play soccer at all; I'm a cop. Yes, I am, with the Federal Preventive Police. No, don't get excited, there's good and there's bad everywhere, you know. There's even good and bad in the police, although I think that if we put it to a vote, we good ones would lose by a landslide. In any case, I was able to take Elías part of the way. I took him from Mexico City to Puebla, and I would have taken him all the way to

Chiapas, except that I had to turn in the patrol car. It would have been good to see the comrades, but I was only able to go as far as Puebla. No, he was not alone. He had a lady with him, or not exactly a lady, but a person dressed like a lady. Elías said her name was Magdalena. Well, what happened was that I ran into Elías, who had come into Mexico City to see the doctor and was now returning, so I offered to give him a lift, even if it was only part of the way. Truth is, I wanted to chat with him. Elías is a very fine person and even if he does talk very funny, he's a great listener and he always comes up with good advice. The Zapatistas? Well, I had heard about them during the uprising. I was just a kid then. Later there was the March of the Indigenous Peoples in 2001, and since I was assigned to protect the Zapatista delegation, I got to hear the speeches by the comandantes in all the rallies. After that, a group of comrades in the police started talking a little about everything and we saw how what they propose is a good thing—the Zapatistas, I mean. No, we don't do anything, we just read the things they say and talk about it amongst ourselves. Yes, I did go to Chiapas once, to one of the Good Governance Board meetings. No, I didn't go as a spy. I went in civilian clothes, but I told the people at the door that I was a policeman. Yes, they did welcome me, and the board members explained all the things they were doing. That was when I met Elías. No, he doesn't belong to the Good Governance Board and he's not one of the authorities. No, he was there because he had been sent on an errand. I was waiting for a car to take me back to the city and we got to talking. I understood everything he said and I liked what he had to say. Yeah, you know, some of the communiqués sent by El Sup are very complicated and I don't always understand what he's saying, because he uses very cultural words.

Elías, now, he talks so we can understand him, a lot like us. When we parted company, I told him that if he ever got to Mexico City and there was anything I could do for him, he should look me up, and what do you know, the day came and he did. No, he hardly talked along the way, but he listened with a lot of attention. Me? Well, I told him about what happened in San Juan Ixtayopan, in Tláhuac. Yes, when they lynched two comrades from the police force and left a third one half dead. Yes, it was in all the papers. Well, so he would tell El Sup about it. Who knows, he might even write a communiqué about it. You see, what happened is not what they say happened. What you got is that there were these people from a TV channel and they were doing one of those things they call a *reality show* or something like that.

These people from that Televosa started talking about the child stealers here and the child stealers there and a lot of people started gathering. Yes, they were in front of that school. And then people started to get all excited and hot under the collar. But it wasn't true at all. They just wanted to film the reaction of the people. Yeah, they were filming a program. No, I don't remember the name. Well, thing is, those policemen were passing by in their civilian clothes and one of the TV people started screaming that those were the kidnappers of the children. No, I suppose they were meaning to explain that it was just a television film and that it wasn't true and that it was just acting, but things got out of hand, as they say, and they just left. Yes, the television people just up and left all those people in a fury. Later, the television owners paid the government a load of money so no one would say what really touched things off. Yes, that's why I get so mad with some of the media when they claim they're really concerned about what happened. All lies! They're the first ones who go around saying that we policemen are all crooks and delinquents, and now they're crying and moaning. Of course, there are some policemen who are worse than the crooks, but then there's others of us who are good. No, they don't care about the dead, just about selling lies. Oh, and it also helps them get officials in or out of office, according to their convenience. And now it's the mass media that's actually governing. Mainly the television channels. You got it: We on the bottom put up the dead bodies and they on the top pay for the commercials. Like to make you vomit. No, I have to give you the ticket anyway because one of your brake lights is broken. Hey, you don't have to insult me. You have to go to the Good Governance Board to pay the fine. To anybody over there. There's one in Oventic, in La Realidad, another in Morelia, another in Roberto Barrios, and another in La Garrucha. Yeah, they know me there. Yes, everyone I give a fine to, I tell them to go over there so they'll learn. Yes, of course.

The Time of Nobody

Now let me tell you about how we met with El Sup to think about all the reports we got together on that Morales person. That was around the 4th or 5th of February of this year, 2005. Now, the thing is that besides all the stuff I got together with Belascoarán on my trip to the Monster—that is, Mexico City—over here in Chiapas they were doing a lot of getting together also and all the information was about this thing, or this case, depending, and it had to do with this one Morales that I got in the distribution of the Bad and the Evil that we had done in that other meeting over in the place where Belascoarán works. One of the information reports El Sup had was sent by Frayba to the Good Governance Board of

Los Altos, which is Oventic, answering the letter sent by the comrades, where the autonomous authorities asked Frayba for help with information about the paramilitary. A few days later, on Febuary 9, 2005, to be exact, on the tenth anniversary of Zedillo's betrayal of the Zapatistas, the Mexican newspaper known as *La Jornada* published part of that report from the Fray Bartolomé de las Casas Human Rights Center, or Frayba, which is how us Indians here in Chiapas call this here organization that's in Jovel—that is, in San Cristóbal de las Casas—and that keeps watch so they won't violate the human rights of the indigenous peoples. So that report was about the paramilitary and how they get support from the bad governments.

So I don't have to tell you what it was they said in that report, cause it's already published in that newspaper called *La Jornada*, but it made it real clear that all the bad governments have an agreement to fuck the indigenous Zapatista peoples using what they call the Dirty War, which means that it's secret, that they don't say it's on and they make like nothing's wrong, but it is and there's killing and disappearing and people displaced and a whole lot of misery for the screwed. So the problem is that they not only did what they did way back in the Zedillo administration, but the guilty ones, they're still around doing the same evil on account of us Zapatistas won't give up and we won't sell out; what I mean is, we don't forget what we're fighting for, and that's why they need to defeat us any way they can.

So like I was saying, we were with El Sup looking over all the reports we had all together and you could see right there that a great evil was, or rather *is*, taking over our country, which is called Mexico. So what we were doing is we were drinking some coffee, only we couldn't really drink it cause it was real hot and it burned our tongues, so while we went on smoking and waiting for the coffee to cool down a bit, we were thinking how the Bad and the Evil were doing all their tricks and cheating and no one ever said anything. And we got to asking ourselves if it was that people didn't notice or that they didn't care. And then we saw how people just don't see the Bad and the Evil, but not cause they're hiding or anything like that, cause they're right out in the open everywhere. So they're not hiding, but people don't see them, like it was magic. And right there I remembered what it was that the magician Alakazam said, and I told El Sup, and El Sup said that that was what it was, that we were all looking the other way. So the powerful, which is the rich, which is the bad governments, have the people looking the other way, and they can't realize things, and that's how the Bad and the Evil come to do everyone harm and we can't even tell. About then I tasted my coffee again to see if it was going to let me drink it, but it wasn't, so I commented to El Sup that they were destroying our country, which is Mexico, and then we're all going to be like orphans: sad, lost, not knowing where we came from, and like forgetting our own selves. And then El Sup didn't say anything, but he took a big sip from his coffee and really burnt his tongue, and that got him to saying some big dirty words and people's mothers and all, and I couldn't really tell if it was cause he got burnt or cause they were killing our country while we were looking the other way. So I figgered that it was like we were watching television while they were robbing the house, and people say they have a lot of information and that they know a lot of things, or cases, depends, but what they don't know is that they're stealing our hearts. Then I remembered how in the news they jump from one thing to another and it kinda hurts your eyes just to keep jumping.

Well, just then we noticed that the coffee was fit to drink and we began to enjoy our coffee without danger of burns, and that's when El Sup said: "As you can see, Elías, it seems the time of nobody has arrived."

Nobody

The strategic location of the Southeastern Mexican state of Chiapas awakened the interest of the world's great powers. Because of this, the governments of the United States, Canada, Japan, Russia, China, and those of the European Union have all posted agents of their respective intelligence services there. If you add to this the agents of the different sectors of the Mexican government, you get what they call *saturation* of the theater of operations. As anyone knows, that saturation brings about what is called *intoxication*, which means that the information compiled is not only worthless, but actually harmful to the intelligence agency in question.

It may be due to these factors of saturation and intoxication that none of those agencies ever caught on that the organizational structure of the Zapatista National Liberation Army contains a branch equivalent to the Special Forces or elite guard of other armies. Its existence is known only to a few: the members of the General Staff of the EZLN and some of the older comandantes of the CCRI. That part of the neo-Zapatista structure is made up of six people who have carried out extremely delicate and important missions, in utmost secrecy, at different moments in the history of the EZLN. One such mission was the protection of Sup Marcos at the time of the betrayal, about ten years ago, in February of 1995. According to some accounts, when the community of Guadalupe Tepeyac was completely surrounded by paratroopers of the Federal Army, it was this group who got El

Sup out of the encirclement and delivered him to a safe place. The special unit was also responsible for finding out, in just twenty-four hours, the truth about the events that took place in Acteal on December 22, 1997. The information they uncovered became the foundation for a series of communiqués issued at the time, which, along with additional data contributed by some of the media and NGOs, discredited the government strategy of representing the massacre as an internecine fight among indigenous peoples. In January of 1998, it was this unit that saved the Supreme Command of the EZLN when the Federal Army tried to take the La Realidad community on the same day that Francisco Labastida Ochoa was sworn in as Minister of the Interior.

While few know of the existence of this unit, even fewer know the names of the members: the members themselves and Insurgent Subcomandante Marcos. And only they know that their code name is . . . NOBODY.

1. Erika. Insurgent. Indian woman. Fifteen years old, going on sixteen. She was four years old at the time of the uprising. Her father was killed in the fighting at Ocosingo and she was brought up by the resistance. She decided to become a member of the insurgent forces in 2001, after the March of the Indigenous Peoples. Elías talked to her, and that's when she lied. She said she was already sixteen, but she was only eleven, going on twelve. She is a radio operator. Sometimes, when El Sup and the Monarca don't manage to get up the radio hill in time, she starts on her own with the transmissions of Radio Insurgente, the voice of the voiceless. She is also reputed to be ready to fight any of the males in the Zapatista troops if they make disparaging remarks about women or make fun of them. Very good with both the mili-

tary angle and the political. Expert in radio communications. Loves poetry, the songs of Juan Gabriel, Los Bukis, and Los Temerarios. In the evenings, she makes illegal use of a lamp to read a tattered book of verses by Miguel Hernández that she found at an old mountain drop point. She goes off-key when she sings the song of the Zapatista *caracoles*. She is NOBODY's radio operator.

2. Doña Juanita. Indian woman. They say she's the widow of Old Antonio, who died in 1994. No one knows how old she is, but she's an adult. She knows a great deal about herbal medicine, has a good clinical eye, and the patience of 500 years. She knows how to make sweet toast and *marquesote*, which is a bread made with sugar and butter. When she speaks at her town assemblies, everyone listens with attention and respect. She was one of the comrades who drafted the so-called Revolutionary Law on Women, and she was the first to state that women can become authorities too. Even the bravest of the men come to her for advice and guidance. She is NOBODY's nurse.

3. Toñita. Indian woman. About ten years old, going on eleven. Daughter of insurgent parents. Her mother was carrying Toñita in her belly when she participated in the storming of Las Margaritas in January of 1994. She is very talented at obtaining and interpreting information. She is handy with disguises and can pass undetected anywhere, and in almost any situation. She loves to draw and to run. There isn't a man among them who can get up a tree faster or shoot more accurately with a slingshot. She attends the autonomous school, and when she graduates, she says, she's going to become an authority and then outlaw mathematics, because she suffers

a lot with her numbers. She's in charge of intelligence for NOBODY.

4. Maa Jchixuch (*Maa* means macaw in Tojolobal, and *Jchixuch* means porcupine in Tzeltal; macaw is also *Moo* in Tzeltal, and porcupine is *ixchixuch* in Chol and *tek tikcal chitom* in Tzotzil). Young mestizo man. Must be close to twenty. Wears a punk-style haircut with his hair up in spikes like a porcupine and dyed a bunch of different colors like a macaw. He has a stand in the Mercado de los Ancianos, in Tuxtla Gutiérrez, Chiapas. He sells anything, depending on which way the wind is blowing. From dealing in fireworks, he became an expert in explosives. He is also a singer-songwriter. Well, he makes up songs and sings them, but he doesn't set them to music. They say he writes the lyrics and sends them off to someone else who does the music. One example is the song known as "Other Caresses," which goes as follows:

> *In some corner of the world/Some skins meet./They speak, they listen./They ask, they answer./They caress each other./For a caress is a question./For a caress is an answer./A piece of flesh asks: Here? Like this?/And another piece of flesh answers: Yes, there, like that./But not always./There are men and women in the world./And there are ghosts as well./The ghosts are very different./The ghosts get wounded when they caress./But that is not the worst of it./Those caresses don't leave scars./Because those caresses never heal./Worst of all is that ghosts devote all their clumsy tenderness/To caressing the whole world/And preventing it from healing the memories./When a ghost caresses/It asks and answers/Rebellion.*

He sent that song to some rockers in Europe and,

according to them, this and some of his other songs will become part of a record they are putting together called *Ghosts*. Maa Jchixuch is NOBODY's explosives expert.

5. El Justiciero. Male mestizo. About forty years old. Black as night. Formerly a plumber's assistant. Presently drives a construction truck. The sticker on El Justiciero's rear bumper reads, *Historical and Dialectical Materialist,* just above the one that reads, *Old, But Still Able*. He got to talking to Elías one night when his truck broke down at the La Garrucha *caracol*, and they say that when the sun rose they were still at it. After that he became a militant Zapatista. He talked to his friends and colleagues and they all registered with the Good Governance Board. He recruited taxi drivers, tortilla vendors, table servers, and even a few soldiers. He is the driver-mechanic for NOBODY.

6. Elías, Investigation Commission. You already know a bit about him. He is the commanding officer of NOBODY.

7. La Magdalena. We already know her background; she was co-opted temporarily, on Elías's recommendation, as the seventh element. She's just barely part of NOBODY.

Cry Me a River

What I did was I talked to Magdalena and told her she should wait till I got back, cause I had to go grab the Bad, but he/she said she wanted to help any way she could, so I took her to meet with the group we call NOBODY.

When we got there, I introduced her to everybody and I told them that he/she was my daughter, or my son, depending on your perspective, and they said hello, and that was about it. I told the unit that we had to make a plan to catch this Morales and that we didn't have much time to do it, cause we had to get it done by February 9, which means right away. So we got to studying the reports we had and looked at them with perspective. Course, I had to explain what *perspective* means, and they all jotted it down in their vocabulary pads. So when we had done the collective analysis of the Morales thing, or case, depending, from all angles, we came up with a plan and an agenda. (I also explained what *agenda* was, and they all wrote it down.) So then Erika started setting up her toaster, which is what we call her communications equipment, and she screwed on the antenna and did all the calibration and tuning so's the signal would reach far's it could, and she settled down to communicating with all the radio bases in the Zapatista towns and insurgent outposts.

Meanwhile, Toñita was writing down the messages Erika was receiving. Maa Jchixuch began to get the things ready that we were going to need to grab this Morales, and El Justiciero did all the checking he always did before a mission so that nothing could go wrong—I mean, if he could avoid it. Doña Juanita filled her knapsack with herbs and *pozol* and toast, cause what if it took longer'n we thought, and Magdalena got together the makeup and clothes she was going to use. Now me, Elías Contreras, Investigation Commission, I was going over and over in my head the plan to catch the Bad and the Evil, this Morales person who was doing his evil things in Zapatista lands. So that's what I was doing, and every time I got a new idea I would tell everybody to stop and listen up. Then I remembered something and I called everybody in and told them to pull out their vocabulary pads and take down the word *aforementioned*, and I explained that in this case, or maybe thing, the *aforemen-*

tioned referred to Morales. Then they went back to doing what they were doing before to get ready to catch the aforementioned Morales—that is, to bring him up before Zapatista justice.

So we did all that in the early hours of the 8th of this month, which is February of 2005, and when the sky was beginning to get gray, Erika and Toñita came to tell me that according to the reports, that Morales person, the aforementioned, had gone to the municipal seat in Ocosingo and was getting all drunk and bothering the women. Besides that, the aforementioned had with him a couple of gorillas as bodyguards, so he was being guarded wherever he went, and I think they even took him to the bathroom. Toñita said how maybe there was very few people and nothing to do in Ocosingo because the feast of Candlemass was already past and people didn't have the money to go on partying, so that was why she thought it might be a good place to grab that Morales person, the aforementioned, without making a really big noise.

El Justiciero came back and said the truck was all ready. Then Maa Jchixuch said he was ready to go. Then Doña Juanita said she was ready to go. Then Magdalena said she was ready, and Erika and Toñita had already said they were ready. Then I said I was ready and that they should wait for me to go to the john, and then I came back from the john and we all climbed in El Justiciero's truck, and we got to Ocosingo when nighttime was settling into the streets. So we got ourselves installed in a little shed on the outskirts of the town called Paradise—the shed was called that, not the town—and Erika set up her radio with the antenna and all and sent back a message that read, *Big eye to old horse. Big eye to old horse. NOBODY is ready. Repeat, NOBODY is ready.* So that was the message for El Sup, letting him know that we were ready to carry out our agenda with a perspective to grab the aforementioned—Morales, that is. Then Toñita dug into her knapsack and pulled out a pack of gum and told me she had some that are laxatives and then went out to take a look to see where the aforementioned, which is Morales, was getting to. And then Doña Juanita went off to talk to her cousin who works in the Ocosingo market and is one of the biggest gossips around and . . . I mean, her cousin is the gossip, not Doña Juanita, so wherever she is, she knows what's going on . . . the cousin. Then Maa Jchixuch got his things together in the yard of the shack and El Justiciero found a place for the truck so's it would be handy, but not really out in the open. Erika got her sound equipment in place and set up a speaker in the yard and another where they put the cars—the driveway, that is. Magdalena was busy getting herself all fixed up. And I started thinking how NOBODY is really good at these jobs that the General Staff of the EZLN gives us every once in a while. Just then, Toñita came back and said that the aforementioned Morales was over in El Infierno, and I asked what the hell he was doing in the inferno when he was sposed to be here in Ocosingo, and how everything was mixed up, and then Toñita just looked at me and said I was right, but that El Infierno was the name of the cantina where we could find Morales, the aforementioned. So I guess it was clear that El Infierno was just the name of the cantina where he was, and Toñita went on explaining that the aforementioned Morales was about my age, that'd be around sixty, and my height, and had gray hair and was a bit fat. And then Toñita said for sure it was him, the aforementioned Morales, cause that's what the bodyguards kept calling him. Then Toñita said how the bodyguards were these really big guys and double-wide, which is real strong like, and how they had their hair real short, sorta like the soldiers of the bad government. And just then Juanita came back and told us that the cousin said that the aforementioned Morales was a little tanked, which is a little drunk, and so were the bodyguards.

So it was time to get together and go over the plan one last time and make any changes we might need, and then we sat back to wait for nighttime to get a little further on, until it was almost morning. Then, in the really dark part just before first light, I put on my hat and everybody understood that we were about to start the mission. NOBODY was ready to move.

Then Maa Jchixuch, Erika, El Justiciero, and Doña Juanita got into their mission positions, and I took off with Toñita and her pack of gum and with Magdalena and her really high heels that were making her stumble every few seconds. And then we got to the doors of the inferno, which is the name of the cantina, which is El Infierno, and Toñita went in with her pack of gum and came right back out again. She said how there weren't that many people, just a few, really, and that the aforementioned was right there—Morales, that is—and that he was completely gone, not that he wasn't there, cause he was, but completely gone cause of all he had drunk, and gone with him were the bodyguards.

Toñita explained how she had given the aforementioned's bodyguards the gum with the laxative and that it would take awhile for it to work, so I told Toñita to get in her position. Then I told Magdalena to go on into the inferno, which was the cantina's name, El Infierno, and I went in after her to make sure nothing happened to Magdalena.

So Magdalena walked on in, doing her thing and moving so. And then the aforementioned Morales was all drooling as he watched Magdalena come in. The bodyguards were doing a bit of drooling themselves. Then the Morales person, the aforementioned, started saying things to Magdalena, like how come a pretty girl like her was all alone, and how she should be having a good time with him, and other things that were kinda dirty and I can't tell you cause who knows if there's women and children listening, or reading, depends. So then Magdalena went over to this aforementioned Morales and told him how she was looking high and low for a man who could do her right, cause she was all woman and there weren't any real men in these parts, and how she was thinking of going over to the Zapatistas to see what they had. And then the aforementioned, the Morales person, said that the Zapatistas were all queer, that's what he said, and the bodyguards laughed.

So just then, Magdalena walked over to this Morales, who is the aforementioned, and stuck her butt in his face as she turned and winked at me and said to him, "Well, from what I can tell, some of them Zapatistas might actually be queer."

And she sat on his lap and started saying to him how come he was there in the inferno when she could take him to paradise, and then Morales, the aforementioned, said, well, why don't you just take me there, honey, and they got up and moved to the door, and I moved out after them, and when they were at the door, the aforementioned Morales began grabbing her all over and she kept saying that they shouldn't do it here and they should go to her room, cause she had all sorts of things there to make him, Morales, the aforementioned, really happy. Well, the aforementioned Morales said that was good and let's go and all, and they went over to where he, Morales, the aforementioned, had his car, and I took off running to get there first. When I got there, I took my position, and just a second later I could see the car lights and then it went into the courtyard. They all got out of the car and one of the guards commented, hey, boss, I think I gotta go, cause something in that cantina didn't go down right. And then the other guard said how he was feeling a little like going to the john. And then Magdalena told them how there was a latrine in the patio, and they both took off trying to get there before the other, but all the time bumping into each other cause they were so drunk.

Magdalena went into the house and told the aforementioned Morales how he should wait for me here, sweetie, while I go slip into something a bit more comfortable that you're really gonna like. And then Magdalena came into the room where we were all crammed. Then I gave the signal.

Then Erika started her sound equipment how they should all surrender and they were all surrounded. Then Maa Jchixuch lit the fireworks he'd set up and it sounded like they were shooting the place up good. So there was a real riot sounding like a lot of shooting and noise. Then the bodyguards ran out, but they couldn't hardly move cause they were so drunk and had their pants down around their knees. Now, a body would have thought that they would be scared shitless from all the shooting and all, and they woulda been, except for the trick gum Toñita gave them. So there they were, all covered with shit, both from being scared to death and from real shit, cause the noise and stuff caught them when they were in the middle of the diarrhea brought on by the gum. Well, all they could think of doing was run, and they did, off into the woods. And then the Morales person, the aforementioned, asked what the fuck is going on, and you could tell the shock scared the drunk out of him, cause he was in control of himself. So that's when we all rushed out of the little back room. And we surrounded him so he wouldn't be going anywhere.

Then I told the aforementioned Morales that he was under arrest by order of the autonomous justice authorities of the Good Governance Boards, and that we were going to take him back so he could account for all his evil. Then Morales, the aforementioned, said, "Nobody is going to arrest me!" and that's when Erika said, "Well, that's just fine, cause it's NOBODY that's arresting you."

So then Doña Juanita was about to tie up his hands, when the aforementioned Morales pulled out a gun and said we should all raise our hands. So that's what we did. And Morales, the aforementioned, said how he was too tough a bone for any pissant Zapatista to chew on, and that no amount of nobodies was going to take him in. And then he pointed the gun at Toñita and said she was a damn street kid, and he pointed at Doña Juanita and said how she was a wrinkled old bitch, and then he pointed at El Justiciero and called him a no-count nigger, and then he pointed at Maa Jchixuch and said he was an earring-wearing punk shit, and then he pointed at Erika and called her a useless kid, and then he pointed at Magdalena and said she was a goddamn fag, and then he pointed at me and said I was a rat-shit Indian. And when he got through pointing—that is, when he had us all in his sights—he said he was just going to kill us and be done with it, cause we're the kind of people there are always too many of and nobody was going to miss us anyways, cause there was too many just like us.

So as this Morales, which is the aforementioned, was getting off his neo-liberal speech, Magdalena, it seems, just got her dander up and went at him and started wrestling hand-to-hand like. And then, as if Magdalena's attack had been the signal, we all went at the aforementioned Morales. And that's when we heard a shot. Course, we got him under control and took the gun from him. And then Doña Juanita, El Justiciero, Toñita, and Erika got up to tie this Morales, the aforementioned, so he wouldn't get into any more mischief. That's when we saw how Magdalena didn't get up off the floor. So I thought it was cause she was beat up. But I went to pick her up and saw she had a bullet wound in her stomach. So I called out to Doña Juanita that Magdalena was wounded.

So Doña Juanita got some herbs out of her knapsack and started packing her wound, Magdalena's, to stop the bleeding. Then I told Erika to radio back urgent that we had a NOBODY down. And I told Magdalena not to worry cause we were going to take her to a hospital to get healed. But Magdalena was getting paler and paler. So I told El Justiciero to get the truck ready to leave. Then I told the others to get Morales, the aforementioned, into the truck to take him to justice. And I said to make room for Magdalena so we could take her to the hospital. So I was there with Magdalena, and she asked me how the mission had gone. So I said it had gone real good, that thanks to her, which is to him, the Bad was in custody. And then he/she asked me if she looked pretty. And I said she looked like a princess. And right there he/she got to crying. So I thought it must be on account of the wound, and I said she/he shouldn't cry cause real soon we were going to get her to be healed. Then he/she said the crying was not on account of the pain but cause nobody had ever called her a princess before. So I said that actually she always did look like a princess, but I didn't say so cause I didn't want her to get me wrong. And just then everybody else came to be with Magdalena. Doña Juanita leaned over real close so's only I could hear her, and she told me how Magdalena wasn't going to make it cause all her insides were torn up. So me, I just stayed with Magdalena and held her hand and tried to cheer her up. And that's when he, or she, asked me if he/she was going to die. And I said no, she/he wasn't going to die. And then Magdalena said how she wanted to be taken to a Zapatista hospital so she could get operated on and finally have the body of what she was, which is a woman. So I said of course we would. And then he/she said that just maybe some Zapatista would fall in love with her when she was a woman and marry her, and then I, Elías, would be the father-in-law. And I said that father-in-law it would be. And then he/she asked, Papa Elías, did we really fuck the Bad and the Evil? And I said, you bet we did, son. And then Magdalena said, listen, Papa Elías, if I die, cry me a river. I said how she/he was not going to die, at least not for a bunch of years. And then Magdalena didn't say nothing else. And then Doña Juanita took her pulse and said that Magdalena was deceased.

Then we all grew really quiet and still . . . like as if we'd all died . . .

The Morales Person Is Not Morales

INQUEST RECORD

Community of La Realidad, Autonomous Zapatista Rebel Municipality of San Pedro de Michoacán, Good Governance Board.

At 10:00 hours, 10 a.m., of the 9th day of February of 2005, a meeting was held by the justice authorities of all the autonomous Zapatista rebel municipalities of the five Good Governance Boards of Los Altos de Chiapas, Tzetal Forest Zone, Northern Zone, Tzotz Choj Zone, and Border Forest Zone, to deal with the problem in the Montes Azules, in the state of Chiapas in our country, which is called Mexico, which is the fault of the bad national and international governments. The problem is that the rich and the powerful are trying to steal the Montes Azules, which belong to all of humanity, and they want to use it for their own benefit and with no thought of the great tragedies they may bring about.

In order to find the alleged perpetrators of those deeds, on this very day a man was arrested and accused of committing that crime with the support of the bad governments. The accused was delivered to the autonomous authorities for investigation. The person who made the arrest is Comrade Elías Contreras, Investigation Commission of the EZLN, who is not present because a relative was severely wounded in the course of the arrest of the prisoner who was presented with the name of Morales, but whose name is not Morales and who has many different names. The prisoner was presented in good health, with no signs of beating or of wounds, except for the marks on his wrists left by the ligatures the arresting parties had to apply to prevent any further mishap, and he is also a little hungover from having been very drunk. Along with the prisoner, the following articles were delivered to the Zapatista authorities as having belonged to the prisoner:

- One hand weapon, an automatic pistol: Colt .45, of the type issued to officers of the Federal Army of Mexico. The pistol has the national emblem of Mexico on the handle and the serial number has been filed off, making it illegible. Along with the weapon came one clip with six unfired rounds.

• Various identification documents and passports, all with the prisoner's photograph, but with different names, as follows:

Diego Manuel de Jesús Cevallos Bartlett y Ortega
Santiago Felipe Creel Calderón y Sahagún
Onésimo Iñiguez Cepeda Sandoval
Roberto Carlos Madrazo Salinas de Gortari
Vicente Ernesto Fox Zedillo
Enrique Mario Renán Cervantes Castillo
Jorge Morales Serrano Limón

[Note: Some are voter-identification documents and passports with the prisoner's photograph and fingerprints; others have only a photograph, such as the membership cards for: Pro-Life, University Movement for Renovation Orientation, National Union of Family Fathers, Integral Human Development, and Citizens' Action.]

• In national currency: 150,000 pesos. In U.S. currency: $12,000. Credit cards from a number of banks.

• One Goldstar satellite telephone (a telephone that allows the user to call from any point on the globe to any other point).

• One small computer of the type known as "handheld" with many names, telephone numbers, and addresses.

All the aforementioned things having been presented before the prisoner, who recognized them as being his, the prisoner was then informed that he stood accused of many wrongful acts perpetrated against the indigenous peoples of Mexico and against all of us who live in this country, that among them are: sale of the natural resources of our nation to foreign interests; and planning to murder Indian brothers and sisters. He was informed that he is accused of doing wrongful business, together with the bad governments and the neo-liberals, by selling the riches from the region of Chiapas known as the Montes Azules.

First preliminary public hearing with the alleged Morales

The prisoner stated that this is not his name, that his name is not Morales, but that Morales is one of the names he uses in his work, and that he no longer remembers what his real name is because he has changed it so many times, according to who he's working for. He further stated that he was detained in the municipal seat of Ocosingo, here in the state of Chiapas, Mexico. He said that nobody had arrested him. He was asked how it was that nobody arrested him, and he said that the people who had arrested him had said that they were nobody. The authorities could not understand what the accused was saying and asked him to provide clear intelligible answers. The accused grew angry and began insulting the authorities and the whole Zapatista movement and stated that he has great influence in the Supreme Court of Justice of the Nation and in the Congress of the Union and in the Presidency of the Republic and with Bush, Blair, and Berlusconi, the Royal Couple of Spain, and other personalities we were not able to copy down because the accused spoke too fast in his fury. The authorities just stared at him and let him finish what he was saying. The prisoner went from super-pissed to super-meek and said he could give us money or drinks or women, but please let him go. Then one of the women authorities known as Lupe began to get pissed on account of the prisoner's disrespect for women, but she held her tongue and waited. Since we said nothing and just stared at him, the accused started crying and asking not to be killed. That took awhile. Between the prisoner's insults and the things he offered to give us and the crying, it came time for *pozol*, and the authorities declared a recess. The accused did not want *pozol*.

Second preliminary public hearing with the Morales who is not Morales

After we'd had *pozol*, we went back to taking the statement from the accused through questions and answers. But he was advised that if his answers were not clear and if he kept on making threats, we would turn him over to the authorities of the bad government in the presence of the press and we would reveal everything we had found on him. The accused said that we shouldn't do that because his bosses would have him killed to keep him from talking, because directly involved in his wrongdoing were a great many powerful people from Mexico and around the world, and they would have him killed to keep him from accusing them all. He said that this was the way the powerful did things: When somebody outlives his usefulness or becomes a danger to them, they eliminate him and find another. The prisoner then said that he was ready to cooperate and answer truthfully.

Authority: Why were you carrying a satellite telephone?

Morales who is not Morales (hereinafter to be referred to as Non-Morales): To speak directly from Montes Azules with my contacts in the United States and Europe.

Authority: Why did you need to speak to those contacts?

Non-Morales: To give them status reports on the Montes Azules deal.

Authority: What deal?

Non-Morales: To get them to privatize the lands in order to sell them. First we had to evict the indigenous communities living there. The plan was to stir up trouble to justify a military occupation of the entire region and clear it of all people. Our plan, and don't you believe I'm in on this alone, was first to plant drugs so as to have a pretext on which to send in the Army, but that fell through because you don't allow drugs. Then the idea was to set forest fires, but that fell through because of the Forest Protection Law. The next plan was to provoke a confrontation among Indians. We had already contacted some Lacandones, the people from SOCAMA, and a few from the official ARIC. We were going to give them paramilitary training, like we did in the north of Chiapas in Los Altos, and then set them against the Zapatistas, but that one got fucked as well because you decided to relocate the communities and you eliminated the pretext. So that screwed our last plan and we had to come up with another. That's what I was doing when you got me.

Authority: Why do you say you're not alone in this?

Non-Morales: Because there's a lot of very rich and powerful people in the deal. Their representatives met with Fox the other day, right there in the Lacandona forest. That was the reason he and his wife visited. The statement about promoting ecotourism is a lie. They went there because powerful men are pressing him to privatize everything so they can buy it up and do their business. Zedillo and Carabias were there. The satellite telephone was precisely to contact a guy who's very close to Fox and who was with him on his tour of Europe. I stayed back here to check out what we were going to do with the lands, and to see about some "pets" they wanted in the Spanish Court, but now they're in for a long wait.

Authority: Why are you carrying all this money?

Non-Morales: To pay for the transportation of the animals to Spain and to pay off the Indians to get them to support us in the privatization scheme. Besides, you have to throw money around with officials: small, medium, and big, as well as municipal, state, and federal.

Authority: Who was going to be in charge of training the paramilitary?

Non-Morales: The weapons and the training were going to be put up by the Federal Army, but the ideas—the vetting and the ideological training—were going to be supplied by El Yunque.

Authority: What is El Yunque?

Non-Morales: It is a secret rightwing organization, extremely rightwing, involved in both the PAN and the Fox administration. But they're also present in other political parties. The members include political figures, businessmen, and bishops. They have spent years following the teachings of their predecessors, Salinas and Zedillo. The plan is to sell everything they can and become rich. They don't care about anything else, not the country, not religion, not the people, even if they say they do.

Authority: Do you belong to El Yunque?

Non-Morales: No. They contacted me because I worked with the paramilitary in the north of Chiapas, and with the people from Paz y Justicia. And also in Los Altos with the Cardenistas and Máscara Roja. And in other places with Los Puñales, Los Chinchulines, Los Albores de Chiapas, Los Aguilares, MIRA, and SOCAMA. And in Montes Azules, it was me who was organizing the PRD people in Zinacantán. El Yunque believes that the Zapatistas are the main obstacle in the way of their plans. It is ready to do anything, even go to war, to eliminate you guys. And now, with the Bush victory in the United States, well, they're ready for anything. The rich gringos want to buy up the whole world, and the politicians here are willing to sell them this part called Mexico. El Yunque is one of the sellers, but there are other groups inside the political parties. Anyone who can, no matter if he's PAN, PRI, or PRD, is going to sell.

Authority: Are the bad governments aware of the things you are saying?

Non-Morales: Of course they are. They're the ones organizing the whole thing. I'm just a hired hand.

[Note: The second hearing was suspended because a messenger arrived from the General Staff with news that they had traced the satellite telephone and discovered that the number was registered to the Vamos Mexico Foundation, headed by Mrs. Marta Sahagún de Fox, the wife of President Fox.]

Third preliminary public hearing with Non-Morales

The accused was asked if he had anything else to declare, and the Non-Morales said that he did and started off on a rambling speech switching from one thing to another and moving from insults to crying, and we could hardly understand what he was trying to say because half the time he would be screaming and the other half speaking so softly that only he could hear himself. From what little could be understood, he mentioned the deceased Pável González, a student at the National University (UNAM) who had been killed, and then explained that the question of the deceased Pável González had been a warning from El Yunque to the authorities who were trying to uncover their activities in the university and other places, and the message was that there was going to be war. That the Digna Ochoa thing had also been a warning. That El Yunque, the far right, uses the same tactic as the gringo administrations—preventive war, which is to kill people before asking who they are or what they want. That successive administrations have to pretend that things change even when they never change, and if not, then it happens all over again. That he, Non-Morales, is just another number and that even if we screw him over, there will be others, perhaps worse than him. That we should please forgive him and he will never do it again. That he wants to go home to his mother. That we should all go home and fuck our mothers. That he hopes no one gets killed. That we should forgive him. That he's afraid, very afraid. Then the Non-Morales went in his pants—that is, he shit and pissed in his pants—and didn't even tell anyone, but just did it and stood there and the session had to be suspended because of the stench. He smelled real bad, so we had to suspend so that the Non-Morales could get cleaned up a little, and then he came back and said that was all he had to say.

THE PRELIMINARY PUBLIC HEARINGS WITH THE NON-MORALES ARE ADJOURNED.

Signatures of the accused prisoner and the comrades of the Honor and Justice Commissions of the different autonomous Zapatista rebel municipalities.

Sentence

The Honor and Justice Commissions of all the autonomous Zapatista municipalities organized under the five Good Governance Boards have met to sentence the Morales who is not Morales.

At 16:40 hours (4:40 p.m.) of the 9th day of February of 2005, the Honor and Justice Commissions of the autonomous municipalities, having presided over the first, second, and third preliminary public hearings with the individual known as Morales, who is accused of selling out the national sovereignty—that is, the country—and planning the deaths of Mexican Indians, and it having been proven that he did participate in the commission of these crimes, the authorities do decree:

1. That the person known as Morales, who is not Morales and has many different names, is hereby sentenced to ten years of community service in the projects of the Good Governance Boards in different Zapatista communities to atone for this great evil crime against humanity.

2. That there will be no parole until he has served his sentence.

3. There being no other matter to be discussed, the sentencing is concluded at 17:00 hours (5:00 p.m.) of the same day and date.

Signature of the accused prisoner, now the condemned prisoner. Signature of the authorities of the Honor and Justice Commissions of the autonomous municipalities.

The Telephone Call

Excerpt of a transcription of a telephone conference call originating in Washington and extending to Rome, Madrid, London, Moscow, and Mexico, intercepted on February 10 by the Echelon spy satellite system and erased from the record on the order of Condoleezza Rice, Secretary of State of the United States of America:

"They caught Morales in Chiapas."

"Have him released."

"Can't do that. He was caught by the Zapatistas and we have no control over their justice system."

"Fuck! He's going to spill everything and the Zapatistas will make it public. Something has to be done. Where do they have him?"

"He was tried and found guilty in the Montes Azules affair and the matter of the paramilitary. He was sentenced to community work among the indigenous peoples. We can assume that they seized everything he had with him. The IDs are no problem because we can say the Zapatistas invented them, but his computer had names that can sink the whole thing."

"He has to be located and terminated."

"Yes, we kill him and blame the Zapatistas."

"Bad idea. No one is going to believe us. If the Zapatistas didn't kill General Absalón Castellanos Domínguez, who was as bad or worse, they won't kill Morales."

"Right! But there are other options."

"Does anyone know where they have him?"

"No, but we can find out."

"Do that, then send someone who can give him something that will make him seriously ill. But it has to be fast, because the Zapatistas won't hesitate to make everything public."

"I'm going to send López, who has been there for some time undercover as a journalist; he's just like Morales, capable of killing his own mother."

"Okay! But remember, if something goes wrong, yours will be the first head to roll."

This Is As Far As I Go

So that's how things went with this case, or thing, when I went into Mexico City, the Monster, to find the Bad and the Evil, and how I got to work with Belascoarán, and the people I met, and what I did over there and here in Chiapas, Mexico.

A while back I sent a letter to Belascoarán telling him that the aforementioned Morales was not Morales and everything else that happened in this case, or thing, regarding the Bad and the Evil. I didn't tell him anything about Magdalena and I might not even tell you, cause it's like I said at the beginning of this story, there are wounds that don't heal even if you talk them out, and it's even the contrary—they just get to bleeding worse than ever when you dress them in words. As soon as I get through with you here, I'm going to take some flowers to Magdalena's grave. NOBODY will be coming along with me. Oh, by the way, on her headstone I had them carve, *Here lies the heart of NOBODY.*

Okay, so I'll be leaving now. This is as far as I go. I still have to go ready the mule, but first I want to thank you a whole lot for having taken the time to stop and give us a look, even for a little while. I already did my part. We still have to find out how things went for Belascoarán over in the Monster, which is Mexico City. But I gotta tell you to be ready for anything, cause we Zapatistas are like that: Just when you think we're through, we come up with another thing, or case, depends. So that's what our struggle is like; what's missing is always missing.

And you know what? Well, it so happens that El Sup's not here cause he went to talk to Moy and Tacho, so I'm here all by myself, and that's how come I have to do the honors of wrapping up our participation in this story about the uncomfortable dead and all those things, or cases, depends. So I'm going to sign:

From the mountains of Southeastern Mexico,
Elías Contreras, Investigation Commission
of the Zapatista National Liberation Army
February 2005

CHAPTER 12

AND I LIVE IN THE PAST

It was the strangest daybreak Héctor had ever seen. He knew because he had followed the process delicately, with almost mathematical precision. First there was the invisible presence of the sun, affecting the shape of the darkness. Then came the gray streaks on the horizon, leading to the unveiling of strangely purple clouds . . . Then, suddenly, there was light. *Smog can do some marvelous things*, the detective told himself. He went down to the place where he often had breakfast to try and wake the waiters out of their stupor. They usually set the morning tables while they were still asleep, and Héctor knew it would take them awhile to serve him some fresh orange juice—fresh out of the refrigerator, because the actual squeezing had taken place about a month and a half earlier in a concentrate plant in Miami.

When Monteverde came out his front door, Héctor was waiting for him.

"Where's the dog?"

"Well, I can't very well take him to the office. The dog stays home."

"Do you know Barney? Barney, the purple dinosaur?"

"Beg your pardon?"

"I think I know who's been calling us," Héctor said, lighting a cigarette. "Jesús María Alvarado had a son, Ángel Alvarado Alvarado, and they tell me he works as a voice-over artist on television: *The Flintstones* and a purple dinosaur—"

"*The Flintstones* isn't on TV anymore."

"Well, that kind of thing . . . Do you know him?"

"No."

"I didn't think so."

When he got back to his office, Héctor discovered that his office mates had left on work missions. Two notes bore witness: *Went to fix a lady's plumbing. Gilberto* and *Went to La Merced to buy materials—Naugahyde and damask. Carlos.* This, of course, meant that along with being a detective, he now had to fill in as receptionist.

For the umpteenth time, he dialed the number they had given him for Ángel Alvarado and listened to the endless rings. No one home. Did this Alvarado actually exist?

He turned to his notes on Juárez's ministers and opened the Yellow Pages. Before trying to cross-reference any of the names with a furniture shop, he called upon the simplest method of logic: Ruiz, Ramírez, and Guzmán were extremely common names. If your name was any one of those, no one would say you have the same name as one of Juárez's ministers, they'd say it was the same as about a million other Joe Schmoes in the book. Furthermore, it had to be a well-known minister, not just any old appointment; it had to be something that sounded like a street or like one of those statues on Paseo de la Reforma. It probably wasn't Melchor Ocampo: too well known and there was a major street with his name. No, he was just a reference point and would not be described as "one of Juárez's ministers." Prieto? Zarco? Santos

Degollado? Lerdo de Tejada? It wouldn't be González Ortega, not unless he used his compound last name.

The telephone book is like what the Bible represents for fundamentalists in Kansas or what tarot cards represent for freeloaders. If you know the questions, you can find all the answers right there in that immense volume of yellow pages. So there were three *Prieto* furniture shops, one *Lerdo* used-furniture salesman, a *Zarco* home-appliance store, and one *Degollado* furniture depot. Six to start with. He jotted down the addresses and celebrated the first step in his desk research with a soda.

Héctor dialed the number for Deep Throat once again and finally got signs of life at the other end of the line.

"Is that Mr. Alvarado?"

"He hasn't come in yet, but he'll be here around 12. He's got a voice-over session."

"I beg your pardon, but where is *here*?"

"You have called the studios, the Gama Studios. We're in the Roma district, number 108 Puebla Street, very close to the Insurgentes metro station."

Barney the purple dinosaur looked more like a hairy-chested, overweight, forty-something Mexican who didn't care much for shaving. When he finished dubbing a very coquettish voice onto one of the three little pigs, they handed him a note from Héctor, who was watching him through the glass partition in the control cabin. The note on the back of one of Héctor's business cards read very simply, *Jesús María Alvarado wants to see you.*

"Good day," Alvarado said a little timidly, holding out his hand formally, a very hairy and homely hand it was. His voice was unmistakable. They had taken seats on one of the benches in a little park across from the studios, and Alvarado-Barney took out a package of old bread to feed the pigeons. Héctor opened a pack of filtered Delicados and proceeded to blow smoke at the animals as they came to eat the bread.

"You must be one of the people who received the calls."

Héctor nodded and returned to his Alec Guinness face. He was going to let this guy tell his story with no pressure.

"It was the only idea that I could think of."

Héctor smiled. He liked this Alvarado character. "It wasn't a bad idea," he said.

"Do you really think so? It's just that talking into a microphone is what I do. What else could I do, shoot the bastard? No, right? Go to the police? No way! What would I tell them? *Hey, listen, I ran into a prick on the street and I'm sure he's the one who killed my father thirty years ago. He's a certain Morales whose name is not Morales. Oh, by the way, he's a policeman too, like you, or was, or maybe you worked under him, or maybe not.* No, right?"

"So why were you calling Monteverde?"

"Who's Monteverde?"

"The one who was a friend of your father in '68, the one with a dog named Tobías, the one who got me into this."

"Oh, I'm sorry. He was just one of the people I called. I found one of my father's address books and decided to call them all. Most of his friends from the '60s were no longer at those old numbers; some had died, others had moved away from Mexico City. I left messages for many of them, the answering-machine messages."

"So why did you call *me*?"

"Who are *you*?"

"Héctor Belascoarán."

"The detective?"

"Sometimes."

"Well, that was funny. I was calling this one guy and leaving the message on his machine, when suddenly he picked up and yelled, 'Stop breaking my balls, buddy! You should call a detective named Belascoarán. I ran into that guy in the National Archives and he was looking for a picture of you.'"

"So?"

"Well . . ."

"And what about Morales?"

"That bastard?"

"Exactly."

"A week ago, I was walking down the Lázaro Cárdenas Central Axis, along a street called San Juan de Letrán, looking to buy some of those pirate videos that go for fifteen pesos and work great, and also to have some chocolate and donuts, and out of nowhere, fuck if I don't see this guy! Just from looking at him I got a bad feeling, a kind of chill. Do you believe in ghosts?"

"Some I do, some I don't," Belascoarán said, not meaning to be enigmatic or anything, just trying to establish the difference between Hollywood and the Holocaust.

"Then I took a good look at him, and there was no doubt about it. It was Morales. It was the man I remember from Lecumberri. The same one who once gave me his yo-yo collection, all friendly like, the prick. The same one who killed my father. And my whole body started shaking, but I calmed down and watched him enter the Latinoamericana Tower and get in the elevator. That was about where I ran out of steam, but I did see that the elevator stopped on 7, 17, and 41."

"And then?"

"I went home and didn't say a word to my daughter. And I spent the whole night awake with cold sweats. In the morning, I took my father's address book and started making phone calls."

"What about the story you tell about how Morales set up a metal barricade on one of the roads to rob coffee from the farmers?"

"Well, that's one they told me."

"And all that stuff about a secret amnesty in this country and how Morales benefited from it?"

"Well, isn't it the truth? Isn't it the pure fucking truth? Aren't the murderers all free and in good health?"

Héctor nodded. "What about the shot in the back of the head?"

"I was seven years old and my father had just gotten out of jail. He was lying in bed reading the *The Bolivian Diary of Ernesto Che Guevara.* I'll never forget that, and I still have the book, the Siglo XXI edition, the binding all broken, but I still have it. He got a telephone call, then put on his shoes and left the house. My grandmother always said that it was Morales who called him . . . And he never came back. They found him in the Tlatelolco gardens, sitting on a bench with a bullet in the back of his head."

Alvarado-Barney's last words were, "Can I keep calling you?"

Héctor was about to answer with an emphatic *no*, but the guy had such a sad expression on his face that he found himself nodding instead. He remained in the park awhile tying up loose ends. None of the furniture places on his list had offices in the Latinoamericana Tower. Well, the guy could have been there on an errand. When Héctor ran out of cigarettes, he realized that he hadn't asked Barney about bin Laden.

He went to look for the taxi he had taken from the failed mugger, almost certain that someone else must have stolen it, but no, there it was, all rusty and powerful.

Winding his way through traffic that was getting heavier as the morning wore on, he visited the addresses on his list. The Prieto furniture places belonged to three brothers, all very young, who had inherited them from their father two years earlier. The used-furniture dealer called Lerdo, in the Doctores district, was actually a Lebanese immigrant who had bought the business from the original Lerdo in the '50s. On one leg of his trip, Héctor's vehicle was hailed by a couple of young newlyweds who wanted a ride to the Toluca terminal. When he refused to charge them, they attributed it to young love and good luck, and Héctor didn't really want to set them straight by telling them that it was a pirate taxi stolen from a mugger, and that he, Héctor, was not a professional driver.

It was getting close to lunchtime. Héctor could tell because his sense of smell was growing sharper and sharper. Ever since he had lost his eye, he could smell things better and at a greater distance. He let the smells guide him and wound up in a Michoacán taco stand that sold meat skewers; it was over in the Escandón district, near the area where he would later look for the Degollado warehouse.

One hour and thirteen *campeche* tacos later, Héctor Belascoarán pulled over on Prosperidad Street, a surprising name in a district that had wallowed in decadence ever since the Revolution seized the estate from Mr. Escandón.

The entrance to the warehouse was a large metal door secured on the outside with a padlock. Héctor knocked three times without really expecting a reply.

A young boy stopped his soccer practice long enough to

tell Héctor, "Sometimes he doesn't hear; the man is half deaf. You can go around the back," he added, pointing to the alley beside the neighboring tenement.

When he got around to the back, Héctor found a courtyard full of rubble and a second door, one that didn't even rate a lock, just some twisted wires. He knocked again, and based on the wisdom that he had never known of any cats actually killed by curiosity, he untwisted the wires and walked in.

When the door closed behind him, Héctor found himself in absolute darkness. In the absence of windows or skylights, he couldn't even guess at the size of the place. Obviously, he had not brought a flashlight with him, so he used his tiny Bic as a sort of proletarian Statue of Liberty to blaze a trail of light in the darkness. He bumped into something he guessed might be a crate and moved off to try and find a wall. When he finally located one, he made his way along it to where he thought another door would be. He found a light switch by pure chance, as it was much lower than it should have been. When he turned on the light—a few old mercury vapor lamps—they revealed a phantasmagoric cemetery of old furniture distributed around the space by category and type: here the metal-frame kitchen tables, over there the archaic console record players, along with a phalanx of about fifty refrigerators that had probably been new thirty years earlier, and all sorts of chairs: dining room chairs, garden chairs, rustic chairs, and a dozen bar stools. In one corner of the warehouse, which must have been close to fifty meters long by another fifty meters wide, there were open crates full of toys.

Once upon a time, in a curiously philosophical aside, a historian friend had told him that it was important to distinguish between antiques and old junk. At the time, Héctor thought it was foolishness, but what he saw here was something different; this wasn't just old furniture, these were the mortal remains of the Mexican middle class that had only made it halfway, the glorious middle class of the '60s that was crushed in the '80s and dead and gone in the new millennium. Or was it? Who knows . . .

In another corner of the old warehouse, a single desk bore witness to what might have once been an office. He found a piece of pipe to break into the drawers, but he didn't have to use it; the drawer was open . . . open and empty. There were no lists, no records, not even a filthy old inventory. There was merely a single box of old business cards with two telephone numbers and addresses—one for the Escandón warehouse, which is where he was, and another for an office on the forty-first floor of the Latinoamericana Tower—both in the name of *Juvencio Degollado, Manager.*

For many years, the Latinoamericana Tower had been the center of Mexico City. The Zócalo was the ceremonial center, the symbolic center, but the place to have an unforgettable tryst was at the foot of the Latinoamericana, on the corner of Madero and San Juan de Letrán. There, in the shadow of the tallest building in Mexico, people intending to commit suicide would congregate, so much so that they wound up fencing in the scenic observation deck. But the place was also frequented by young couples visiting the sky bar, from where you could see almost to the edge of the known world. By now, however, the Latinoamericana Tower was no longer the tallest building in the biggest city in the world. And some people were saying that it was not even the biggest city in the world anymore, that Tokyo and Buenos Aires were bigger. In any case, with all the pollution there were precious few days when you could see anything at all from the observation deck. And in the final rat-shit analysis, just to finish fucking it completely, Mexico City had lost its center . . . there was no center at all—what had been the center was now a collection of neighborhoods whose inhabitants didn't know their neighbors and rarely even went outside to contemplate the dangerous splendor of the urban world.

The office had a little sign to one side of the entrance: *Degollado Furniture*. There was no lock on the door, so Héctor just turned the knob. There was a single room with a desk at the end on a dirty green rug, and Morales, sitting on an executive chair with a very high back, his hands on the curiously bare desktop, just staring at him.

"You're the one who's been following me. I knew it."

"No. I'm a friend of the one who's been following you."

Héctor looked around for another chair to sit on, but there was nothing. Just a refrigerator, an old umbrella stand, and two horrendous Velasco reproductions—his *Valley of Mexico* and a landscape from the Porfirio Díaz period—hanging on the wall.

Morales wore very thick glasses and his nearsighted gaze followed Belascoarán's eye as it explored the room.

"Piece of shit of an office, isn't it?"

Héctor nodded.

"Years ago, the elegant thing was to have an office in the Latinoamericana Tower. There were the big-time lawyers, the money lenders, the dentists who made gold fillings, agents for German machinery companies."

"That was a long time ago," Héctor said, resting on his good leg. He could walk for hours on end, but standing around really hurt a lot. In about half an hour, the pain in his lower back would be murder.

"Would you like a soda?" Morales asked, pointing to the broken-down 5'10" Westinghouse. Héctor opened the refrigerator and found it almost empty. There was a single Coke and half a dozen Sol beers.

"I never left. I stuck it out in this stinking city. And every once in a while, someone would stop and stare at me, kind of recognizing me, but nothing would happen. They were all afraid, so they turned around and went the other way. Sometimes it was me who chickened out; I'd rush into the nearest metro station and spend the next hour with my ass dripping sweat, looking over my shoulder."

Morales was wearing a blue suit that needed cleaning and a red tie on a light blue shirt. He had no one to iron for him and he had never learned to do it himself. Héctor opened the soda with the end of a stapler he found on top of the refrigerator and took a long swig. It tasted awful. Was Morales trying to poison him? He spit it out on the table. Morales, shocked by Héctor's behavior, jumped back and reached into a drawer. He would have brought out his old gun if Belascoarán had not whipped around and stomped the drawer shut, crushing his hand. Over the din of Morales's unintelligible obscenities, Héctor couldn't help feeling a little proud of the ballet step that had swept him to the drawer in time to kick it shut with his bad leg. Not bad for a one-eyed gimp. Though now he was going to have a sore back for the rest of the day. He pulled out his own gun and showed it to this character, who was trying simultaneously to dry his soda-spattered shirt and rub life back into his mangled hand.

"What did you put in the Coca-Cola?" Héctor figured it was about a dozen Valiums. Morales didn't look like the arsenic type. Maybe a hundred grams of rat poison. Did they still sell that shit?

"What the holy fucking hell do you think I put in it?"

"It tasted like shit," Héctor said, a bit apologetic for the commotion he had started.

"It must have been stale."

Héctor motioned toward the huge window in the corner of the room. Now that was a great window. And forty stories down, there was the city. Morales moved over to the window and Belascoarán, wasting no time, flopped into his chair. Not bad at all.

"You are Morales," Héctor said into open space, not even acknowledging the man holding a hand attached to a wrist that was rapidly turning purple. He took Morales's pistol from the drawer and slipped it into his jacket pocket. "You killed Jesús María Alvarado."

"No way. I was just tailing him. I swear by Our Lady of Guadalupe. I was merely the finger-man. It was Ramírez who killed him."

"No! You were there and you killed him!"

"I swear I didn't. I was there, and I fingered him, but I wasn't even carrying a gun that day. I said, *Look, there's Alvarado*, and that's all. I fingered him, but fingers don't kill. I didn't even know they were out to kill him."

"You were a torturer in the '70s."

"Is that what they told you? Is that what those pricks said?"

"You ratted out your own wife, and because of you they almost killed her."

"We had already separated. We were no longer together and she was suing me over some paintings and jewelry belonging to her grandmother, which she claimed I stole from her."

"You were in the White Brigade."

"Yeah, I was into that, but I wasn't giving the orders. The

orders were coming from the real pricks. Whenever an operation got interesting, they'd send me out for sodas."

Morales began to sob. He pulled off his glasses and threw them on the floor. Then he wept two huge tears.

"I'm just a poor jerk. I'm nothing. Do you know how I made a little money? The shittiest way you can imagine: by stealing refrigerators and stoves from the homes of the people we kidnapped and later disappeared. It was easy; we were going to kill them anyway. What the fuck would you want a stove for if you were going to be tortured for three months, and if you didn't die from the torture you were going to spend years in the cooler? What? Was I supposed to leave them for the supers? Or the landlords? Because none of those people ever dared return to a house we had *taken*. There was a smell of death in them. They were *burned*. So here I am, selling ranges and fucking Formica dining room tables and easy chairs with cigarette burns on the arms. That's how I made money. But not much."

He was a poor slob, a minor scumbag. Héctor had no doubt that in the torture sessions, he was the pinch hitter, or that he stole records, or that every once in a while he did pull the trigger or push the dagger, or pour the bottle of Tehuacán water up a prisoner's nose to suffocate him, or that he occasionally kicked a naked and bleeding detainee lying on a floor.

What was he supposed to do with this character? Who was he supposed to turn him over to? In Mexico?

"Let's go down to the street," Héctor blurted out.

The hallway was empty. Héctor pointed to the stairs: forty-one floors. Not a bad punishment at all—punishment for his bad leg.

"So where are you taking me?" Morales asked with half a smile. "Where are we going?"

"You are going to fuck your mother!" Belascoarán barked, with all the rage evoked by the memory of a certain Jesús María Alvarado—whom he had never met, but whose ghost kept talking to him on the phone—as he stuck his foot in front of Morales's, clipping him with his shoulder and watching the man tumble head over heels, down and down, probably all forty-one stories of the Latinoamericana Tower, right out into San Juan de Letrán, also known as Lázaro Cárdenas, and known to some as the Central Axis. Down to the very end. Down into the bowels of hell.

THE END

EPILOGUE

On his way home, Héctor Belascoarán thought he saw two or three Moraleses. One of them was getting out of a car in front of a hotel on Reforma Avenue. He tried to get rid of this paranoid syndrome, to shake it loose like you do with a bad thought accompanied by chills, but he only managed to make it worse.

He walked by a woman who was crying silently, without a fuss, and trying to cover her face with a bluish Kleenex.

He talked about soccer with a lottery vendor.

He ran across a couple of peasants who were lost and guided them to the bus stop by the Chapultepec metro station. The man was carrying a saxophone and the woman a bag of stale bread.

The city had a peaceful ambience today, but Héctor was unable to tune in to that peace. Moraleses kept turning up in the most unlikely places: in the middle of the stolen kiss of two adolescents parting at the trolley stop, in the doorway of a jewelry shop that was closing its curtains . . .

Was he going crazy? Or was he more lucid and sharper than ever? Was he living with ghosts from the past because he was lonelier than a dog?

The thought of the dog reminded him that he had to call Monteverde and tell him the end of the story. He also had to bring the dog a present. Tobías had liked the *chorizo*. A pound of *Toluca* sausage? The poor dog would die, but what a way to go! He decided that old Tobías could get along fine on half a pound of *Toluca* sausage; that would leave the other half a pound for his own breakfast, with a few scrambled eggs.

He took off his shoes and nudged them into the middle of the room, tapping them with his big toe. The room was as empty as always. He had never been able to buy furniture, nor had he ever even thought about it. He had his rug, and in the corner of the room a floor lamp, his easy chair where he went to think, and the telephone perched beside it on top of his collection of Mexico City telephone books, past and present.

He went to the refrigerator to get himself a drink and found an unopened three-liter bottle of Lulu's Red Currant Soda. What a windfall! When had he bought it? When had he gotten the idea of having a feast of red currant soda, cigarettes, and Mahler? Out on the street, the teenage yuppies had invaded the neighborhood to dine in the local restaurants. They made big noises, little noises, laughing noises, brake-screeching noises, and horn-blowing noises. He wondered what Elías Contreras might be doing at that moment over in Chiapas. Over there, everything was probably a lot clearer, the air more transparent, enemies more defined, things simpler, traps more evident, potholes easier to evade. He poked his head out the window and gazed over the rooftops, over many, many streets, in the direction of the invisible Ajusco, toward the pale lights of Chapultepec Castle, beyond the jungle of television antennas.

The thought occurred to him to send Elías Contreras a telegram, but if he sent something like, *My Morales, fucked,* it would get censored.

Suddenly his telephone rang. Héctor stared at it with mistrust. It was one of those old telephones with the cradle on a slim neck, the kind you could hold between your ring finger and your middle finger without being double-jointed. He'd inherited it from somebody who had stashed it away when they changed over to the ugly modern ones. He let it ring a few more times. Finally, the answering machine kicked in.

> *Belascoarán, this is Jesús María Alvarado. Well, what do you know? If you were intending to catch Morales and snatch Juancho from him, you're too late. He already sold Juancho to the gringos, who took him back to Burbank. Juancho would have been very well-off if he had stayed here in Mexico; he could have kept on making commercials for Gansitos Marinela on Channel 2:* Osama bin Laden says that the best chocolate-covered tarts are . . . *I'm just telling you so that the next time you see that guy reading a communiqué on* CNN, *you can check out the mark under his right eye. It's a little scar, and the thing is . . .*

Héctor let the voice ramble on until the minute and a half of recording time was up. Then he moved over to the telephone, picked up the receiver, and dialed a number at random. A pre-recorded voice picked up, speaking for International Financial Investors:

> *All our representatives are currently busy with other customers and will take your call in the order it was received. If you want to leave a message, press 1; if you need personal attention, press 2; if you want to be transferred to our main menu, press 3—*

Héctor pressed 1.

"Listen, this is Jesús María Alvarado, and I'm calling to let you know that if you have a certain Morales on your staff, be very careful because the guy is a delinquent, an expert in fiscal frauds designed to screw the overwhelming majority of the people for the sake of a minority. Well, that's more or less what you do already, but he does it illegally. Bottom line: Morales is bad news."

He hung up feeling immensely satisfied, like a kid with a new ball, like a teenager who's discovered his father's secret *Playboy* collection. He picked up the receiver again and dialed another number at random.

"*You have reached the home of Susana Quirós,*" a youthful voice said. "*If you wish to send a fax, start now; if you wish to leave a message, wait for the beep . . .*"

"Listen, this is Jesús María Alvarado and I've called to tell you . . ." began Héctor Belascoarán Shayne, independent detective.

THE [SECOND] END

Mexico City
Late winter, 2005

Also from AKASHIC BOOKS

JOHN CROW'S DEVIL by Marlon James
232 pages, hardcover, $19.95

"A powerful first novel . . . Writing with assurance and control, James uses his small-town drama to suggest the larger anguish of a postcolonial Jamaican society struggling for its own identity."

—*New York Times*

"*Pile them up,* a Marlon James character says repeatedly, and Marlon does just that. Pile them up: language, imagery, technique, imagination. All fresh, all exciting. This is a good book and a writer to watch out for."

—CHRIS ABANI

ADIOS MUCHACHOS by Daniel Chavarría
***Winner of a 2001 Edgar Award**
245 pages, trade paperback, $13.95

"Daniel Chavarría has long been recognized as one of Latin America's finest writers. Now he again proves why . . ."

—WILLIAM HEFFERNAN

BECOMING ABIGAIL by Chris Abani
****Essence Magazine* Book Club selection**
128 pages, trade paperback, $11.95

"Compelling and gorgeously written, this is a coming-of-age novella like no other. Chris Abani explores the depths of loss and exploitation with what can only be described as a knowing tenderness. An extraordinary, necessary book."

—CRISTINA GARCIA

SOUTHLAND by Nina Revoyr
***A *Los Angeles Times* bestseller**
348 pages, trade paperback, $15.95

"What makes a book like *Southland* resonate is that it merges elements of literature and social history with the propulsive drive of a mystery, while evoking Southern California as a character, a key player in the tale."

—*Los Angeles Times*

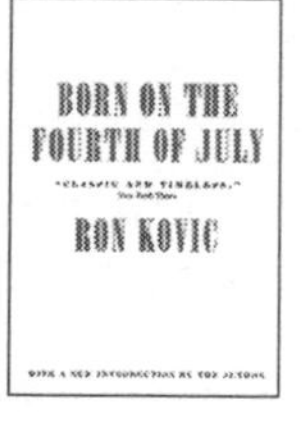

BORN ON THE FOURTH OF JULY
by Ron Kovic
218 pages, trade paperback, $14.95

"[A] classic of antiwar literature . . ."

—Howard Zinn

"Classic and timeless."

—*New York Times*

PLAYING PRESIDENT: My Close Encounters with Nixon, Carter, Bush I, Reagan, and Clinton—and How They Did Not Prepare Me for George W. Bush
by Robert Scheer, with a foreword by Gore Vidal
308 pages, trade paperback, $14.95

"With these observations on a section of our history, Scheer joins that small group of journalist-historians that includes Richard Rovere, Murray Kempton, and Walter Lippman."

—Gore Vidal, from the foreword